THE LAST ARTIFACT

A TRILOGY BY GILLIAM NESS

Toronto, Canada.

POLYMATH PUBLISHING and the portrayal of the letter "P"
within the box are trademarks of Polymath Publishing.

ISBN 978-0-9917265-9-2

January 2016

BOOK TWO

THE LOST LABYRINTH

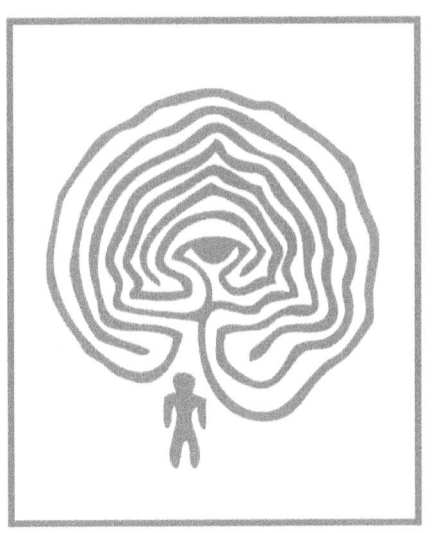

CHAPTER 1

Gibraltar.

Major Richard Roberts, aide-de-camp to the Governor of Gibraltar, sat at his desk, his task book open before him. He was a ruddy faced man, a little on the plump side but powerful and tall, with a stamina on the field that could put soldiers half his age to shame. He wore simple khaki barracks fatigues, had never once lost his temper, and possessed the kind of relaxed, confident demeanor that put people at ease.

He reached over and took hold of his mug without taking his eyes off his work, sipping the milky tea and wincing.

"Bloody hell," he muttered. "It's gone cold..."

It was only six hundred hours, but Roberts already knew what kind of day it was going to be. Along with the latest terrorist strikes in Spain had come an endless list of security tasks that needed to be accomplished, and the governor himself was of absolutely no use.

The old man had been bedridden for three days now and was showing no signs of improvement. His doctor had been the first person to call that morning, insisting the old man be taken to the naval hospital at once.

"You will please understand that I have insisted, Doctor," Roberts had said, his right eye winking nervously. "Sir William will have nothing of it. He seems quite content to die in his bed rather than be transferred to any hospital."

The military doctor had not offered much resistance. He knew the governor's stubborn streak. He had instead scheduled another visit for later that day, hoping to at least be able to collect some urine samples. The prognosis did not look good.

Major Roberts shook his head in exasperation as he looked over his agenda. What had been described to him as a ceremonial role was turning out to be the most challenging position of his career.

Since 1704, a governor had always been appointed to Gibraltar as a representative of the British monarch. He was the de facto head of state, responsible for the swearing in of the chief minister, who was officially the man in charge.

The trouble was that of the few duties still assigned to the governor, Gibraltar's defence was one of them, and during times of terrorist threats such as the ones of late, the governor's administration had been a very busy one to say the least.

The governor's residence, or the *Convent,* as it was also known, was located at the southern end of Gibraltar's busy main street. It was a majestic stone and brick building that had originally been built by Franciscan friars in 1531. Since 1728 it had been the command centre of the Royal Gibraltar Regiment and had not seen any military action since the Second World War. It was more of a ceremonial place than anything else, its dining room renowned for the most extensive display of heraldry in the entire British commonwealth.

"I understand, sir," said Roberts into the phone, "but you must understand that this change in policy will have far reaching implications for Gibraltar. To be told with no warning whatsoever—"

He paused to listen.

"Yes, sir, I understand, but you must see that it comes as quite a shock."

Another pause.

"No sir, I'm afraid the governor's truly quite sick, sir. No, the doctor is not sure what it is. Very well sir, I'll let him know."

Roberts hung up the phone, a look of disbelief blanketing his ruddy features. He could feel his right eye blinking as it always did when he was nervous, but he knew that this time it had good reason.

In the span of just two minutes, Gibraltar had been pushed from her imperial nest, and it had happened on his watch. Roberts made his way down the long corridor to the governor's suite, knocking softly on the heavy wooden door when he arrived.

"Come in," said a voice from within.

Roberts entered quietly. A clean-shaven old man lay in a large bed before him, a stack of snow-white pillows propping him into a semi-seated position. Behind him was a prominent, oaken headboard. It was carved with the crest of the Gibraltar Regiment, a castle and key under a crown. It gave him an air of regal importance.

The room itself was spacious and brightly lit, the curtains drawn aside to reveal a view of the lush gardens outside. The chirping of birds made its way in through the open window.

"Good morning, Major," said the old commander in chief from beneath his blankets.

He had a Roman nose, dark hair, and deep-set blue eyes that still twinkled despite his poor health. He had always held a deep fondness for Roberts, and never seemed to tire of his company.

"Good morning, sir. How are you feeling? Do you sense any improvement?"

"Perhaps a little," smiled the old man, lying. "The new nurse only just left. She was quite pretty, really. Quite nice.

And speaking of pretty women, how is that little wife of yours, Major? Is she managing the renovation well? You must remind her to be very careful. A woman in her condition should not tax herself."

"I tell her that every day, sir," said Roberts. "Anita decided that she wanted to renovate the oldest house in Andalucía and have a baby all at the same time. Even still, I think she's managing remarkably well, sir. Thank you."

"It will be a seaside retreat to be reckoned with," smiled the governor. "Only yesterday she was telling me all about her new kitchen."

"The one she had to have custom made in England," said the major, exasperated. "It cost a fortune, but if it makes her happy it's well worth it, I suppose."

"Indeed, it is, Major. Indeed, it is."

The governor's voice trailed off. His tone was more serious when he spoke again.

"What news have you for me, Major?"

Roberts looked down for a moment to choose his words.

"I only just got off the telephone with Lieutenant Williams in London, sir. The news is not good. I'm afraid they've cut our military support. We'll not be seeing any British security forces here any time soon, sir."

"No, of course not," said the governor nodding. "Well, I do say this does not come as much of a surprise, now does it?"

"No, sir," said the major. "We both feared it would happen someday. Given the state they're in after the strikes, we've been told to do our best with what we've got. The lieutenant hinted that there would soon be a need for all His Majesty's forces in a retaliatory strike. Against whom or what, I'm not quite sure, sir.

"The truly shocking news is that Britain's completely given up its directorate. Gib's become her own republic, sir, at least for the time being. I was told to inform you that the Gibraltar Regiment is now under your exclusive command."

"Oh, my," said the governor, groaning in pain.

He had attempted to change his position on the bed but failed. He motioned the major to come closer.

"Richard," he said softly, patting the major's hand. "My faithful aide-de-camp. It has begun. For the time being, you must take command of this ship. I know you've got it in you. You were born and bred on the Rock, and you're my best officer. If anyone can protect Gib, it's you."

"Surely you'll be fine in a few days, sir."

"We will see, Major," said the old man weakly. "Now off you go and get to work. Remember everything I taught you."

The governor closed his eyes and immediately fell asleep, leaving Roberts sitting quietly in his chair. The major hoped against hope that the old man would recover soon. He was a true gentleman, the last of a dying breed.

Roberts walked through the Convent in a state of disbelief. The many events that had transpired that morning were still turning over in his mind. Not only was Gibraltar on its own, but in a matter of minutes, the governor had completely handed over the responsibility of its defence to him. This was no small thing, yet oddly enough, he felt up to the task. For the past three years the governor had been more a teacher and mentor to Roberts than anything else.

"Richard, I will tell you a secret," he often said. "There are powers behind the throne that seek to dominate the world by destroying it first. When they rebuild it, things will not be the same as they were before. Dark times will come, and Gibraltar will be left to defend herself. She must be prepared for the worst."

Roberts had always taken the old governor's warnings with mixed feelings. On the one hand he knew of the governor's vast political experience and his high connections. He was, after all, a Duke, and an influential one at that. But on the other hand, he was also an old man who, like many old men, thought the world was going to its destruction.

One thing was certain, however. The governor had always been in love with Gibraltar; her people, her history, and her culture. The Rock's best interests were always at the forefront of his mind. He would often refer to Gibraltar as a big magnet.

"No matter where you go," he would say with a fond wink, "she's always pulling you back to her."

Today it would appear that the governor's gloomy projections had been proven correct to a certain degree at least. Only yesterday they had received orders from England to be on high alert, a terrorist strike imminent.

The major shook his head. They were truly on their own now, and as if to punctuate his thoughts, he heard the pounding thunder of jet engines overhead. The RAF was wasting no time in bringing its fighters home.

Roberts felt a vibration in his pocket and pulled out his phone. It was his young wife calling.

"Hello, cookie," he said.

"Oh, darling," said Anita caringly. "I just got your message. What's wrong?"

"The UK's left us high and dry," he said. "Just like that. No more military support. No more governmental support. Listen, cookie, it looks like it's going to be a long day, I don't think I'll be able to make it over tonight. Why don't you come down and we'll have a nice dinner here?"

"All right," she said. "Oh, no, I can't Richard. The plumber's coming to connect the appliances. You know how long it took to get him to come. I simply can't cancel now."

"Don't even think of it," he said. "You're better off in Spain anyway. The *Levante* is terrible today."

"The bane of Gibraltar," said Anita, referring to the easterly wind that often formed a somber cloud over the Rock. "Are you sure?"

"I wouldn't have been much company tonight anyway. I'm bogged down with work. How's our little soldier?"

"He just gave me a kick," she said. "I think he knows I'm talking to you."

"Well, tell him to take it easy, and you do the same. He could come any day now."

"He's still three weeks away, you worry wart."

Roberts reached down into his pocket and produced a beeping two-way radio.

"I've got to go, darling. I've got a call coming in. We'll have a nice lunch tomorrow."

"I'll miss you."

"I'll miss you more. Now run along, I've got a million things to do."

Back at his desk, Roberts ran a hand through his short-cropped hair. He picked up the receiver of an old military telephone and used the back of his pen to punch in some numbers, giving a sigh of resignation.

One step at a time, Richard. One step at a time.

Renewed strength was pouring into the major as the shock of the news wore off. Things were not that bad. He had a full battalion of superbly trained men and plenty of ammunition and supplies, much more than would ever be needed to stave off a few random terrorist strikes. He heard the phone line engage.

"Captain Brown," he said in a commanding voice, his right eye giving a quick twitch. "I want all the officers assembled in the mess for lunch today."

There was a short pause before he continued.

"Stop asking questions. Make the necessary preparations. As of now we're on high alert. Don't screw it up."

CHAPTER 2

Sierra Nevada Mountains, Spain.

"We're on our way to visit some friends in Marbella," said Gabriel to the Spanish Guardia Civil agent.

The latter was poking his head into the car, eying Natasha as she slept. It was the third time Gabriel had been asked where they were going, and he was not about to tell them the truth.

Three hundred years after Gibraltar had officially become a British colony, the Spanish were still silently disputing its ownership. Gibraltar was not a good word to be saying to paranoid soldiers. Gabriel watched the ensign walk away and then looked over at Natasha, glad she was getting some sleep.

Having left Toledo far behind, they had been driving through a mountain pass north of Granada when they encountered the checkpoint. It had been set up at a toll station, something that did not normally occur.

The lieutenant had returned Gabriel's documentation, but for some reason they were not allowing them to depart. Having been stopped for over half an hour now, Gabriel was beginning to grow impatient.

"What a load of crap," he muttered quietly, pushing back his shaggy hair.

His eyes followed the ensign who had just been questioning them. He was walking over to speak with one of his commanding officers. Gabriel heard Natasha stir.

"What's going on?" she asked sleepily.

"They've declared martial law in Spain, and most of Europe by the looks of it."

He pointed out the commanding officer.

"That guy over there says that all foreign plated cars need special permits to circulate. Our plates are Italian. He also says that we need to produce papers that confirm our reservations in a hotel tonight. There's a curfew in effect. Nobody's allowed to be on the streets past ten."

"Gabriel," said Natasha, looking out her window. "I'm scared. This has never happened before."

"Sure, it has," said Gabriel. "Curfews were in effect during the entire second world war."

Natasha chewed her lip.

"Is that what this is? Another world war?"

"I don't know if it is technically, but if it isn't yet, I'd wager it's going to be soon. There appears to be a global crisis developing. The agent was just saying that Islamic militias have surfaced all over Europe. He says they're armed and aggressive. The newspapers published those cartoons again, and this time all hell broke loose."

"So, what'll happen now?"

"We'll wait and hope the lieutenant gives us a break," said Gabriel, turning on the radio and searching through the stations.

"You're listening to the Galaxy Network News International Radio Broadcast."

He turned up the volume. They were giving a report on the latest developments. Another nuclear suitcase bomb had detonated, this time in a Boston university. It had incinerated more than a thousand people. China had invaded Taiwan, simultaneously declaring war against the United States coalition, and condemning their attacks on Iran. Already there were scattered skirmishes happening between Chinese and American troops all over the Middle East. Many had been killed on both sides, and Russia had officially sided with China.

"This is so strange," said Natasha, still trying to come to grips with the dread she was feeling. "All our lives we've feared this would happen, and now it's happening. It's World War Three."

"It sure seems that way," said Gabriel, looking over at the ensign who had just been questioning them.

He was a few stalls over in the next toll booth and Gabriel could see him talking with his commanding officer. There was a white van parked beside them, and it had just become surrounded by half a dozen agents, their assault rifles poised and ready. By the large tarpaulin-covered load it was carrying, Gabriel guessed that it was Moroccan.

"What's that strapped to its roof?" asked Natasha.

Gabriel kept his eyes on the scene as it developed.

"Moroccan men will often head up to France and work there for several years," he said. "They save up their money to buy a van and a bunch of stuff to sell back in Morocco. With the money they make they can usually buy a small piece of land and move up in the world. It looks like they're being given a hard time."

Gabriel caught a glimpse of the driver's hardened face and in an instant knew that something was terribly wrong. He had friends who were Moroccan merchants. They were good, family-oriented people. They did not look like that.

The momentary appearance of a weathered, bearded face in the passenger seat only served to confirm his suspicions. These men were militants. He was sure of it. What they were doing here in Southern Spain he could not even begin to guess, but he did not like it in the least.

"Look," said Natasha. "Someone's getting out."

A man emerged from the back of the van just then. There was a large pack strapped to his back, and heeding his intuition, Gabriel slipped the car into reverse, glancing into the mirror to see if the way behind them was clear.

Who wears a backpack while they're on a road trip?

Gabriel pushed the accelerator to the floor and popped the clutch, keeping his eyes glued to the van as the sportscar lunged backwards. The man with the pack had just closed his eyes. He reached over and pushed Natasha below the safety of the dashboard.

"Get down!"

The rest unfolded rapidly. Seeing the terrorist's intentions, the civil agents had opened fire immediately, but the bomb detonated nonetheless, sending broken bodies and shards of metal in all directions. A second later the van itself exploded, its hidden store of ammunition igniting to produce a massive, mushroom cloud of fire and smoke.

The sportscar continued to speed backwards, shaking under the force of the blast. To the right of the van that had exploded, a delivery truck came about with squealing tires, its doors opening as several masked men spilled out. They too were armed, and they immediately opened fire on the remaining Guardia Civil troops. In a matter of seconds, a small war had erupted; a war that Gabriel wanted no part of.

"Hold on!" he said, slamming on the brakes and throwing the car into first gear.

Natasha peered up cautiously. Instead of driving away from the melee, Gabriel was heading right into it. He was accelerating directly for the tollbooth.

"Are you crazy?!" she screamed. "You're going to get us killed!"

"Not if I can help it!" barked Gabriel, flying through the narrow gate at full throttle.

The engine roared and dozens of bullets zipped past them on all sides as they flew from the toll booth, not one finding its target. In an instant the rattling machine guns had been left behind, and before them, stretching out like a promised land, lay a sunny, traffic-free autoroute. Gabriel released a long breath of relief and set the cruise control.

"Are you all right?" he asked, looking over to Natasha.

"I think so," she said, sitting up in her seat.

Gabriel shook his head.

"That was close. Sorry for screaming at you like that. I guess I got a bit spooked."

"Well, that makes two of us," she said, fixing her disheveled hair. "That was fast thinking, Gabriel."

"I just wanted to get out of there as quickly as possible. Besides, we've got to make it to Gib. Hopefully we can still get across the border."

Gabriel turned up the radio. The journalist speaking sounded more like a sports commentator than a correspondent. He shook his head again, but this time in disbelief. There were crises unfolding across the entire planet.

"This just in from the Middle East: U.S. and Pakistani forces have been overwhelmed by rogue militants in Islamabad. There are no confirmed reports, but it is feared that the entire Pakistani nuclear arsenal has fallen into terrorist hands. London Heathrow Airport has been destroyed by a series of missile attacks launched from somewhere in the United Kingdom."

Gabriel lowered the volume and used the car's voice control to dial a number.

"Boss," said Amir. "Where are you guys?"

"We'll be in Malaga soon," said Gabriel looking at the GPS.

He tapped the screen.

"If we can keep up this pace, we should be in Gib within two hours."

"Head to Estepona," said Amir. "We'll send a launch to pick you up. The Gib border's a mess. I doubt you'd get through."

"Where in Estepona do you want to meet?"

"Bar Jimmy."

"Done," said Gabriel.

"Boss," said Amir. "Are you guys all right? There are skirmishes happening everywhere in Spain. It's one of the most unstable regions in Europe right now."

"Tell me about it," said Gabriel. "We only just managed to slip out of a gun fight about fifty clicks back."

"Just take it easy. You're doing great for time. Everything's ready on this end. I'll send out a boat right now. It should be there waiting for you when you arrive."

"Amir."

"Yes, boss."

"Put a bottle of Johnny Black in the launch, would you? I'm dying for a drink."

"No worries, boss."

Gabriel terminated the call and let out a sigh. The day was turning out to be beautiful. They were heading due south now, descending out of the mountains. Straight ahead and far below the Mediterranean shimmered like a gemstone. Above them a wide-open sky cradled a warm, yellow sun.

"Look at it out there," said Gabriel. "I'd roll down the windows but at this speed we'd probably get sucked out."

They drove along the rocky coast for about an hour, the autoroute eventually winding around the city of Malaga and heading south-west along the arid Costa del Sol. The day was well under way now, and the growing traffic prevented them from achieving the speeds they had reached up to that point.

At long last they exited the autoroute and made their way into the *Puerto Deportivo* of Estepona. It was a nicely constructed marina complex, filled with bars and restaurants, and nestled amongst groupings of shady palm trees and spurting fountains.

Gabriel steered off the main path, navigating the car through some low buildings and into a hidden area where fishing boats were docked. He parked in front of a crowded little bar, filled with darkly tanned fishermen and their families. The lively sounds of *Sevillana* music filled the air.

"Bar Jimmy," said Natasha, reading the sign.

Gabriel shut off the engine and unhooked his seatbelt.

"If we didn't have to storm a castle, I'd treat you to some *Chanquetes*."

"What are *Chanquetes?*" asked Natasha, climbing out of the car with bright eyes.

"They're tiny little fish, no bigger than minnows," said Gabriel, exiting the car as well.

He opened the front hood to take out their equipment.

"They pass them through flour and deep fry them. It's all very illegal," he added with feigned severity.

"Why?" asked Natasha, stretching her body after the long drive.

Gabriel was taking up the bags, but he could not help watching her out of the corner of his eye. He loved the ballet and could recognize a schooled dancer when he saw one. Even in the simple act of stretching, Natasha's movements were elegant.

"Because the fish are just babies," he said, turning his attention back to the luggage, "and babies should be allowed to grow into fish before you eat them, I suppose. But if you know the owner of the bar, you can usually get them. It's always been like that, and they've never run out of fish."

Natasha reached for her backpack, but Gabriel shouldered it first.

"We'll have some next time," he said, leading her forward. "That and some *tinto con gaseosa.*"

"That I've had before," said Natasha, walking close by his side. "Red table wine with carbonated sugar water. It is a Spanish staple!"

They squeezed their way through a crowded dining room and around an equally busy bar. It was clad in the ornate blue and white tiles typical of Andalucía. The countertop was stainless steel and cluttered with countless varieties of tapas, its perimeters delineated by hanging legs of ham and other cured meats.

At the rear of the establishment, they passed through a door that opened onto a beachfront patio. Gabriel scanned the shore. There was no launch in sight. He looked at his watch.

"I think we might have made it here faster than Amir thought," he said. "Come on. We can grab a table and keep an eye out for them. Looks like we might have time for a little bite after all."

Gabriel pulled out one of the aluminum patio chairs and invited Natasha to sit down.

"It's so beautiful here, Gabriel," she said, scanning the shady terrace and breathing in the fresh sea air. "It seems you know this place well."

Gabriel waved at a waiter and then sat down.

"I used to live close by," he said. "I came here almost every day."

When the waiter arrived Natasha could see he was not lying. The two embraced like old friends, dealing heavy blows to each other's backs.

Gabriel spoke to him in fluent Spanish, introducing Natasha and ordering their food. In no time they were dining on the tiny fried fish he had promised. They came piled on a large plate and looked more like thinly shaved potato frites than fish. Gabriel took a big lemon wedge and squeezed it over top of the dish.

"Give them a try," he said, skewering half a dozen of the *chanquetes* with his fork.

He popped them into his mouth along with a chunk of crusty bread, leaning back in his chair as he chewed with delight.

"You eat the heads and tails too?" whispered Natasha in surprise.

Gabriel gave her a wink and took a gulp of his *tinto con gaseosa*.

"Trust me on this one," he said.

Natasha took a tiny fish on her fork, looking down at its two little eyes. They were not even the size of poppy seeds, and all was covered in light, golden batter. Her eyes lit up the moment she had placed it in her mouth. It was light and crispy and the most delicious seafood dish she had ever tasted.

"Wow," she said, tearing off a piece of bread. "I see what you mean. It's so simple, and yet so good!"

They ate contentedly, with Gabriel telling Natasha all about the time he had spent in Estepona. He had found the town while looking for a base to head up a treasure hunt. The objective had been to locate a sunken ship just off the coast. The story was fascinating.

"It was a tenth century Moorish patrol boat, about a kilometre out and thirty meters down," he said, pointing to sea. "The research we did said it was carrying twenty kilos of plundered Visigoth gold. It took us the better part of a year, but we found it."

Natasha was captivated the entire time that Gabriel told the story. She had never met anyone even remotely similar to him. His tale was engaging, his voice almost musical, and with no trace of pretension. He gave most of the credit to Amir, or to the local fishermen they had contracted to help them. In this way he related their fantastic accomplishments without seeming even remotely boastful.

Natasha laughed at the predicaments he described, and listened intently, making the occasional comment when she felt she had something to add. In the end their lunch together proved one thing to Natasha: Gabriel was a true gentleman, in every way. When her glass was empty, he filled it. Once, when her napkin had blown from her lap, he had retrieved it for her. He had even stood up when she left the table to use the restroom, and done it again when she had returned. This was unheard of.

There was only one problem with Gabriel, and it plagued Natasha the entire while. He showed no signs that he was sexually interested in her. Gabriel's indifference took her off guard and she began to feel self-conscious.

"Do you have a girlfriend, Gabriel?" she asked when a gap appeared in the conversation.

Gabriel shifted slightly in his seat.

"I have friends," he said carefully, "but nothing serious."

Natasha smiled.

"What about you?" he asked. "Have you got a *ragazzo* waiting for you in Florence?"

Natasha looked down.

"I did, but we split up a few months ago."

Gabriel nodded.

"You left him."

"I did," said Natasha. "How did you know?"

Gabriel looked out to sea.

"Only a dummy would give a girl like you the boot, and you're way too smart to date a dummy..."

Natasha arched an eyebrow.

"Was that a compliment?"

Gabriel shot her a wink.

"Simply an observation."

Natasha smiled and rubbed her chin pensively. Gabriel seemed pensive as well.

"He was a jerk, right?"

Now it was Natasha's turn to look out to sea.

"And a liar, and a cheat."

Gabriel was scanning the horizon to the southwest.

"Even though you tried to fix him."

Natasha looked over at him in surprise.

"It seems you know me well."

Gabriel shrugged.

"I've known one or two pretty women before."

"So, you're saying we're all the same," said Natasha, a little perturbed by his remark.

Gabriel remained silent.

"In what ways do you think we *pretty women* are all alike, Gabriel?"

He turned to face her, his expression serious.

"Do you really want to know what I think?"

"Yes, I do."

He poured himself some more *tinto con gaseosa* and drained the glass before speaking.

"Pretty girls always move from one boyfriend to the next," he said. "If they've been more than a month without one, they start coming apart at the seams. But that never really happens because there's always a long line of guys waiting for their turn."

Gabriel sat back and put his feet up on a neighbouring chair. Despite his best attempts to remain indifferent he could already feel old resentments coming on. He grimaced slightly.

"The only time a pretty woman ever feels good about herself is when she's got a fancy man at her side to make her feel that way."

Natasha was shocked by Gabriel's words. He was making sweeping generalizations, but despite her reluctance to admit it, they were bitingly true, at least in her case.

"Is that so," she said peevishly.

"I'm pretty sure it is," continued Gabriel, masking his bitterness with a yawn. "But instead of giving the asshole the boot, pretty girls always try to fix him. Turn him into a real man. You see it makes a girl feel noble to be so selfless. Really all she's doing is trying to compensate for the guilt she feels for having betrayed herself in the first place."

"Betrayed herself?"

Natasha could not believe Gabriel was saying these things, but she wanted to hear him out regardless.

"Sure," he said. "She betrays herself by needing to be dependent on a jerk to make her feel good about herself. She acts confident and self-assured, but she's not, and she knows it. That's why she punishes herself."

"Punishes herself?" blurted Natasha.

Gabriel was blind to her exasperation. He just nodded and looked out to sea.

"By rejecting the real guy when he comes along."

The pain in Gabriel's voice was unmistakable, and Natasha felt her anger slipping away, despite her indignation. Gabriel obviously had issues with past relationships, but this still did not give him the right to say what he had just said, as though it were true of all attractive women.

"It seems to me a pretty girl once broke your heart."

Gabriel ignored her remark and continued to look out to sea. At length he spoke, voicing a thought that had only just occurred to him.

"Maybe deep down inside pretty women don't think they're worthy of real love. So they reject the real guys, and keep trying to change frogs into princes…"

He glanced over at Natasha and then back out to sea. There was no cynicism in his words anymore, just a desire to understand. Natasha knew she had been right about his broken heart.

"So naturally, you'd never get involved with a pretty girl then."

Gabriel sat up in his chair. He had just spotted a boat coming towards them.

"I don't get involved with *any* girls," he said over his shoulder. "Period. Life's simpler that way."

Natasha cocked a suspicious eyebrow.

"You don't seem like the celibate type to me."

"That's because I'm not."

Natasha frowned. His words had opened a painful wound.

"So, you're *that* type of man, then."

"What type of man?"

"The kind who uses women for sex. The kind who are liars and cheats."

Gabriel turned and looked directly at Natasha, mirroring her frown.

"Now wait a minute," he said, leaning forward in his chair. "If I offended you, it certainly wasn't my intention. You asked for my opinion, and I gave it to you. There's no reason to be insulting."

Natasha clasped her hands over the table.

"Generally speaking," she said in earnest, "if a man wants to sleep with a woman, he has to make her believe it might go somewhere. In your case, that would be a deception, and that would make you a liar. You'd become a cheat the moment you seduced more than one woman in this way."

Gabriel held her gaze. He could see he had offended her, and it only confirmed what he already knew. Wonderful women like Natasha were off limits. Something in him prohibited them, though he could not say what it was.

"Listen, Natasha," he said. "I'm not going to tell you I haven't done what you're saying. I have, but I stopped it a long time ago. There was always someone getting hurt or feeling used, no matter how well they hid it. It got ugly."

He could hear a boat approaching behind him. By the sound of its engine, and the hull slapping against the waves, he knew it was a fast launch. The smugglers had finally arrived, but he did not want to turn away from Natasha until he had explained himself.

"So you stopped seeing women then," she said, smiling curtly. "Somehow I doubt that."

"No," said Gabriel bluntly. "I started paying women to have sex with me instead. Things have been working great ever since."

Natasha had to consciously stop her jaw from dropping. She was speechless. She would never have guessed that this would have been his response. She could only stare at Gabriel as though he were a stranger.

"I'm a whoremonger, Natasha," he said. "I know that must disgust you, and I don't blame you. It's just what I am."

He rose to his feet and Natasha followed him up, her eyes wide the entire time. She was surprised by her reaction.

Since when did I become so innocent?

"What kind of prostitutes?" she heard herself ask.

Gabriel looked at her with strained patience.

"The expensive kind, Natasha. Does it make a difference?"

They heard Amir cry out and turned to see the launch coming up on the beach. Its engine roared louder for a moment as the prop was pulled from the water.

"If it makes you feel any better," said Gabriel, looking at the boat, "you're not the typical pretty girl anyway."

"I'm not?" asked Natasha.

Gabriel shook his head.

"You're more like a plain girl who happens to be pretty."

Natasha frowned in confusion and came up speechless. Gabriel pointed to the fast launch to change the subject. It was coated in matt black anti-radar paint, and it had a stealthy, military look to it.

Together they watched Amir hop onto the sand and jog towards them, his dreadlocks contained by an Indian print bandana. He was wearing khaki cargo pants and a dark, loose-fitting sweater. A pair of military goggles hung from a strap around his neck and there was a combat knife strapped to his belt.

A serious, black-dressed pilot remained in the launch behind him, scanning the coast through a pair of binoculars.

"I can see you made good use of the downtime," said Amir, scanning the empty plates on the table as he arrived.

He and Gabriel clasped hands and embraced heartily.

"You're late, my friend," said Gabriel.

Amir shrugged and gave Natasha a courteous nod.

"A pleasure to make your acquaintance, Dr. Rossi," he said, taking her hand regally. "Gabriel failed to mention your beauty..."

Natasha smiled, still coming out of her earlier shock.

"He also failed to mention your charm, Amir."

"Jealousy and envy," he said with a charismatic wink. "He's always had a burning desire to be just like me."

Gabriel tossed a lemon wedge at him.

"What the hell took you guys so long?"

Amir shook his head in trepidation.

"It was a close call, boss. We ran into some trouble with customs boats. Two of them chased us for over an hour. The entire coast is crawling with Guardia Civil. Something's up."

Gabriel was reaching for his wallet when the owner of the establishment appeared. He was a large Andalusian man, with a generous belly and a jolly countenance.

"Dr. Parker!" he said in a thick Spanish accent, smoothing down his apron as he approached.

He propped his big hands on his hips.

"Thinking of taking off without paying again, are you? I'll have to keep that fancy car of yours!"

Gabriel laughed and gave the fat man a wholehearted embrace.

"Could you do me a favour, Jimmy?" he asked quietly.

He passed him the car keys and some folded bank notes.

"Could you put her somewhere safe for me until I get back?"

Jimmy took the keys but refused the money.

"She will be safe in the boat shed," he said. "Would you mind if I take her for a spin?"

"Go crazy," said Gabriel. "Just stay around the port. We ran through a check point back near Malaga. They might still be looking for the car."

"Some things never change with you, Dr. Parker," he said, rubbing his chin and frowning. "Always with somebody at your heels. I think I will pass on the ride, old friend, but thank you just the same. The Guardia Civil are back in their fascist element again. I want no trouble."

CHAPTER 3

Los Picos de Europa, Northern Spain.

The sun was setting rapidly as Isaac hurried to finish setting up the tent. He could see Shackleton lying next to the fire and he marvelled at the dog's ingenuity. Earlier that evening he had disappeared for twenty minutes only to come back with a plump goose in his maw, the same goose that Isaac was roasting over the fire.

It had been a full day of hiking and they had covered much ground. That morning, having eaten a good breakfast, Isaac had found himself feeling much better and strong enough to follow Shackleton's lead. Putting his trust in the dog, he had followed him faithfully, never once doubting that he would lead him to safety.

"That should do it," he said, securing the final stay and moving to the fire.

He rolled down his sleeves and put his suit jacket back on. Shackleton opened an eye as he approached.

"Shall we eat, old boy?"

Shackleton sat up immediately, licking his chops as Isaac pulled the piping hot goose from the skewer. He divided it and placed half of the steaming carcass before the dog.

"There is nothing like a barbeque to lift the spirits."

Shackleton responded with a round nod, and a lick of his chops. It was clear that he preferred his food cooked, but as the bird was still too hot for him, he laid his head down before it, his snout resting on his two paws while he waited for it to cool.

The sun dipped down and out of sight as the two of them ate, until at last they found themselves engulfed by night. Above them the Milky Way hung like a snug blanket, growing brighter with each passing minute. They had made camp in a sheltered pocket on the side of a crag, and the fire crackled merrily.

After dinner, Isaac fought back his sleepiness and took out the notebook that he had found in Father Franco's pack along with the tent. He hoped he might find some explanations in it. He desperately wanted to know why all this was happening. He produced a flashlight and shone it down on the book, opening it to its final entry.

Wednesday, December 5. — Santander — Waiting to board the floatplane.

I feel somehow comforted to know that regardless of what shall happen to us, the professor's Cube journal is safely in the post and on its way to Bishop Marcus. There have been many unexpected turns of late, and I cannot guess what awaits us at the island. The professor seems optimistic, but I fear the worst. Dark and powerful forces are at work here, and I doubt very much that they will allow us to bring an end to their sinister plan without considerable resistance.

The body of the hermaphrodite has already been loaded onto the plane, along with all the equipment we will need for both the burial, and our hike to the monastery. Mr. Rodchenko was nowhere to be found when we departed. I am convinced that his mental illness is a blessing in disguise. How could any man live with the knowledge of having conceived a child through such abominable means?

Isaac looked up from the book, a sickening dread welling in the pit of his stomach.

What does he mean?

He shrugged off his drowsiness and flipped through the book, finding many entries pertaining to something referred to as the Compostela Cube. It was not long before he came upon a loose sheet of paper. It was a photocopy of a child adoption form. Isaac had worked extensively with church orphanages before his illness. He was no stranger to their paperwork.

"This comes from the Istanbul orphanage..." he muttered, his brow furrowing.

He scanned the document. He could see that it was dated the same year that his own son had been born. He would have been in Istanbul at that time, working at the very orphanage from which the document had originated.

What are the chances of this happening? And why are two names on this paper circled?

"Gabriel Parker and Natasha Rossi..."

He had only just seen these names in one of Father Franco's previous entries, and even then, they had sounded familiar to him. He flipped back through the book until he had relocated the entry.

With these latest developments, any remaining reservations we have held concerning the connection of Gabriel and Natasha to the Compostela Cube have now been put to rest. Every element of the Ascender's Prophecy has been fulfilled.

Isaac pocketed the book and crawled into the tent. As strong as his desire to know more was, his exhaustion from the day's travels won out in the end. He could no longer keep his eyes open.

"We'll have another look tomorrow," he said, giving a gaping yawn.

Seeing that Isaac had retired, Shackleton moved to the threshold of the shelter and laid himself down. He gave the night one final sniff and then lowered his head onto his paws, loosing a long sigh before abandoning himself to sleep.

CHAPTER 4

The Atlas Mountains, Morocco.

Najiallah Nasrallah sat at his desk, his unwashed hair pulled back into a tight ponytail. He was wearing a designer suit, its shiny black material expensive, but as gaudy as his mustard-coloured shirt. He was in the act of examining an ancient map that was spread out before him.

"Where are you hiding?" he muttered.

The richness of the chart's Islamic illuminations sent thrills of excitement through him, but they also filled him with pangs of frustration. It had been this very scroll that had led him to the Compostela Cube, but despite all his efforts, he had been unable to locate the second treasure marked on its surface: A fabled Islamic codex known as the *Book of Khalifah*; an artifact he knew was inextricably bound to the Cube.

Nasrallah ran his fingers over the ancient parchment. At its centre, surrounded by Islamic texts, was an ornate diagram of the Strait of Gibraltar, showing the location of a secret cave hidden somewhere beneath the Mediterranean Sea. In that chamber resided the Book of Khalifah, hidden for centuries and impossible to locate.

He picked up the jewel-encrusted cylinder that housed the scroll and marveled at its workmanship. Even if he could never use the map to locate the Book, the scroll itself would fetch him a fortune when a buyer for it had been found. His mobile phone rang and he answered it with a curse.

"Everything is ready, Master," said a man's voice.

"Where is Bahadur?" he hissed, remembering his anger.

"He is somewhere in the plaza, sir. I do not know his exact location. We determined where we should position the snipers over the phone should Parker decide to flee."

"He is to call me immediately. He is consistently out of coverage!"

Nasrallah terminated the call.

My captain is keeping something from me...

He got up from his desk and crossed the room. These were troubled times. Each of his last hashish shipments had been intercepted by the police, and he had lost hundreds of thousands of Euros as a result. His mind raced. Who had tipped them off? There was a rat in his organization. Nasrallah rolled up the scroll and carefully inserted it into its bejeweled cylinder.

I will try to sell this to Antov along with the Cube...

Not ten days had passed since he had been approached by three Dutchmen while dining in a Tangiers hotel. They had somehow learned of his acquisition from the museum of antiquities the year before and were curious if it might still be for sale.

"Our employer has a mild curiosity for artifacts belonging to that period and would find it entertaining to purchase it from you."

Nasrallah had gone into dealings with them immediately, and by the end of the evening had settled on the cool price of one million Euros. They had arranged to make the exchange the following week, but Gabriel Parker had robbed him of the Cube before this could happen. Nasrallah ground his teeth.

He came into my home and stole from me. He will pay dearly.

Nasrallah passed a light hand over his slick head. He would not mention the scroll until the deal with the Cube had been finalized. He could not help feeling ill at ease about the transaction. His original contact, a Catholic priest named

Adrianus, had been replaced by a cold and unpredictable man named Christian Antov.

Nasrallah could not afford to make any mistakes. Already his men were complaining. They had not been paid in months, and the treasury was empty, the last of his money being diverted to settle an overdue account with furious Afghani suppliers.

Nasrallah paced around his office, unable to concentrate. There were too many things going wrong. He left the room and marched along a corridor until he arrived at a small balcony. Below him lay the boundless majesty of the Atlas Mountains. For anyone else it would have been a breathtaking view, but for Nasrallah it meant nothing. He grasped the iron railing as one of his mobile phones rang again.

"What is it?" he barked.

"Word just in from Tripoli, Master."

The man's voice was trembling nervously.

"Speak up, imbecile!"

"Our operation there has been raided," he said. "Interpol has seized everything."

A rage consumed Nasrallah. He had already arranged to sell that operation. Everything was now resting on the sale of the artifact; an artifact that he still did not possess. Unable to control his anger, he hurled the phone over the railing and into the sweeping gorge.

CHAPTER 5

Central Jerusalem, Israel.

"The Compostela Cube is not in Rome, Mr. Nasrallah," said Christian into his phone. "My predecessor might have trusted in your abilities to find it, but I do not. I'll be using my own men from now on."

Christian made his way along a sunny atrium in the Vanderhoff Group's bustling Jerusalem complex. A tired Dr. Bennington followed two paces behind, struggling to keep up.

"But there is no need, sir," implored Nasrallah, knowing that he would receive no payment if Christian's men were to find the relic first. "I have confirmation that the Cube is in Rome. My men will intercept it at any moment."

"The Cube is in the south of Spain, you imbecile!" snapped Christian, his voice tight with impatience.

"But that's impossible...," said Nasrallah. "I can assure you it is in Rome."

"You can assure me of nothing!" hissed Christian angrily. "I, however, can assure you of one thing. If you don't produce the Cube in twenty-four hours, you'll be taken prisoner and tortured."

Christian pocketed his phone. After Bennington's hypnotic trance, he had not only become fully aware of the Cube, but also of the previous Nautonnier's dealings with Nasrallah to obtain it. No sooner had their plane landed than he had called the drug lord and demanded its delivery. His father's urgent whispers were commencing in him again, fueling a frantic desire to complete the transaction.

Christian and the doctor were now descending a broad, spiraling corridor, its paneled walls lined with beautiful works of art. Below them lay a massive underground complex, housing hundreds of employees, each working in departments ranging from finance to advanced biochemical research.

This was the Vanderhoff Group's central hub of operations, a maximum-security control centre buried deep beneath the city of Jerusalem. What had emerged in the late nineteen-fifties as a crude operations fallout shelter, had grown into a state of the art, and exceptionally elegant, corporate fortress.

Christian led the doctor to the door of an elevator, oblivious of the respectful nods he received along the way. He blinked into a retinal scanner and stood aside as the doors slid open.

"After you, Doctor," he said, ushering him in.

Minutes later the elevator doors slid open again, this time revealing a luxurious lobby, flanked by two walls of heavy glass shimmering under a rippling film of water. Directly before them was the beautiful young Cynthia. She stood behind a reception desk of polished granite.

"Good morning, Mr. Antov," she chimed as he approached. "All are present and waiting for you in the main boardroom, sir."

The thirteenth level was also the deepest level and reserved exclusively for the members of the Vanderhoff Steering Committee. Here could be found not only their offices, but their living quarters as well, along with all the amenities of a five-star hotel.

Christian proceeded at a relaxed pace. He felt truly in command of himself now and was possessed of a confidence that he had never known before. As he had expected, they arrived at the boardroom to find its occupants in an outrage.

Being ordered to the Jerusalem complex on such short notice was utterly unacceptable for the venerable committee members. They had barely had time to pack. In addition to this, the current state of the geopolitical arena was spinning out of control. Global chaos was bad for business, and this fact, coupled with Christian's irrational orders, made for a very hostile environment.

All rose in anger as Christian appeared, each one reprimanding him with heated words. They were the ones who gave the orders here, not some inexperienced boy with an ego the size of Manhattan.

Christian moved to the head of the sprawling table with Bennington a pace behind, a tranquil smile on his face. All could immediately sense that their angry words were having no effect on him. This was not the same novice they had met in Amsterdam. He exuded a confidence and strength that was illusive, yet undeniable, and there seemed to be a latent power in him that struck fear into their hearts, no matter how vehemently they denied it. Within a few moments their strong words had trailed off into a murmur of muttered curses.

"I thank you all for arriving on such short notice," said Christian, inviting Bennington to sit next to him as he spoke. "I can understand that it must have been difficult for you and your families."

He gestured towards Bennington.

"This is my personal advisor, Dr. Bennington."

"Just what are you getting at, Antov?" barked an old Texan on the opposite side of the table. "Where do you get off ordering this relocation without our approval? We're on the verge of a bloody world war, boy; one that's five years ahead of schedule!"

"I have arranged both this war and this relocation with perfect timing," said Christian dryly, "and if you give me an opportunity, I will explain."

The room burst into surprised dialogue. Who did this man think he was? It had not been two weeks since he had taken his new position. What did he know that they did not? Christian waited patiently for everyone to become silent and then continued.

"As you all know, our organization dates back far beyond the fifty years that the Vanderhoff Group has been in existence," he said. "It was founded by a society that is traceable to the time of Herod, with roots that go as far back as Ancient Egypt and Mesopotamia."

All were silent. Christian knew this would not be easy, but an explanation would have to be given in order to facilitate the next stages of his agenda.

"Throughout history many have tried to wrestle our power from us, but we have never given it up, and we never shall.

"There was, however, one man who succeeded in threatening our retention of power in a way that no other has been capable of doing. Despite our greatest efforts to undermine him, he continues to be a thorn in our side. He is a threat to our ultimate plan of world domination; a plan that we have been working to fulfill for more than two thousand years."

The group of octogenarians listened intently.

"His name, my colleagues, is Jesus Christ."

At the mention of the name the room burst into a series of guffaws and outright laughter. Had this debutant lost his mind? Next, he was going to force them all to attend Sunday school. This was preposterous. Several men stood up with the intention of leaving.

"You will sit down," said Christian with icy severity, "or everything you hold dear shall be stripped from you."

So poignantly malicious were Christian's words, that the old men fell immediately back into their seats.

"It matters not whether you wish to believe in Jesus Christ or not. This is of absolutely no relevance. What is of relevance, are the original teachings that this historical figure spread; teachings that our society has been very successful in repressing and distorting over the centuries.

"As you all know, if we are to remain in power, fear must be maintained in the masses. Unfortunately, a dangerous political and spiritual movement is about to be born, and it will undermine this fear if it is not stopped."

"Christian," said an octogenarian seated close by. "Please be more specific. What movement do you speak of? Surely, you're not referring to the Christian faith?"

"The Christian faith offers no threat to us," continued Christian. "On the contrary, our alterations have made it an invaluable vehicle through which to spread the fear and guilt needed to secure subservience.

"No, gentlemen. I am not referring to Christianity, but rather to the pre-Egyptian body of knowledge that was promulgated by the upstart Jesus Christ more than two thousand years ago. A body of knowledge that will be delivered to the entire world if the Compostela Cube is not recovered and destroyed at once!"

Again, the room burst into a frenzy, but this time one of utter disbelief. The lost Compostela Cube was a name familiar to them all. It belonged to a legend that was as old as their society. It was the harbinger of their doom. It was their nemesis. But this was only a legend, nothing more.

"With all due respect, Christian," said an old man, attempting to be reasonable. "You are now going too far. How can you expect us to take you seriously? The Cube is a myth."

The man looked around at his counterparts.

"Next you'll be telling us that the extra-terrestrials are coming."

They all laughed.

"The Cube of Compostela has been found," announced Christian amid their jeers, and in a split second every mouth had become silent, their faces aghast with disbelief.

Like any secret society, theirs too had its traditions and ceremonies, but they had lost their original meanings long ago. For generations the same words had been uttered: Ahreimanius, the Zurvanites, the Compostela Cube; but only as one might utter the name of an obsolete god. They were not real. They were stories. Fictions.

Nevertheless, many eyes fell on the coat of arms inlayed in the centre of the sprawling conference table. It bore an image of Set, the Egyptian god of chaos, surrounded by fourteen red eyes. Under Set's foot was the Cube of Compostela, and in the demon-god's upraised hands a spherical cage could be seen, with the fettered earth within it. It was from this image that the symbol for the United Nations had originated.

To all but very few, the secret society of Set had long ago become a society of business and politics, the Vanderhoff Group becoming its new face. Even still, in their vows of initiation, each member was made to swear a pledge of allegiance to their lord and master, Ahreimanius.

In this pledge, a promise was duly made to recover the Cube and destroy it. This was the first mission of every priest upon inception, a ceremonial rite that appeared, only now, to be revealing its true purpose.

"The Compostela Cube is a legend!" asserted a baldheaded man, breaking the silence. "It does not exist!"

"It is as real as this table!" affirmed Christian, bringing his fist down on the dark wood. "Our deceased Nautonnier, the late Father Adrianus Vanderwerken, was on the verge of acquiring it when it was stolen from under his very nose! It currently resides in the south of Spain and is in the possession of *The Two*!"

"Impossible!" exclaimed another man.

The Two had been mentioned in the legends as well. They were the sworn enemies of their society.

"Oh, come now!" exclaimed yet another. "Enough of this nonsense!"

"What proof have you got?" demanded the old Texan.

"The appearance of the Zurvanites is proof enough," replied Christian more quietly now.

"The Zurvanites?" balked the old man. "Are you mad?"

Christian watched as the men at the table began to whisper and chuckle quietly amongst themselves. He could sense the fear that lurked beneath their laughter, and as the merriment increased, it became clear to Christian that they were all in denial.

"Why, we're the Zurvanites!" cried one of them in jest.

"Be silent!" bellowed Christian, and his fury silenced them all. "I am the new Nautonnier!" And just as the prophecy foretells, I come to lay waste!"

With Christian's final words, there came an end to the merriment. Any remaining smiles had now vanished from the faces of the committee, replaced by their usual dry expressions. Time was money, and the destruction of the earth was bad for business. Their new director had obviously lost his mind.

In unison, every member of the group rose to his feet and proceeded to make ready to leave, shaking their heads in disbelief.

"If you're the Nautonnier, then I'm Peter Pan," said the old Texan.

"We'll be contacting the extended Vanderhoff group and informing them of your resignation, Christian," said another. "You've been reading too many of the initiation books, son."

"They're just stories, boy!" said a member who must have been in his nineties. "What you need is a nice long vacation."

Christian had anticipated such a response and had made the necessary preparations. He produced his mobile phone and sent a text message. Within seconds, armed security guards appeared at the door, sending a wave of surprise through the group of old men.

"Have you lost your mind?" exclaimed one of them. "Have you forgotten who we are?"

"You are nothing!" snapped Christian.

"This is madness!" cried another, holding the side of his head.

He had attempted to make his way past the guards and been delivered a backhanded blow.

"You will receive no assistance from us!" said another of the group, outraged.

"Oh, but I will," said Christian, growing calm again. "Of this you may be certain. You see gentlemen, you all possess something that I do not: Loved ones. Every one of you has family members who happen to be my guests in this facility, is that not correct?"

"What are you getting at, Antov?" said the old Texan. "By God, if you do anything to them—"

"I will rape your little virgin granddaughter before your very eyes, you arrogant fuck!" said Christian viciously. "You will all comply! The Zurvanites have come, and together we will destroy the earth! And when it lay in waste, we will build it up again as the Great Prison Planet of Ahreimanius!"

"You're mad!" cried out several of them in unison.

All eyes found Dr. Bennington.

"What have you done to him?" they demanded. "You're responsible for this!"

Dr. Bennington looked back at them pleadingly. It was true. He was responsible. Had he not hypnotised Christian, none of this would have transpired. He had awakened a slumbering fiend.

Bennington's eyes scanned the group of octogenarians. They were surrounded by security personnel, and he could not help but feel a certain compassion for them. As unscrupulous as they might be, they did not deserve to be used as pawns in the destruction of human civilization. The doctor hung his head in defeat.

"The Vanderhoff Group will lead the world into oblivion," said a fully composed Christian. "And just as the masses are molded by our media, so will the extended Vanderhoff Group be molded by those in this room. Like the rest of humanity, they too will serve our needs, ushering in a New World Order that will secure our dominion forever."

Christian moved to the centre of the table and planted both hands down on it in a dictatorial pose.

"I am the new Nautonnier," he said through steely eyes, "and from the ancient chamber of the *Kadosh Hakodashim* I shall rule the world. You will all bow to me."

And looking past their pale faces, Christian directed his attention to the head guard.

"Take them away," he said, yawning. "And bring me wine."

CHAPTER 6

Gibraltar.

Major Richard Roberts opened the throttle of his motorcycle and accelerated past the traffic that clogged Winston Churchill Avenue. It was always a busy route to the Spanish frontier, but today it was at a standstill. A foreboding dread had engulfed the Rock that morning, and it was not just the growing storm clouds that were responsible for it.

Roberts squinted into the gloom. Gibraltar, it would appear, was on the verge of being invaded.

"Major," came the crackling voice over his radio. "More Guardia Civil forces are arriving."

"Keep them on their side," he said into the receiver, his right eye twitching. "Form a line if necessary. Under no circumstances are they to cross the frontier. Is that clear?"

"Yes, sir," said the officer. "We will hold them back."

The major traversed the long stretch of tarmac that comprised the airport runway and blasted through the gates, racing alongside a queue of pedestrians. Thunder assaulted him as he arrived at the frontier, and even though he had known what to expect, seeing so many Spanish agents so close to the Gibraltar side of the border sent a wave of surprise and anger through him.

They've gone too far this time.

He navigated his motorcycle through the crowds until he arrived at the main border crossing. It was there where he found Captain Brown. Just like Roberts, he was clothed in dessert combat dress and body armour.

THE LAST ARTIFACT

"Where's their commanding officer?" asked Roberts, dismounting.

"He's standing beside the customs entrance, sir," said Brown, pointing to the place.

Roberts nodded and turned to see several Gibraltar Regiment troop transports approaching fast. They were on the runway, their engines roaring as they raced towards them. Roberts put his hand on Brown's shoulder.

"Follow me, Captain."

"You will remove these men and let us pass at once!" ordered the Spanish officer, gesturing to the two dozen Gibraltar regiment troops that blocked the way.

"We'll do nothing of the sort," replied Roberts. "You've no authority to occupy positions on Gibraltar soil."

"We have been authorized by the European Union to deploy anti-terrorism forces throughout the entire Spanish Peninsula!"

The officer handed Roberts an official looking document stamped with the seal of the Spanish Civil Guard. Among many things, it stated that being a geographical part of the peninsula, Gibraltar fell under Spain's anti-terrorism jurisdiction.

"This does not originate from the government of Spain," said Roberts, returning the paper. "It comes from the Spanish Civil Guard. You have no authority to be conducting this operation."

"Yes, we do!"

Roberts shook his head in disbelief.

"I will consult with the E.U. concerning this issue. Until then, stand down. This is an official border crossing, and it must remain open."

"Spain's border is closed! It will only be reopened when we have occupied our positions!"

A violent clap of thunder shook the air.

"This is British soil," said Roberts, turning to leave. "I won't have it occupied by fascist paramilitary forces."

He had no sooner said this than things changed very quickly. A man emerged suddenly from the crowds on the Spanish side, not ten meters away. He wore a backpack and was crying out in Arabic. Before anyone could react, he had crossed the border and moved into the crowds on the Gibraltar side.

"Get down!" bellowed Roberts.

A deafening explosion shook the earth, and the crowds dispersed in both directions, leaving a mass of mutilated bodies littering the tarmac. Seconds later, a deluge of rain exploded from above, the coursing water mixing with the blood of the victims.

A handful of Guardia Civil agents took advantage of the resulting mayhem to cross into Gibraltar, taking up positions in one of the customs buildings along the frontier. Shots were exchanged, and within seconds a small war had erupted.

With the arrival of the Gibraltar Regiment troop transports, defensive positions were immediately established. All knew exactly what to do. The defence against a possible Spanish invasion at the frontier was one of the first scenarios to be learned by any new soldier in the regiment.

In a matter of seconds, the major and captain had retreated to a defence post that they knew would be there when they arrived.

"Captain!" bellowed Roberts over the rattling gunfire and thunder. "Relay these orders! Full deployment of *Siege Defence 1704*, effective immediately across the entire Rock perimeter!"

"Yes, sir!" bellowed Brown through the downpour.

Roberts watched the captain disappear into the tumult and made his way to where the temporary command post would soon be set up. He arrived to find it almost entirely assembled.

In the ten minutes that had passed since the skirmish had begun, tents had already been set up with important equipment rolling out of trucks, and a flurry of military technicians buzzing about.

The countless drills had proven effective, and in another five minutes the command post would be fully operational. As it was, they had already set up Roberts' field desk.

"Good work, boys," he said, watching as a battery of monitors lit up before him.

They contained feeds from cameras along the entire frontier, as well as from up the rock. Roberts studied the images more closely, not liking what he saw.

A dozen Guardia Civil agents were installed in the Gibraltar customs building. By taking this position, they had flanked the first defence post, and were currently exchanging fire with them. Roberts knew that it would not be difficult to flush them out. The tricky part would be doing it with as few casualties as possible.

They had been fired upon, and one of their men was down. He had the legal right to retaliate. The surveillance cameras would prove it. But this was not about killing. He wanted no more blood spilled. At that moment Captain Brown entered the tent, breathing rapidly and drenched from head to foot.

"Major Roberts, sir," he said. "The perimeter is now secured. We have isolated the forces in the customs building. What are your orders?"

Roberts pointed to one of the monitors.

"It looks like they could be planning a frontal attack to the west of the frontier," he said, and just then a violent thunderclap shook them. "I want that customs building hit and hit hard. Flush those bastards out of there immediately. Use delta tactics. I want them taken prisoner before the Guardia Civil gets any ideas of what to do with them."

"Yes, sir!" said Brown, turning to leave.

"And Captain," said Roberts, his right eye giving a quick wink. "Get me a casualty report."

"Yes, sir."

Roberts sat back in his chair and took a deep breath. It was imperative that he think clearly. As additional monitors were set up, he could see more and more of what was happening around the entire Rock. Gib was no stranger to attacks, and it was now fully mobilized.

Historically, Gibraltar had always been a bastion of British sea power, controlling virtually all naval traffic into and out of the Mediterranean Sea. The six square kilometre rock had been designed to withstand attacks from land, sea, and air, and housed a labyrinth of more than eighty kilometres of internal tunnels.

There were also massive caverns blasted out of the limestone. They comprised what was, in essence, a small underground city; barracks, mess halls, theatres, offices, a fully equipped hospital, and room for all of Gibraltar's thirty-three thousand residents. Roberts released a long breath.

Calm, cool, and collected, Major.

On the array of monitors before him, Roberts could see as much activity happening within the rock as without. Scattered over much of Gibraltar were gun installations. The Rock was literally bristling with them. Dozens were housed within heavy fortifications, many others cut into the sheer cliffs themselves, and all were fed by an extensive network of supply tunnels that were coming to life as he watched. Roberts could not help but smile.

The complex was extensive, boasting heavy ordinance, anti-aircraft guns, and state of the art surveillance systems, not to mention huge caches of ammunition, food, fuel, and medical supplies. Over the past three years the governor had worked diligently to revitalize the tunnels and bring the underground city back into a fully functioning military complex, something it had not been since the end of the Second World War.

"There are hard times coming," the governor had always said when asked about his tunnel restoration project. "When the crisis arrives, we must be ready to meet it."

It had been the governor's personal assets that had funded most of the renovations, including the excavation of residential galleries in the new lower level. Having never had a family of his own, the governor had adopted Gibraltar as his heir, and could see no better way to use up his enormous fortune than to prepare her for a storm that he was convinced would come.

"Casualty report, Major," came a voice from behind Roberts. "One KIA. Three more WIA."

"Who did we lose, Private?" asked Roberts, turning to face the soldier.

A series of lightning blasts lit up the tent, followed by an earth-shaking clap of thunder. Roberts saw the man's lips move but heard nothing.

"Who?"

"Private Morrison, sir!" he repeated.

Roberts slumped back in his chair, running his hands over his face. Morrison had only been twenty-one years old. He looked up at the monitor in time to see the customs building falling under attack. Tear gas was being used to flush the enemy out.

So far so good.

Roberts looked down at his pocket. His mobile phone was ringing.

"Is everything all right?"

It was Anita who spoke.

"Where are you?" asked Roberts, sitting up with concern.

"I'm still here," she said. "Gibraltar was just on the news. Everyone in town is talking about it. They're saying there's been a terrorist attack at the frontier. What happened?"

"Just that, cookie," he said, rubbing his eyes. "A suicide bomber. The problem is that the Guardia Civil are using the attack as an excuse to try and put anti-terrorism troops on our soil."

"Are things very bad?"

"Not really," lied Roberts. "They could be a lot worse. We'll have things set straight soon enough."

"Oh, darling," said Anita. "I'm scared."

"Don't be, cookie," said Roberts. "Everything will be fine. I'll call you later today and let you know how things are going."

"Be careful."

"I will."

CHAPTER 7

In the Strait of Gibraltar.

"Something's up," said Gabriel to Natasha.

They were sitting at the back of the fast launch. He had to speak into her ear to be heard over the roaring engines.

"I'll be right back."

Although unsure of the cause of the disturbance, Natasha was certain that something was not right. They were in open seas now, and the distant coastline was barely visible under a mass of angry black clouds. Amir was with the pilot at the front of the launch. He was talking on the radio.

Natasha watched Gabriel make his way to the bow of the lurching boat, his shaggy hair flying in the wind. Amir had just put down the radio. She could see them talking and could feel Gabriel's sudden concern.

Far to the right she could make out Gibraltar, rising from the sea like a faint triangular mountain. Above it, black clouds rippled with lightning. The Rock was under a massive stormfront. Perhaps this was why they were so far from the coast.

"There's been a change in plans," said Gabriel when he returned.

"What's happened?"

"A renegade branch of the Guardia Civil has used a terrorist strike as an excuse to occupy Gibraltar. The government of Spain's denouncing them, but they can't do anything about it. They can't spare the troops."

"That's insane. Did they get in?"

Gabriel sat down next to her.

"A dozen or so are holed up in a customs building. The border's closed and a Gibraltarian soldier's dead."

Natasha looked out at Gibraltar's grey-blue form. It seemed more like a ship of war than a land mass.

"So what happens now?" she asked. "That looks like a dangerous storm."

"It's coming from the south and moving northwest," said Gabriel, squinting into the wind. "We should be all right if we stick to our heading. Bahadur and his men left the Rock as soon as the trouble started. The sea around Gib is crawling with patrol boats now. It's a full-blown siege."

"Where's Uncle Marcus?" asked Natasha with concern. "And Suora and Fra?"

"They're in Gib but I wouldn't worry. That rock is the ultimate fortress. It's never been taken."

"And Bahadur and his men?"

"Moving towards the Moroccan coast as we speak. Our paths should intersect in about forty minutes. There's good news though, a chance we might be able to get the hostages out without doing any fighting."

"Really?" asked Natasha. "How can that be?"

"It would appear Nasrallah's belly up," said Gabriel. "He's broke. Hasn't been able to pay his men in months. Bahadur's already started secret negotiations to hire them all."

"Bahadur must be rich."

"He hasn't got a cent."

"Where will he get the money?"

"It looks like my father gave Marcus a stash of unstamped gold coins to keep for him," said Gabriel, shaking his head in amazement. "He'd found them in a sunken Roman merchant ship back in the day, and as they had no historical value, he decided to hold onto them. They were going to use them to buy the Cube, but since we've already got it—"

"We can use it to hire Nasrallah's men out from under him," interjected Natasha.

Gabriel shrugged.

"The gold should get Amir's family out safely," he said. "And some of those new recruits could help us get up to that labyrinth."

Natasha nodded in understanding.

"Spain's become a very dangerous place these days. An escort would be good."

Gabriel frowned.

"Marcus also hinted that some powerful people want us dead."

Natasha's expression mirrored his.

"They want the Cube..." she said, looking out to sea.

She recalled an entry she had skimmed over in the professor's journal. It had spoken of the existence of a dark organization, sworn to destroy the Cube. When she turned back to face Gabriel, he was holding two glasses and a small bottle of whiskey.

"Would you like a cocktail?"

Natasha remembered how he had asked Amir to bring it along and smiled at his foresight. She hated whiskey but a drink would probably do her good.

CHAPTER 8

The Mediterranean Sea, North-African Coast

It was only when they were right upon them that Natasha could make out the dozens of launches speeding over the sea to the south. She saw Amir point to them just as the pilot aimed the boat in their direction, its hull responding with an explosion of foaming seawater.

Unbeknownst to her, they had converged precisely as planned, not two kilometres from the city of Tetouan, their designated landing point.

Covered in their light absorbing anti-radar paint, the smuggling launches were difficult to see at first, even in the broad daylight. As they drew closer, Natasha was at last able to study them in more detail, observing the many occupants that filled them.

"Look, Gabriel!" she cried out, pointing to the launch at the head of the pack.

Sitting at its stern were three tiny figures, oddly out of place among the pirate-like men surrounding them.

"What the hell are they doing here?" exclaimed Gabriel, laughing with surprise.

It was as if the unexpected occupants had heard him speak. No sooner had Gabriel cried out than he could see them waving happily. Bishop Marcus, Fra Bartolomeo, and Suora Angelica, all smiling excitedly.

In fast launches, and on open seas at that their age? Have they gone insane?

Despite their concern, Gabriel and Natasha's hearts were filled with joy at the sight of them. In a matter of seconds, the boats had drawn together, their hulls bobbing up and down in the mid-sea swells.

"Ahoy!" cried the old bishop. "Well met, my dear ones!"

"Uncle Marcus!" cried Natasha in delight. "You're crazy!"

The bishop feigned consternation.

"Do you think I was going to let this man run away with all of our gold?" he exclaimed, resting a hand on Bahadur's massive back.

His response was deep and booming.

"Never have I met three more delightful bankers! Now follow our boat! The sooner we land, the better!"

They were soon speeding their way into Tetouan, its shining white beaches drawing nearer with every passing second. It was a small city, ancient by all standards, and built at the feet of the Atlas Mountains. Its clutter of whitewashed walls and green tiled roofs could be seen perfectly from their vantage point, a tangle of tight little streets and ornate balconies covering the hilly terrain like a textured quilt. The sky was clear and blue.

"What happens now?" asked Natasha over the roaring wind.

Gabriel shrugged and looked her way just as an explosion of seawater came up to douse them both. Natasha was having to hold on tightly now. The waves were getting choppier as they approached the coast, and it seemed like the speeding launch was spending about half its time in the air. Gabriel moved a little closer.

"We'll land in some dodgy place, no doubt," he cried, studying the lie of the approaching land. "Then we'll be shuttled off to Nasrallah's digs by a pack of cutthroats and pirates!"

Natasha beamed.

"How wonderful!" she cried. "And where exactly might these *digs* be located?"

"Up there!" cried Gabriel, pointing to the towering peaks, "About a three hour drive in from the coast!"

Gabriel's prediction proved to be more accurate than he had expected. After entering a sheltered fishing port, the procession of launches was soon taxiing into a grouping of dilapidated boat houses that stank of fish.

They were greeted by a motley group of rogues, the leader of which spoke only to Bahadur. Ten minutes later the same men were leading the way into a neighbouring garage where several Land Rovers were parked. Gabriel, Natasha, and the three elders entered one of the trucks, with Amir taking the driver's seat.

"Together again!" exclaimed the old bishop from the back seat, adjusting his vestments.

He reached forward, excitedly rubbing Gabriel and Natasha's shoulders.

"It would appear the adventure continues!"

"I'd say," said Gabriel, turning in his seat to face the three of them. "And what made all of you decide to come along?"

"I'm afraid it was my idea," said Suora timidly. "I felt that Mother Mary wanted us to come along. Why, I cannot say..."

"I only hope that we will not be a burden to you," said Fra, squeezing the old nun's knee. "When this woman gets set on something, there is no changing her mind."

"You could never be a burden, Fra," said Natasha. "And I'm glad that you acted on your intuition, Suora. An inspiration from the Blessed Virgin should never be ignored."

Compared to the strife that plagued the rest of the world, Morocco was a bastion of peace and tranquility. As they made their way up into the fertile mountains, one would never have suspected that the world was at war.

They were entering into Berber country now, home to an ancient people who lived in ways little changed from their original culture. The keepers of these lands spoke the same language and farmed using the same methods they had used since the times of ancient Egypt.

"The home of *Taric el Tuerto*," said Gabriel, rolling down his window to let in the mountain air.

"Taric the who?" asked Natasha.

"Taric the one-eyed," he said. "At least, that's what the Spanish called him. He was the Berber general who led the conquest of Visigothic Spain in 711, one of the greatest generals in history. His invasion was the best thing that could have ever happened to Spain, and to the rest of Europe for that matter."

"Why's that?" asked Natasha.

Gabriel surveyed the passing countryside, his shaggy hair blowing in the wind.

"The Moors brought everything that was needed to pull Europe out of the dark ages," he said. "No small feat considering the stranglehold the Vatican had on everybody at the time. It's thanks to the Arabs that European culture is what it is today."

As they bounded and bumped up the twisting mountain road, Gabriel talked about the Golden Age of Islam, an age of freedom and enlightenment, and he outlined some of the numerous influences that would eventually find their way into every culture on the planet.

For seven hundred years, he explained, Islam would cultivate art, science, philosophy and literature in Spain, making monumental advances in agriculture, law, medicine, technology, astronomy, and economics.

"It's no small coincidence that the Renaissance coincided perfectly with the re-conquering of Spain," he added. "As each of the Moorish cities fell into Christian hands, so did their vast libraries. Think about it. The world would never have known about Plato, and all the ancient Greeks for that matter, if it wasn't for the Arabic translations the Christians had captured. The Church had destroyed everything heretical centuries before."

Their convoy plodded its way higher and higher into the mountains. Behind them, and across a shimmering sea, lay a spectacular view of the Spanish mainland, with a storm enshrouded Gibraltar standing majestically at its prow. It would not be long now before they arrived at Nasrallah's castle. Its structure could be seen directly above them, a small square of timeworn stone atop a ragged peak.

"I sure hope Bahadur fixed things right," said Amir, a cinnamon toothpick clenched in his teeth. "I'd hate to have to get into a gunfight now. It would ruin our little trip."

Gabriel looked skeptical.

"I saw them loading an arsenal of weapons into the Land Rovers back at the boat house."

"Bahadur doesn't like taking chances, boss," said Amir. "But things'll go smooth. Gold makes people pretty friendly when they're passing it around."

Amir pulled up behind Bahadur's truck. The convoy had come to a stop and a pack of thirty or so armed ruffians had already assembled on the road, kicking up dust and checking their weapons. Bahadur approached Amir's side of the Rover, motioning for them to remain inside. Moments later his big head was poking in through Amir's open window.

"I trust that everyone has had an agreeable ride and that my cousin's driving was not too unpleasant?"

"He has done an excellent job," said Suora, her face lighting up at the sight of the giant.

Bahadur smiled tenderly at the old nun.

"It pleases my heart to hear that, Sister."

He turned his attention to Gabriel and Amir in the front seat.

"I will be continuing on foot with my men," he said, his voice taking on a deep and serious tone. "Amir, you will come with us. The rest of you will remain here until we send word. Please do not leave this truck."

"What are you talking about?" asked Gabriel. "I'm the one who caused this whole mess. You can't expect me to just sit here and do nothing."

"Dr. Parker," said Bahadur in earnest. "I can understand your wanting to help but your presence would only confuse the men. This is not about the Cube or my family for them. It is about changing their loyalty. You have done enough by financing this endeavor. Stay here and leave the rest to me. This is more a political exercise than anything else."

"Listen to him, boss," said Amir, clasping Gabriel's forearm. "He knows what he's doing."

"If all goes as it should," said Bahadur, "we will meet with our contacts outside the castle and show them the gold. After that, the only remaining objective will be to capture Nasrallah. For that we have more than enough men."

With that Bahadur reached in with a massive hand and gave Gabriel a heavy pat on the shoulder. He bounded off before Gabriel could respond.

"Stay put," said Amir, tying back his dreadlocks and leaving the truck. "Everything will be fine."

From their vantage point in the Land Rover, they could see Bahadur strapping guns and ammunition to his bulking body. Though he was by far the most powerful man in the group, his authority was founded more in respect than in his physical size. Bahadur was not like the other smugglers. He was intelligent and well-spoken, and would have led the life of an academic if the fates had been more kind. As a boy, he had dreamed of becoming a university professor, but being the son of a smuggler captain had made that impossible.

Having watched the armed party disappear into the rugged terrain, Natasha turned in her seat to face the old bishop.

"Gabriel and I only had a chance to skim through the professor's journal on the way down. Did you read it all, Uncle Marcus?"

"I did, my child," said the old bishop. "I spent all of last week studying it but I could hardly say I know it well."

Gabriel turned in his seat and told them everything he and Natasha had learned from the old gypsy woman. He explained the extinction level event that would soon take place, and told them of their impossible mission to find the Labyrinth of Sarras before the crossing of the Dark Rift occurred.

Suora immediately began to pray silently, but Bishop Marcus seemed more concerned with the note that had led them to the *Bodega Del Pi*.

"I must have missed it entirely," he said, baffled. "And I was of the belief that I had visited every page in the journal. It is a good thing that it found you."

Natasha could not bear the suspense any longer.

"Where is the Labyrinth of Sarras, Uncle Marcus?" she asked. "Did the professor know?"

The old bishop frowned.

"Yes," he said, "but that information died with him and Father Franco I'm afraid. All that we know is that the entrance to the Labyrinth is located on the same island where the tomb of St. James the Just was found."

"Yeah," said Gabriel. "We already figured that part out."

"So how do we find the island?" asked Natasha. "And even if we do find it, and we somehow manage to return the Cube to its original resting place, how are we supposed to pass through the labyrinth and open all the seals?"

With the day moving on, the sun fell heavily on the truck. The bishop looked over and spied a shady patch of grass beneath the cover of some trees. It was not far from where they were parked.

"What say you all to a picnic?"

"But your Excellency," said Fra, his Italian accent particularly thick in his distress. "Bahadur has told us not to leave this vehicle."

"Oh, come now!" said the old bishop, nudging the brother with his shoulder. "Don't be a stick in the mud! Since when were you one to follow orders from anyone but our divine Father in heaven?"

"Fra," said Suora, delivering a weak blow to his other shoulder. "A picnic would be lovely."

"Well," said the old brother reluctantly, thinking of the cooler in the back of the truck. "I did pack a bit of lunch before we left Gibraltar. Now would be a good time to eat it I suppose…"

"Done!" exclaimed the bishop. "Bring out that journal, child! We shall study it over a nice bottle of wine and some food. I am certain that it will yield all the answers we require!"

CHAPTER 9

Central Jerusalem, Israel.

Dr. Bennington followed Christian through the complex, but he was hard pressed to keep up with his pace. In the fifteen minutes since the boardroom meeting had ended, they had done nothing but walk. During that short span of time the doctor had witnessed a drastic change come over Christian.

It was as if a metamorphosis were taking place before his eyes. Gone were the subtle traces of Christian's self-doubt and fear. They had been replaced by a cold wickedness that seemed to radiate from every pore in Christian's body. Even his facial features had altered to suit, his paleness intensifying, and his eyes becoming hard and cruel.

Bennington battled his fear with professionalism. The dark self that Christian had spoken of had clearly taken over. It was difficult to pinpoint, but there was something about Christian that reminded him of a reptile, a cold-blooded predator. It was as if Christian's inner-demons were altering his physical appearance. Bennington had seen similar transformations in patients before, but never to this extent.

"Please, Christian," he said, breathing rapidly. "I cannot keep up this pace."

Christian made no reply but in that instant the doctor felt as though something were suddenly pushing him along, as though a strong wind were now at his back.

This is uncanny. Is it possible that he has developed telekinetic abilities? What other powers has he been given? Where is he taking me?

"I have been given nothing that was not mine to begin with," said Christian. "And in answer to your second query, I am taking you to a laboratory. Our scientists have been working on a virus for more than fifteen years now, and it has come to my attention that they have at last been successful with it."

They arrived shortly at an elevator and used it to ascend several levels, moving past a crowded reception desk and into a broad and sterile looking hall. To their left were the entrances to the employee decontamination rooms. Christian did not pass into these chambers, but instead approached a door situated directly next to them.

On the wall was a glowing hologram, a semi-spherical dome about the size and colour of an orange, positioned at head level. Christian stopped before it, a series of pulsating lasers scanning his face to confirm his identity. Seconds later he was leading the way through a thick metal door. It opened into a long glass tunnel, and Dr. Bennington was amazed by what he saw.

A dozen meters below them was an enormous underground cave, teaming with bustling scientists amid batteries of equipment.

"This is where some of the world's most advanced scientific research is conducted," said Christian, resuming his brisk pace as they made their way along the tunnel. "As you just saw with the facial scanner, we have already perfected the holographic interface, but there is much, much more."

"Why have you brought me here?" asked Bennington, struggling once again to keep up.

"Because I enjoy your company, Doctor," said Christian dryly. "I need to be here, and I thought you might come along."

They walked until they came to a second door of thick steel.

"This is the executive decontamination room," said Christian, blinking into another holographic scanner. "Here we will not have to remove any of our clothing. Instead, we will be exposed to a mild radiation. I assure you it is completely safe."

They entered what looked like a perfectly normal waiting room, containing several armchairs and a sofa. Christian invited the doctor to be seated, and then sat himself down as well. The only thing that seemed out of the ordinary in the room was a monitor over the door. On it were digits counting down from ten minutes. Bennington made himself comfortable in his chair. He was thankful for an opportunity to rest.

"Tell me, Christian," he asked. "How is it that you can know my thoughts?"

Christian raised an eyebrow. The answer to Bennington's question had only just occurred to him.

"Thoughts inhabit a field that exists outside of physical parameters," he said. "You might compare this field to magnetism. Both are invisible yet detectable by other means. If the mind is free of its own thoughts, it can sense the thoughts of others.

"Your thoughts appear to me as if they were my own, but as I know that I am not generating thoughts in my mind, it becomes clear to me that these thoughts belong to you.

"Like your thoughts, I can also feel your emotions. You are becoming more interested in me, Doctor. You are puzzled at how I can be so congenial, and yet so wicked at the same time."

"Yes, Christian, I am," said Bennington. "You've changed, and I'm hopeful that you'll now choose to use this newfound power to aid humanity instead of destroying it."

Christian smiled coldly.

"Humanity will be aided through its domination. This is what humanity wants and needs."

"How can that be, Christian?" asked the doctor. "The wish for freedom resides in the heart of every man, woman, and child."

"Yes," said Christian, "this is true. But the wish to obtain this freedom without paying the price for it also exists in every man, woman, and child."

"What do you mean? What price?"

"The price for freedom is responsibility, Doctor. I would think you would have discovered that by now. Humanity does not wish to be responsible for itself. It wants to do as it pleases, much like a child, and suffer no consequences for its actions. At best, people want an efficient government to carry the burden of their lives, at worst, they yearn for some god that will serve them like a magic genie. What rubbish."

Bennington was amazed. In all the years he had treated Christian, he had never heard him speak like this.

"The irony is that every living person could have all the freedom they desired, if they only took their lives into their own hands, but they are too lazy and frightened to do so. Because of this humanity requires a master, and a master it shall have in its new government."

"But your new government is built on lies and deception, Christian. How could that be good?"

Christian laughed coldly.

"In this world there is only one thing that is good," he said. "The good that comes from holding power over others. This is Earth, Doctor, not some fairy tale land. Wake up. Your god is dead, and even if he does live, he doesn't care about us. The state of the earth, with all its poverty and injustice, offers clear enough proof of that."

Bennington considered his words before replying.

"Faith, hope, and perseverance empower us to evolve out of these conditions."

"There is no hope!" asserted Christian. "There is no faith! There is only survival. You and me and every other pathetic creature on this planet belong to only one master.

We vowed allegiance to him aeons ago. His name is Lucifer, and he is our jailor."

Christian produced a cigarette and lit it, inhaling deeply.

"This is our lot, Doctor," he concluded, releasing a cloud of smoke. "Domination is our only saviour, not some weak little man hanging from a cross. Not some Indian telling us to weave our own clothing. What nonsense!"

Just then a chime sounded, and Dr. Bennington looked up to see that the time on the clock had elapsed.

"Come with me," said Christian rising. "I will show you the future."

CHAPTER 10

Los Picos de Europa, Northern Spain.

"How I would love to know where you are taking me, my friend," said Isaac, looking above him to see Shackleton standing at attention.

The dog was perched atop a large boulder not ten meters away, and at first glance it seemed to Isaac that there was an aura of light surrounding the animal, one that disappeared the moment he attempted to verify its existence.

"Just give me a chance to catch up," he complained, resuming the climb. "A slave driver is what you are…"

Considering Isaac's weakened state, they had made very good progress. Two days had passed since they had left the island behind, but instead of making their way down to the coast, Shackleton had been leading them higher into the mountains. Isaac followed faithfully. It was clear the dog had a plan, and that he would soon be finding out what it was.

In the meantime, Isaac was simply content to be alive. He could not help but marvel at how quickly his mental health had returned since he had stopped taking the medication. Everything sparkled with clarity, and it seemed to him that both he and the world had been reborn. He found himself perplexed as to why Father Adrianus had been so insistent that he never miss a dose. The old priest had been adamant about it, and for the first time in his life, Isaac felt an unmistakable distrust for the man.

He had spent the better part of the day going over all the events that had transpired since the plane had crashed, giving particular attention to the tribulations he had suffered at the hands of the demons. He recalled how Ahreimanius had mentioned a Cube, and how he had told him that he would never allow him to assist the Two in their endeavors. Ahreimanius had clearly been referring to the same Cube that Father Franco had written of, but who were the Two? Isaac looked searchingly at Shackleton as he arrived at his side.

"Who are you, my friend?" he asked. "And why did you come to save me?"

Shackleton looked back at him playfully, as if telling him to stop thinking and enjoy the scenery. They had been following a narrow goat herder's path for most of that day, and it was clear that the dog was enjoying the trek tremendously.

Isaac looked out from their perch. Around them the land had taken on a barren and rocky character, foreign to the lush green that had been their surroundings up until now. Here the earth was dry and of a russet colour, with only tangled and brittle shrubs dotting the otherwise barren sections of rock. Isaac used a hand to shield his eyes from the sun and gazed far into the south and west. There was not a village in sight.

Abandoning his search, he saw that Shackleton had decided to lie down and take a break. He joined him happily, and after sharing some water with the dog he pulled out Father Franco's diary, deciding to have another look at a map he had found there the night before. He used the sleeve of his tattered suit jacket to wipe the sweat from his brow.

There simply must be a way of locating our position in these mountains...

Over the past two days Isaac had found many puzzling things in the notebook, but none more so than the existence of the two orphans named Gabriel and Natasha. After much struggling, he had remembered why their names seemed so familiar. It had been his secretary who had first called his attention to them, more than thirty years before, when he was still in the employment of the church.

"This is very peculiar," she had said, holding up a document. "Have you seen this week's adoption summary?"

Isaac had been gazing out the window of his office at the time, lost in grief. It had not been a month since his young wife had died and he was still reeling from the loss.

"It says that two newborns were admitted into our agency this morning," she told him. "A boy named Gabriel, in our Taiwan orphanage, and a girl named Natasha, in the Argentine shelter. The bizarre thing is that both of them were born in comas, just like your child, Mr. Rodchenko. What a strange coincidence, wouldn't you agree?"

"Yes, indeed," he had said. "And the circumstances?"

"Unwed teenage mothers. Both gave birth to their babies on the same day that your child was born."

Isaac looked out over the mountainscape, turning the event over in his mind. Gabriel, Natasha, and his own son had all been born at precisely the same hour. The church document confirmed it beyond a doubt. What was more, all three children had been in rare coma vigils at the time of their births. The chances of this happening were incalculable, and that they should all be connected directly to him made the coincidence impossible to ignore. Isaac frowned. What did it all mean?

Flipping back to the map, Isaac could see that it covered a section of the north coast of Spain. At its centre was a circle marking the general vicinity of the island where they had just been, as well as another mark a good distance from it that was labeled *Monastery*. Isaac squinted at the page. Scribbled beside the map was an itinerary.

Day 1: Final rites and burial at the island.

Day 2: Make camp and rest.
Days 3-5: Expedition to the Rex Angelus Monastery.

Isaac was baffled.
What monastery?
He looked up from the book to see that Shackleton had risen again. He was sniffing at the air, scanning the horizon and growling at what he saw. A wall of heavy cloud had amassed in the east. It was advancing like a great curtain, its darkness accentuated by the white gulls that flew up against it. Isaac rose with a groan. What approached them was nothing short of a tempest. They would need to find shelter at once.

CHAPTER 11

The Atlas Mountains, Morocco.

Bishop Marcus insisted on not uttering a single word about the mission until they had each had at least one glass of wine and some of the crustless cucumber sandwiches that Fra had brought along. The day was turning out to be magnificent, and from their shady picnic blanket beneath the olive trees they could easily reach the nearby Land Rover should a speedy retreat be required. Bahadur would not be too upset with them.

"I must apologize for my initial reluctance," said the old brother as he proceeded to slice a leg of lamb. "Your Excellency has once again made a wonderful suggestion. This is beyond a doubt the most glorious spot in all of Morocco. Thanks be to God."

Everyone watched as the old brother worked on the lamb.

"After all," he added, "it could be hours before Bahadur returns, and why not have a nice lunch in the meantime?"

"We will be sure to save him a portion!" chimed the bishop, popping the cork from a second bottle of wine.

The birds sang happily in the trees above, and the lazy afternoon soothed their bodies like the best of tonics. Gabriel breathed in the fragrant air. He was sitting with his back to an olive tree, in one hand a glass of wine and in the other a savory hunk of brie folded into a piece of crusty bread.

"How about it, Marcus?" he asked, languidly looking over at the old bishop. "You've got the Cube and the journal sitting right there, and you've already had two glasses of wine. No more excuses. Tell us about our mission."

"Most certainly," said the bishop, draining his glass. "Now is the time."

Hearing the bishop say this, Natasha came over and sat down beside Gabriel. Suora began to cry with happiness.

"For more than thirty years I have prayed to the Blessed Virgin to see them together," she said, and immediately Fra rose from his place and came to comfort her.

"Their love is true," he said, caressing her back. "Blessed be their union."

Natasha turned to look at Gabriel only to find him frowning into his glass of wine. The bishop noticed too but said nothing. Suora was meanwhile letting Fra guide her to their place on the blanket. They sat down side by side and continued with the preparation of the food.

"Well," said the bishop. "Let us speak of your mission, no?"

"Sounds good to me," Gabriel said petulantly, snapping out of his reverie. "How do we find the Book of Khalifah? How do we open the seals?"

The bishop held out his hands in a gesture of patience.

"Before I can attempt to answer those questions," he said, "you must first understand what your overall objective is. You said that you have gone over the journal's contents?"

Natasha shook off her funk and sat up a little.

"We've only skimmed through it, Uncle."

"Very well," said the bishop, nodding. "We shall begin at the beginning. Are either of you aware of the philosophical concept of the Divine Spark?"

"Of course," said Natasha. "It's our higher-self. The Cosmic Consciousness. Our God-self. It resides in all of us."

Gabriel rolled his eyes.

"Indeed," said the bishop, noting Gabriel's reaction. "And all these names refer to our true, albeit forgotten identity; the very essence of ourselves. Put simply, your primary objective is to re-establish contact with this inner-being."

"And how are we supposed to do that?" asked Gabriel. "That sounds a bit abstract, don't you think?"

"That is where your mission comes in," said the old bishop. "As you move to the centre of the Great Labyrinth, so too will you move to the centre of your own being. With every passing stage, communication with this perfect inner-being will become less and less obstructed, until your higher-self will finally and completely express itself through you."

"And then we'll know all the answers and we'll be able to pass them on to everyone else," said Gabriel in a disbelieving tone.

"Yes," said the bishop. "That is more or less the idea."

"Well, excuse me for being so blunt, Marcus, but what's the point? Why do we need to establish contact with this inner-being in the first place? Everybody seems to be getting along quite fine without it. What's the big deal?"

The bishop paused to consider, sipping at his wine and looking up into the trees. A nice breeze was rustling through the leaves now. It sent fragments of golden sunlight over their picnic blanket.

"Connecting with the higher-self is the most empowering thing that anyone could ever possibly do, my son," he said, bending towards Gabriel and lowering his voice. "It is the true meaning and purpose of life. Anything that we have ever accomplished that has had any value has always come from our higher-self."

He leaned back and studied Gabriel's face.

"The trouble is that most of us are only connected to a fragment of our higher-self at best. Making a full and unobstructed connection to it is the reclaiming of a long-lost, god-like power."

Gabriel moved his glass into a shaft of sunlight, watching the little pool of wine shimmer and glow.

"That sounds really great," he said. "Too bad it's all nonsense."

The old bishop smiled patiently and turned to Natasha.

"Did you have a chance to study Gutierrez de la Cruz's version of *The Great Fall of the Angels*?"

Natasha shook her head.

"Very well," said the old bishop. "I will quickly go over it then. There are many variations of this story in cultures around the world, but Gutierrez's version explains our human condition quite well."

The bishop reached for the bottle of wine and filled Gabriel's glass, topping up his own as well.

"According to the story," he began, "the souls that constitute humanity originally abided in the higher spheres, or in heaven, if you will. Countless worlds existed there, with an endless variety of experiences to be had.

"You see, God had given to each of his created beings tremendous power, and the free will to use this power as they saw fit. He had also, however, warned them against using certain aspects of this power, stating that they ran contrary to his universal laws, and that they could ultimately be destructive."

"And this is a myth, right?" said Gabriel. "We're not supposed to take this literally."

The old bishop nodded patiently.

"These things can only be related through myth, my son. What actually happened would be impossible for us to understand. The spirit world is quite simply inconceivable to us. The function of this myth is to embody the essence of the event of the Great Fall so that it might be understood. In this respect it is very truthful."

Gabriel nodded and motioned him to go on.

"According to the story," continued the bishop, "the first to test out the forbidden powers that God had warned us about was one of God's highest angels. His name was Lucifer, and he was the *Archangel of Illumination*, also called *The Morning Star*.

"Lucifer had shown great promise and was destined to be one of the greatest beings ever created. The trouble was that he had long been questioning Christ's supreme position and wondered why he should have to occupy a place inferior to that of the Christ.

"None of the other angels thought there was much danger in Lucifer's observations, but over time, like a bad seed, Lucifer's contentions grew into pride and envy, and were the eventual cause of the fall."

"And exactly what was this fall?" asked Gabriel. "Mythically speaking, of course."

"It was a mass exodus of spirit entities from paradise, my son. Spirit entities that would later incarnate on earth as human beings. To put it simply, Gabriel, we are all the once fallen angels. Every human being ever to have lived was an angel in heaven before he or she was lured away by Lucifer's lies and promises.

"You see, by tapping into the power that God had warned him not to use, Lucifer generated a force that ran in an opposite direction to divine law. He used this dark power to tempt us into following him, and of our own free will we did just that.

"The tragic consequence of this power was that every divine aspect of God was turned automatically into its opposite when it was used. New *dualistic* universes were created as a result.

"In these spheres, harmony gave birth to disharmony, light created darkness, love spawned hatred, and so on. After that, wholeness split further still, and the more the pull of temptation proceeded, the worse the fractured state became. Eventually, the spheres of Hades came into existence."

"I remember reading an entry in the professor's journal that mentioned this," said Natasha. "It said that the fallen angels made hell for themselves."

"How does that work?" asked Gabriel.

"A universal metaphysical construct," said the old bishop. "According to Gutierrez, every spiritual entity creates his or her own physical world, and that world expresses the state of mind they happen to be in.

"When like-minded entities gather together, their collective states of mind construct the worlds in which they collectively live. One world may be heavenly, while another may be hellish; it all depends on how spiritually evolved the entities abiding there are."

The bishop took another sip from his glass.

"In the case of hell," he said, "the spirits abiding there had fallen to such a degree that the world they created was utterly opposite to that which could be found in heaven. It was a reptilian sphere, and utterly evil. The darkness there was so complete that they could not even conceive of having once been creatures of the light."

Natasha looked over at Gabriel.

"In the journal, your father said that countless spheres exist between the extremes of heaven and hell. He said that the earth sphere is one of them, but that what makes it unique is that it's perfectly in the middle. Humans are equally exposed to good and evil forces here. That's why our world is the way it is."

"It is precariously balanced, my child," said the bishop. "One push will send it spiralling either upwards or downwards, and that push will come at the time of the crossing of the Dark Rift. The outcome will depend on the mindset of humanity as a whole."

"That's a crazy concept..." said Gabriel, thinking. "It basically states that the physical exists as a result of the spiritual.

He looked over at the bishop.

"It's the opposite of what everyone thinks."

The old man smiled.

"The spiritual is nothing other than a state of mind," he said. "It is the state of mind that creates the state of body, and all things material."

Gabriel paused to consider the implications.

"Consciousness creating the physical world," he pondered. "It reminds me of the double-slit experiment."

The bishop and Natasha both gave Gabriel a puzzled look.

"It's a quantum mechanical experiment," he said with a shrug. "It's boggled the minds of scientists since the beginning of the twentieth century. It uses an electron gun and two slits in a metal barrier to isolate the basic principles of what you're talking about.

"In a nutshell, the experiment points to a conclusion that states that it must be our minds that create the physical universe, and that we do this simply by *observing* things; by being conscious…"

The bishop nodded.

"Can you both now see the connection that Gutierrez is making?" he asked. "If our state of mind creates the world in which we live, then it would be necessary to possess a more evolved state of mind in order to create a better world for ourselves to live in."

Gabriel rubbed the stubble on his face. As mind boggling as it was, the concept seemed logical enough, even on a personal level.

"Like good days and bad days…" he said, thinking. "The world seems to literally transform around you when you're in a good or bad mood. The natural tendency is to blame the day's events for the mood you're in, but what if it was the other way around?"

"Moods are born from mindsets, my children," continued the bishop. "And mindsets are what heaven and hell are made of, along with all the worlds that lie between them. The higher spheres are simply societies of purified entities living together in heightened states of mind.

"Whether we are aware of it or not, it is the goal of everyone on this planet to restore these forgotten states of mind and return to the paradise we left long ago. It is your mission to unlock the knowledge that will help everyone to achieve this goal. That knowledge resides in the Cube."

"And we release it by re-establishing contact with our inner core being?" asked Natasha. "With our Divine Spark?"

"Precisely!" exclaimed the old bishop. "This will happen as you make your way through the seals and into the centre of the labyrinth."

"Opening up a stairway to heaven…" said Gabriel, shaking his head. "Pardon me for saying this Marcus but that sounds absolutely ludicrous."

"If you say so," said the bishop, smiling. "But keep in mind that the heaven we search for does not lie outside in the clouds, as Michelangelo would have us believe. The true heaven lies within and is a very long journey away for most.

"Heaven is arrived at one step at a time, and according to Gutierrez, humanity is now ready to take its next step towards it. Let us concentrate on moving humanity to the next higher sphere, shall we? No need to go barging straight into heaven. There will be time enough for that."

"And what will this next sphere be like?" asked Natasha. "Does the journal say anything about it?"

Fra and Suora had by now finished preparing the lamb sandwiches. They placed a tray of them on the blanket and the old bishop's eyes lit up.

"It says that the next higher sphere, or the next *inner* sphere, depending on how you decide to look at it, will be much like it is here, only better," he said, picking up a sandwich and biting into it. "There will be no more war. Neither will there be greed or envy. There will be abundance for all."

He took a sip of wine.

"People will live in peace and prosperity," he said, "and the situation will be such that greater, and more purified states of mind will be achievable. More and more people will understand the universal laws and live by them. Our upward cycle of evolution will continue."

"And what about death?" asked Natasha, taking a sandwich. "In the higher spheres do people still die?"

"Nobody ever dies, child," said the old bishop with a gentle smile. "Death is truly an illusion. Gutierrez does, however, state that reincarnation will still be necessary in the next sphere, as will the death of the physical body, but aging will occur at a much slower rate. People will stay younger longer."

"And what about sickness?" asked Natasha.

"Sickness will take on different forms, but it will not entirely disappear either. Gutierrez states that physical sickness is a direct result of spiritual sickness, and while we are evolving, it is sure to exist, even in higher spheres.

"Pain and suffering will also continue to exist in the next higher sphere, for they are a necessary means of spiritual purification. Even still, our tribulations will be looked at very differently once we have made the transition. They will be accepted and embraced with maturity, because the truth behind them will be fully understood by all. Humanity will see things differently by and large. We will be more evolved."

"Gotta like that," said Gabriel, rising to his feet with a pessimistic smile. "I think I could really get into accomplishing this mission.

"Become my inner god-self and then move up to a higher sphere where everybody's chilled out and enjoying life to the max. Sounds like a blast."

Natasha glanced up at Gabriel only to see the smile vanish from his face. Coming from very close by could be heard the roar of engines, and the rattle of automatic weaponry.

Gabriel frowned when he saw two Land Rovers speeding past on the road below them, one in the lead and another giving chase under heavy fire. As they passed, he saw a hand emerge from the leading truck and lob something into the window of their parked Rover.

"Incoming!" he cried, pushing Natasha and Suora to the ground and covering them with his body.

The ensuing explosion shook the earth. Luckily, the hillock on which they had laid out their picnic gave more than adequate protection from the blast. Even still, their ears rang painfully.

Gabriel jumped up and ran to the roadside in time to see the Rover that was giving chase lose control and swerve off the mountain road, its wheels destroyed by the blast. The sick crunching of steel was soon followed by a massive explosion, the flames of which engulfed the entire switchback below.

It was from out of these flames that Gabriel saw the leading Rover emerge unscathed. It roared past the wreckage and sped off and out of sight.

Returning to the picnic spot, Gabriel saw that although everyone was considerably shaken, no one had been injured. Natasha ran to him.

"What happened?"

Gabriel was trying to collect his thoughts, his head still reeling from the explosion.

"I don't know for sure," he said. "My guess would be that Nasrallah was driving the truck that got away. The guy at the wheel was too well-dressed to be a guard."

"And who was in the other Rover?" asked Natasha.

"I don't know..." said Gabriel, a shadow of worry engulfing his features. "I couldn't see them clearly, but one thing's for sure. They were our guys."

"Bahadur..." said Suora, bringing her hands to her face.

"I don't think so," said Gabriel. "I would have recognized him by his size."

"What about Amir?" asked Natasha with concern.

Gabriel did not reply. He squeezed Natasha's arm and ran off in the direction of the flames.

CHAPTER 12

Bahadur made his way into the safety of the castle amid the incessant clatter of gunfire. He moved briskly but silently, scowling with worry.

Nasrallah knew we were coming. There must have been an informer.

He played the events out in his mind as he hurried forward, thinking back to when he and his men had first arrived at the rendezvous point.

As arranged, they had been met by a small group of smugglers who had taken a handful of gold coins to show the others. Not twenty minutes had passed before they had returned, stating that all had gone well, and that the men were now officially under his charge.

Bahadur had been delighted. To make such a change in command with absolutely no bloodshed was unheard of. He had followed his men to the castle's entrance where they were happily greeted by all.

"We have locked Nasrallah in his quarters, Captain!" said one of the smugglers, slapping him on the back. "There he will remain until you decide what to do with him!"

What happened next had shocked everyone. They had no sooner entered the courtyard than three guards began to open fire on them from the watchtower above. Most of the men had scattered into the shelter of the surrounding arcades, but two had been killed instantly.

Bahadur had managed to find cover behind a column, while Amir, along with three other men, had taken shelter beneath a large bronze basin, located in the centre of the courtyard. There they had remained, trapped beneath the gurgling fountain amid a rain of bullets.

Perched as the snipers were, it had been impossible for the men below to strike back at them, and all were forced to remain under cover, unable to retaliate.

With his enemies trapped in the courtyard, Nasrallah had appeared outside the castle gates. Accompanying him were three men, but the hostages were nowhere to be seen.

From their respective vantage points, both Amir and Bahadur could see that Nasrallah was on the verge of getting away, but to pursue him would be suicide. The snipers in the tower would cut them down before they were halfway out.

Bahadur saw Amir talking to his men. They appeared to be studying the round basin under which they were hiding. Something was afoot.

"Free our family!" bellowed Amir to Bahadur.

Seconds later, he and his men had given the basin a consolidated shove, succeeding in separating it from its stone base. In moments they had perched it on its side, effectively creating a moveable shield. Bullets bounced off the heavy bronze as they rolled it out of the courtyard, making their way to the front gate where they exchanged fire with Nasrallah and his men. The villain had only just boarded one of the many Land Rovers parked there, and in seconds he and his men were off, with Amir and his team in pursuit.

After seeing this, Bahadur wasted no time. With Nasrallah gone there was only one thing left to do: Find his family. Screaming orders to his men, he disappeared into the castle, an intense feeling of dread filling him to the quick. Nothing was going as planned. Why would Nasrallah not have taken the hostages with him? Was his family already dead?

Bahadur arrived at the entrance to the lower levels and descended into the dungeons at full speed. The surroundings were familiar here, and he thought back on his life as a smuggler. Everything seemed so different now.

The fact that his dealings had reached a point that the lives of his very own family had become endangered had changed everything. What had he been thinking? Stealing, lying, killing, cheating. How could his actions not have come back to him? As it was, the people he most dearly loved were in tremendous danger, if not already murdered, and it was entirely his fault.

Bahadur rounded a corner and knew instantly that he was in the right place. It was not the dark stone arches and crudely hewn ceilings that gave him this certainty, but rather the damp stench in the air. It was an odour that only years of incarcerated humans could create. There was a pungent density about it, one that could be sensed on the tongue.

Making his way slowly forward in the dim light, Bahadur tripped over something lying on the ground. It was a smuggler, the body still warm. He squatted down, checking for a pulse. There was none. In the shadows by the door he spotted yet another body, a pool of dark and glossy blood spreading out around its head.

Bahadur readied his gun. To his left he could see a looming passage and he suddenly realized how Nasrallah had appeared outside. The passage led to a secret exit, one that opened onto the castle grounds not a stone's throw from the main gates. It had been built by the Moors centuries before as a means to flank enemy forces attacking the castle. Today, Nasrallah had used it for his own purposes.

Bahadur inched his way forward, pressing his massive body up against the damp stone. Caution would be necessary. If Nasrallah had been able to secure the loyalty of the men in the watch tower, he could easily have left a guard or two behind.

Bahadur was in the process of berating himself for not having brought a few men along when he heard a faint moaning coming from just ahead. He rounded the corner, inching his big head out to see a man sitting on the floor, his back against the wall. He was holding his stomach, and his shirt was soaked in blood.

"Elakhdar…" whispered Bahadur, frowning.

He was Nasrallah's second in command. He was a good man, and Bahadur had known him since childhood.

"My dear friend," he said quietly, kneeling at his side. "You have been hurt."

Elakhdar winced in pain.

"He asked me to betray you but do you know what I said?"

"What did you say, my friend?" asked Bahadur, smiling tenderly.

"I said that you were too big and too ugly to betray."

Bahadur frowned at the joke. There was too much blood.

"Where are you hurt?" he asked, looking for the wound.

"Nasrallah's a dirty swine," said Elakhdar. "He wanted to kill your family one by one until you gave him the Cube and the gold. He sent three of his men down the tunnel to prepare the escape and ordered me to kill your Jadda and leave her body hanging for you to find. When I refused, he ordered his men to shoot me, but I shot them first."

"It would appear they shot you also," said Bahadur, finding the wound and attempting to staunch the flow of blood.

"When I looked up to kill that pigdog, I saw him running away into the tunnel like a coward. I shot but I did not strike him."

Elakhdar swallowed hard. He was fighting to stay conscious.

"Bahadur," he said quietly. "We are not murderers. Perhaps we are criminals, and mercenaries too, but we are also fathers and sons and husbands. We are just men. We do the best with what we have been given."

At this point the captain began to tremble uncontrollably, the blood welling up into his mouth. Bahadur knew there was no hope for him. He held his shoulder, his other hand pressing down on the gushing wound.

"My dear friend…" he coughed.

"Quiet now," said Bahadur in a voice as soothing as he could muster. "Do not speak."

"Go to your family, Bahadur," he said. "They are well. They will be happy to see you."

Bahadur looked up hopefully, peering into the dimly lit tunnel where he knew their cell would be. When he returned his gaze to his friend he saw that he was dead.

Passing a hand over his open eyes, Bahadur bowed his head and thanked him silently. If his family was alive, it was because of Elakhdar's great sacrifice. It would never be forgotten.

CHAPTER 13

Central Jerusalem, Israel.

Dr. Bennington peered out into the adjoining space. A second door in the decontamination room had just slid open, revealing an expansive laboratory beyond. He followed Christian out into it, and immediately noticed the quality of the air. It was utterly clean, bereft of even the slightest odor.

Around them milled dozens of scientists dressed in white overcoats and wearing face masks and head coverings. They nodded respectfully to Christian as they passed, some even bowing.

"It is just up ahead, Doctor," said Christian, leading the way into a high security area labeled *Biological Defence*.

Christian approached a heavy glass door secured by a holographic scanner. Its pulsating lasers mapped his face and then sounded a soft chime, opening the way before them. Within they passed through a maze of blinking machines and apparatuses, arriving at last at what looked to be a large holding tank situated in a corner of the space.

Although it was covered by a thin curtain, Bennington could still see motion within, and he immediately sensed that something dark and sinister was at play. When they were approached by a white-robed scientist he knew his fears were about to be confirmed.

"Mr. Antov, sir," said the scientist, excitedly pulling aside the sheet. "Your timing is perfect."

Having caught a glimpse of what lay within, Bennington instinctively turned and walked away.

"We were only just going to call you, sir. I can now state quite confidently that we have at last perfected the virus."

Christian raised an eyebrow.

"Its genetic propagation has been stabilized?" he asked, moving towards the glass container.

"Why, yes sir, it has," said the scientist, surprised by Christian's knowledge of the project. "The dead tissue has been fully reanimated. By modifying the double-stranded RNA to suit this specific species, we have completely eradicated any traces of DNA polymerases, thereby increasing the mutation rate. The virus is in a constant state of healthy propagation, sir. This is quite unique, given the highly irregular host environment."

Bennington moved towards the tank reluctantly, knowing that a ghastly sight awaited him, but unable to curb his curiosity.

Dead tissue reanimated? What on earth are they talking about?

He arrived at Christian's side in time to see a savage attack occurring. Within the glass tank could be seen a line of seven monkeys, each one chained securely to its base, yet free enough so as to be able to make contact with its immediate neighbours.

Whereas the monkeys to the right of the tank seemed healthy, those to the left appeared to be wounded and rabid. They jerked and strained against their bonds in savage bursts of energy.

What in God's name are they doing to these poor animals?

There was something very unsettling about the enraged monkeys. Their eyes were bereft of life, and the many wounds they had were grey and bloodless. Their emaciated lips were drawn back like those of a corpse, and there was something utterly unnatural about the way that they jerked and twitched, something that seemed completely alien to the natural fluidity of motion characteristic to their species.

"You will be amazed to know, Doctor," said Christian dryly, "that the monkeys to the left of the tank are all clinically dead."

Dr. Bennington was speechless. The evil he was witnessing had left him trembling, yet he could not avert his eyes. The three animals to the right of the tank were clearly still alive, their eyes wide with panic. Directly to their left however, one monkey lay dying, its face utterly destroyed. The grey-faced beast responsible for its wounds was straining against its bonds, licking frantically at a pool of blood that was emerging from the dying monkey's head.

"Watch," said Christian. "The virus will propagate the moment the monkey's brain dies."

To Dr. Bennington's horror, no sooner had the wounded monkey ceased its death rattle than its eyes opened once again, a new savage energy beginning to imbue its body. In a matter of seconds it had leapt to its feet, savagely attacking its healthy neighbour until it too lay dying at the base of the tank.

"What have you done?" gasped the doctor, looking to Christian pleadingly. "What madness is this?"

"We have raised the dead," said Christian, smiling coldly. "Just like Jesus did. It is a miracle. By introducing a specially engineered virus into the dying tissues, we have in essence genetically reprogrammed every cell in the body to conduct itself according to very specific criteria.

"By extracting energy from the host's very own cells, the virus propagates itself into all tissues, mutating them in a way that they begin to function once again, only this time without the need of blood flow or a brain to command them."

"But how is this possible?" asked the doctor. "What is giving them the innumerable orders needed to maintain life?"

"There is only one order to obey, Doctor," said Christian casually. "That is the order to feed. As long as the monkey can introduce more cellular fuel into itself, it will not need to consume its own cells. As far as the intelligence needed to govern cellular activity is concerned, this has been programmed into the virus itself. Virally secreted neurotransmitters mimic the brain's natural messages throughout the organism."

"But how can this be?" asked the doctor, aghast.

"Technology," said Christian dryly. "Technology and dogged perseverance."

He turned to face the scientist.

"Show me the humans."

"Yes, sir," stammered the researcher, surprised by Christian's demand. "We have set up the experiment, but we were waiting to conduct further tests on the monkeys before proceeding."

"There is no need," said Christian. "We will conduct the experiment at once."

* * * * * *

Dr. Bennington sat in his armchair. Above the door he could see the clock counting down from forty minutes.

"I apologize for the length of this decontamination," said Christian, "but leaving the facility is considerably more dangerous than entering into it. I am sure you can understand why."

The doctor looked at Christian but did not reply. He was still in a state of shock. What he had witnessed was more than any man could possibly be expected to endure.

Those poor people. What had they done to deserve that?

He sat shaking in his armchair, unable to remove the grisly images from his mind.

"Why, Christian?" he heard himself asking. "Why are you doing this?"

Christian yawned.

"The earth's population must be culled to a more manageable size," he said plainly. "The virus will help to kill off two-thirds."

Bennington could not muster the will to respond. Christian continued.

"The spirit of the world must be broken as well, Doctor. All hope must be annihilated. Seeing the dead walking and consuming the living will aid in this endeavor. A new age is dawning, one that has been meticulously planned since the creation of this pathetic planet. When all hope has been destroyed, the world will bow to its true master."

"You won't succeed," said Bennington at last. "God won't allow it."

"God has no choice in the matter," said Christian gravely. "His laws require that we use our own free will to liberate ourselves. This will not be possible when all hope is lost."

Christian crossed his legs casually.

"You see, one cannot ask for liberation if one does not know what liberation is. And if one does not ask, one cannot receive. Total darkness will once again return. God's foolish plan of salvation will have failed, and what was once Lucifer's, will return to Lucifer, only this time he won't make the mistake he made before. His new prison will be made inescapable."

"You will never succeed in destroying all the love and hope in this world, Christian."

"Even love and hope will eventually die in the absence of light."

"There will always be light!"

"Maybe so, my good doctor," said Christian, "but not for those on Earth. My society is making very sure of that."

"What do you mean?" asked the doctor. "What are you saying?"

"I'm saying that dark days are coming. They are already upon us. As the decades pass, more and more people will forget what it was like to be free."

"Nevertheless, there will always be scores who will oppose you," said Bennington. "How will you do away with all of them?"

"The only way to truly destroy your enemy is to make him use his own power against himself. In this way you guarantee his complete demise."

"And how do you propose to do that?"

"Propose?" smiled Christian. "Yes, perhaps at one point we did propose, but now things are much further evolved than that. Where should I begin? Perhaps in the protocols that our founders laid down. Each of them revolves around the same basic principle: *Take the best in man and distort it so that it becomes the worst in man.* The desire for freedom, for example, is the strongest desire, but it is prone to corruption by its very nature."

"Is that so?"

"Yes," said Christian. "Because along with the desire for freedom, comes the dread of slavery, and when threatened by this fear, a man can be made to destroy the very freedom he longs to preserve."

"And how would you make everyone on the planet feel so threatened?"

Christian smiled.

"With the mainstream media," he said. "We have already done it as a matter of fact. We have changed the content of traditional entertainment and shifted the trends in pop culture so that they reflect the decline of society. We have given the masses antiheroes instead of heroes; vampires instead of angels. We have made innocence and purity look sickly, and wickedness look strong and sexy.

"We have flooded them with a regular stream of scandal in the government, pointed out every lie, every deception, every lowly act by our leaders, and turned it all into cynical humor on night-time talk shows. We have shown them the hypocrisy that resides within the very political institutions that were once deemed the envy of the free world.

"We have begun to destroy the dream, Doctor, and replace it with the image of a fallen nation; a fallen world. People will soon long for a return to the Golden Age. They will hunger for it."

"And that's why you've given us President John F. Abbot," said Bennington. "You even used JFK's first two initials. Our President is a false King Arthur…"

"You are beginning to understand, Doctor," said Christian, smiling coldly. "In his false attempts to restore freedom, the President will dissolve the constitution and extinguish the last of what used to be the United States of America. He will officially usher in the North American Union, and this union will be a police state.

"There will be no elections of any consequence, and he will remain in office as a dictator. Biometric technology will monitor everyone. There will be no more freedom. This is the birth of the Fourth Reich, Doctor, just as it was planned to be. It will be a New World Order."

"But how can this be true?" asked Bennington. "You are telling me that our demise has been planned since the beginning of the world itself. That there is no hope…"

"Hope for power over others, Doctor," said Christian, "and learn to hate me, for you will soon have great cause to do so."

With these last words the chime announced the end of the decontamination period. Dr. Bennington watched Christian rise to his feet and leave the chamber. Very slowly the old doctor forced himself to stand. He would follow his captor. He had nowhere else to go.

As he made his way down the long glass corridor, he could see the scientists milling about below him, and the memory of the horrific human experiment came flooding back into his mind.

"They have no idea what they are a part off... God forgive them."

CHAPTER 14

The Atlas Mountains, Morocco.

Natasha pushed open the door to see Gabriel sitting next to the bed, his eyes glued to Amir. The latter lay there unconscious, his head wrapped in blood-soaked bandages. His face was severely lesioned, and his naked upper body was covered in burns and lacerations.

Gabriel's dear friend was dying and there was nothing anyone could do about it. The nearest hospital was in Tetouan, over three hours away, and the signs of internal bleeding were everywhere. He would never survive the bumpy ride. He had but hours to live.

Gabriel looked up at Natasha and the events played out in his mind again. He had sprinted down the perilous incline, taking a direct route to the burning truck. Before reaching it, he had found Amir on the ground, his head dashed against a stone. There had been no breath in his lungs, and only the faintest trace of a heartbeat. In a matter of minutes another Land Rover had arrived, and working together, they had loaded Amir into it and sped him back to the castle.

Natasha laid a gentle hand on Gabriel's shoulder, looking down at Amir's battered face. There was a regular flow of clear liquid coming from his ears and nose, and his pupils were dilated to different sizes. These, among other things, were indisputable signs of a brain hemorrhage.

"We're losing him," said Gabriel, his voice choked with grief.

Natasha sat down next to him. She could see he was battling with anger and frustration. In the little time she had known Gabriel, she knew he was not one to sit around idly, but this time there was absolutely nothing he could do.

Natasha remained silent. She was holding the professor's journal in her lap, trying to find the right way to tell Gabriel what she had just learned.

He'll never accept what I must tell him. He'll say it's nonsense...

Even still, she knew it was Amir's only chance.

"Gabriel," she said slowly. "Would you try anything to save him?"

Gabriel nodded silently, reaching over to wipe some of the fluid that oozed from his ear.

"There's nothing we can do, Natasha," he said, smiling sadly. "He's a goner."

Natasha opened the book.

"I was just talking to Uncle Marcus," she said gently. "He believes that there's a way to save him."

Gabriel looked over at Natasha, his haunted eyes penetrating hers.

"Praying isn't going to do it this time."

"Uncle Marcus was saying we could use the Cube to make Amir well."

Gabriel's expression changed. He frowned in confusion but there was a trace of hope in his eyes.

"What are you saying?"

Natasha opened the book to the page she had marked.

"He showed me an entry your father made several years ago. It speaks of the Cube's power to heal."

Gabriel glanced down at the book but remained silent.

"It says all we have to do is intend to heal him and the Cube will make it happen."

Gabriel sat up in his chair and then rose to his feet, his mind beginning to awaken. The Cube harboured a strange technology, this was indisputable. It could respond to their thoughts, but was that enough to perform miracles?

He recalled how it had exploded with energy when Natasha had kissed him in the Chamber of the Sphere, and it dawned on him that he could not begin to explain how any of that had happened. The hologram the Cube had generated was beyond any present-day technology as well. He stopped pacing and looked hard at Natasha.

"Tell me what I have to do."

Natasha smiled gently. Gabriel truly was a fighter. She proceeded with caution, knowing he would not like what she was going to say.

"We'll have to spiritually merge."

Gabriel fell back into his chair, his frustration returning with increased intensity.

"I can't make myself believe in unicorns and fairies, Natasha," he said through clenched teeth. "Just forget it."

He turned his back on Natasha and bent over Amir, his eyes filling with tears.

"Maybe it's not like that, Gabriel," he heard her say. "Maybe it has something to do with the neuro-feedback technology you were talking about."

Gabriel jerked his head around to face her.

"What are you saying?"

Natasha swallowed. Gabriel had frightened her.

"I'm sorry," he said quickly, seeing the effect his words had had on her. "Tell me what you're thinking."

Natasha looked down at the journal.

"When we were having our picnic, Marcus said there was no difference between what's called *spiritual* and what's called *state of mind*. They're both the same thing. The Cube seems to be able to sense our state of mind, so maybe if we both shared the same state of mind, that might be like spiritually merging…"

"And what state of mind would that be?" he said, his pessimism returning.

Natasha remained patient.

"Perhaps one where we are open to each other and not guarding ourselves so much?"

Gabriel frowned angrily.

"I'm not guarding myself against anyone!" he snapped.

Natasha sighed in resignation and stood up wearily. It seemed to her that she had been in this kind of conversation a hundred times before, and it had always gone nowhere. This time she had finally learned her lesson. She would never try to change a man's mind again. It was pointless, even if someone's life hung in the balance. She walked towards the door.

"I'm so sorry, Gabriel," she said gently. "Really I am."

Gabriel looked up.

"Wait. What did that gypsy woman mean when she said that we had been infected with demon parasites?"

Natasha turned around to face him. The room was dimly lit but she could see his eyes in the light of the bedside lamp. There was a tragic desperation in them, and Natasha had to fight back her tears. Gabriel seemed to her like a proud lion who had just been fatally shot. He was giving up, but there was something so dignified about his surrender. So noble…

She looked at Amir and wondered if he was not already dead. He seemed to have stopped breathing. She moved to Gabriel's side and knelt beside him, placing his father's journal on the bed.

"I think the gypsy woman was using a metaphor when she referred to the parasites," she said, opening the book again. "She was probably referring to a psychological malady that effects everyone to a greater or lesser degree."

Gabriel glanced down at the book and saw an illumination of a serpent above ornate Latin script.

"*Vermis Eorum Patebit Indignitas*," he read aloud. "The Worm of Unworthiness."

Natasha looked up at him.

"That's what your father called the demon parasite. I've got it pretty bad, Gabriel. I never realized it until recently, but I've never felt I deserved to share a true connection with a man. I always felt myself unworthy of that kind of love."

Gabriel looked over at Amir, torn between his concern for his friend and for what Natasha was saying about herself.

"You're wrong, Natasha. You're more worthy of that kind of love than anyone I've ever met."

Gabriel was silent for a while, thinking.

"To be honest," he said at length, "I've always felt that way too, although I don't think I ever realized it until just now. It's so strange…"

Natasha was still kneeling beside Gabriel. She put a hand on his leg and looked up at him.

"What is it, Gabriel? Tell me."

Gabriel looked deeply into her eyes.

"I've lied to myself this whole time. You were right when you said that a pretty woman broke my heart. I always blamed her, but the problem was me. I sabotaged it all. I didn't feel I could actually have that kind of love."

Gabriel got up and began to pace. He needed time to digest all this, but he did not have that luxury. Amir was dying. If the Cube was truly their only chance at saving him, he had to get to the bottom of his neurotic behaviour quickly.

"For some reason I always felt I was prohibited to have the things I longed for," he said. "Love, riches, fulfillment… The way I dealt with it was to rebel. If I wasn't allowed to have riches, then I'd just steal them and the world could go to hell. That's why I do what I do, Natasha. I'm a grave robber. I do the same with love. Sure, I tried to make real love happen, but when I couldn't do it I decided to steal love as well, this time by paying women to love me."

Gabriel continued pacing.

"But lately it's all been falling apart," he said after a moment. "There's been this nagging emptiness in me, and my way of dealing with things hasn't been working anymore. All those girls, all that treasure… They couldn't help me…"

Natasha rose to her feet and peered into his eyes. She had never seen him looking so vulnerable.

"How do you feel right now, Gabriel?"

He shrugged and looked away.

"You make the emptiness in me go away somehow," he said, shaking his head in confusion. "I know I'm not worthy of you. I can't even consider... You're good and true and I'm... I'm a creep..."

Natasha smiled gently and took hold of his hands.

"You are many things, Gabriel Parker, but a creep isn't one of them. I think you're wonderful. And you're not a grave robber. You find things that were lost and you put them in museums where everyone can see them. You're the most amazing man I know. Can't you see? It's just this thing that we've been infected with; this *worm*. It explains everything."

Gabriel looked back at her in mild astonishment. He could sense the truth in her words but something in him still refused to accept them. Natasha continued before he could reply.

"And you were right when you said I wanted to punish myself for betraying myself. I always rejected every good man that came along. Can't you see, Gabriel? This is the parasite. There's no reason why either one of us doesn't deserve to love and be loved. We're both more than worthy of it."

Gabriel looked over at Amir, his brow furrowing.

"I can't let him die, Natasha. Not like this."

"Then we must make him well again. I know the Cube can do it."

Natasha walked over to her pack and brought out the artifact.

"Let's at least try, Gabriel."

Gabriel nodded and moved to stand facing her. Together they held the Cube and looked into each other's eyes.

"What do we do now?" he asked.

Natasha glanced over at Amir and then brought her attention back to Gabriel.

"Maybe we let ourselves love each other?" she asked timidly.

Gabriel could not stop himself from smiling with affection, despite his grief and concern.

How could I not love you?

"I suppose I could give that a try…" he said instead.

Natasha smiled back and in that moment it became irrefutably clear that something extraordinary existed between them. Neither could say exactly when the love had surfaced, or where it had come from, but it was here now and there was no denying it.

"Let's do this," said Gabriel in earnest. "Let's light up this Cube and fix Amir once and for all."

Natasha nodded slowly; her eyes misty as Gabriel's lips met hers.

In that moment the Cube exploded with energy. They could both see its light through their closed eyelids, but they paid it little heed. There was something far more magnificent igniting within and between them. It was an indescribably potent force of the purest and most passionate love imaginable; an erotic, pulsating, elevated vibration, exploding with the vigour of life itself. It seemed to them older than the universe, yet fresh and blooming, and it coursed through them with the strength of a thousand quasars.

* * * * * *

In the very same room that Amir had witnessed a man getting shot by Nasrallah, a meeting was taking place between Bahadur and the smuggler captains. On one side of the table sat the Moroccan contingent, on the other, the Gibraltarian.

Among them were Bishop Marcus, Suora Angelica, and Fra Bartolomeo at the insistence of Bahadur. It was they, after all, who had made the rescue of his family possible by providing the gold needed to contract Nasrallah's small army. Bahadur had not forgotten the agreement he had made with the old bishop before they had set out from Gibraltar.

"Gentleman," he said in his deep basso.

He was standing like a battered stone buttress at the end of the long table, his dark military fatigues stretched over his bulging muscles.

"Our mission is accomplished. The hostages have been liberated and Nasrallah has fled in defeat. We shall soon be back in business!"

In an instant the smugglers were on their feet, raising their glasses and sounding a cheer. When all were done drinking Bahadur motioned them to sit down.

"We will now have to restructure our new organization," he said, remaining on his feet. "This will prove to be no small task."

"That's why we brought you along, mate!" said Scotty Roberts.

He was reclining in his chair, his feet propped on the table as he casually lit one of his cigarillos.

"Just don't screw it up!"

Bahadur looked over at the unruly smuggler. He sat next to the old bishop, an infamous Gibraltarian, hated and adored but known to all. His ash-coloured hair was shoulder length, and a solid gold bust of Jesus Christ hung from his neck amidst a tangle of thick gold chains.

He drained his wine theatrically, breaking into a grin that would have made his worst enemies smile. Like the best of criminals, Scotty Roberts was extremely charismatic, and even the old bishop could not help but like him.

"I will try to not disappoint you, old friend," said Bahadur, crossing his arms and looking at the colourful smuggler with a twinkle in his eye.

"You'd better not," said Scotty, a deadpan expression on his face. "Or I'll have to take you outside and give you a sound thrashing."

The idea that Roberts could have given the giant a thrashing was ludicrous, and all burst into laughter. Bahadur feigned a worried frown and chuckled merrily.

It was amidst the laughter that Gabriel and Natasha made their entrance, and their effect on the gathering was considerable to say the least. No sooner had their faces been seen than the gaiety in the room ended. The old bishop rose to his feet.

"How fares that good-hearted soul?" he asked, his voice strong, but bereft of hope.

Gabriel and Natasha looked at each other and smiled.

"I think he's going to be all right," said Gabriel slowly.

Immediately the group burst into yet another cheer, rising to their feet and laughing aloud.

"It's a miracle!" cried someone.

"It'll take more than a bashed skull to stop Amir!" cried another.

When the cheers had died down, Bahadur addressed Gabriel and Natasha.

"Sit down, dear friends," he said, pointing out two empty chairs at the table's end. "You have brought news that I would never have dared hope for."

Gabriel shrugged and pulled out a chair for Natasha.

"He's completely healed," he said, sitting down and glancing over at the bishop. "There aren't even any scars."

No sooner had he said this than everyone became silent. These were tough men. Their lives were hard won, and if one belief tied them all together, it was that nothing in life was easy. Good things came at a price, and miracles belonged in fairy tales. Gabriel's words had filled them with disbelief. Scotty Roberts seemed to be having the most difficulty with the news.

"Now just hold on a bloody second, mate," he said to Gabriel, swinging his feet off the table and leaning forward in his chair. "Just what are you saying? I was there, comrade. I held his bloody crushed head in the Land Rover and he was as good as dead. What do you mean he's got no scars? That's bloody bullshit!"

Natasha could feel Scotty's fear and doubt. Before Gabriel could respond she stood up and spoke.

"Scotty Roberts and one of the Moroccan captains will come with me to inspect Amir's wounds. I would invite all of you, but I think it would be best to leave Amir as undisturbed as possible."

Scotty remained seated. He seemed to be struggling with himself.

"Come along, Mr. Roberts," said Natasha, crossing her arms. "I'll take you to him and then you can tell everyone what you've seen."

"Don't be frightened, my boy," whispered the old bishop with a wink. "This is just the beginning."

Roberts glanced over at the old bishop and stood up, his brow furrowed.

"Very well, Princess," he said, regaining his composure. "Let's go take a look at the Lord's handiwork."

"I will accompany them," said the Moroccan captain named Bahaddine. "I will bring word of the gifts of Allah."

The group remained silent until the three returned. Bahaddine appeared calm and collected, while Roberts' face was white, and clearly distressed.

Noting the silence that had befallen Gibraltar's most boisterous smuggler, all knew that something very important had transpired. Gabriel's earlier words seemed to take on a much more mysterious quality now.

"Well?" asked a Moroccan captain seated next to Bahadur. "What have you to tell us, Mr. Roberts?"

All watched intently as Scotty looked back at his questioner. He produced a cigarillo and lit it under the flash of a wooden match, his eyes still locked with the man.

"Bloody Christ in heaven," he said quietly, breaking at last from his silence. "If I hadn't seen it with my own eyes, I'd have never believed it was possible."

"Believed what?" asked another from the Gibraltar side.

He stood up and leaned over the table.

"Speak up, man! What did you see?"

"He should be dead," said Roberts, turning to look at his countryman. "I saw his head pissing blood all over the bleeding truck. His skull was crushed, man. I loved him like a brother but there's no way he could have survived that injury."

"What did you see?" demanded another.

An impish smile appeared at the corners of Scotty's mouth; his cigarillo still clenched in his teeth.

"By my word, mates," he said aloud. "I just saw that son of a bitch looking better than he has in years! When he gets home, he'll have a good shag waiting for him to be sure! Bloody hell, he looks so good I'd shag him myself if I'd had enough to drink!"

All remained silent, puzzled by his odd humour.

"I'm telling you, you thick headed rogues! It's just as our good archangel Gabriel here says, goddamn it! Amir's as right as rain! Sleeping like a bloody baby he is!"

In an instant the table exploded into excited amazement, each and every captain bursting into dialogue with his neighbour. Scotty's repeated affirmations rode over top of the din like a broken record.

"I'm not taking the piss, man! He's just like new! The son of a whore! He's as right as rain!"

Bahadur was the first to call for silence, and slowly the ruckus came to an end. Everyone gave him their undivided attention.

"My dear friends," he said, a great smile spreading over his broad face. "I can think of no better gift than having Amir back with us. I will not say I understand, but I am sure there is an explanation for what has happened, as sure as there is a sun in the sky.

"We will listen to what Gabriel and Natasha have to say, and we will begin to understand. Of this I am sure."

All looked to the couple, but Bahadur had not finished.

"Before I let them speak," he added, holding up a bearlike hand, "I will remind them that we are all in their debt, and that we will help them in any way we possibly can. Are we all in agreement?"

"Aye!" cried Scotty, bringing his fist down on the table.

And then looking to the bishop, and then to Gabriel and Natasha he said:

"Whatever you need, I'm at your service!"

"As am I," said Bahaddine, coming to his feet.

"And I!" said yet another, rising. "Long live our new captain!"

One by one, as was the way of their band, they rose and swore their loyalty to Bahadur, offering their help to Gabriel and Natasha as well. An unprecedented feeling of union and trust was being shared among the normally bickering smugglers. Something magical was in the air.

"So how about some explanations, mate?" asked Scotty, exhaling a billowing cloud of smoke. "And best try to keep the wording simple on account of all the numbskulls present, myself included," he added with a wink.

Gabriel and Natasha then told them all about the Cube, and how they had used it to heal Amir. They gave a detailed account of its history, and all the things that had happened up to then. They told the smugglers of the ancient myth that surrounded the artifact, of the Cube's mysterious powers, and its ability to unite the world in a new modality of peace and prosperity.

They also told the men of Nasrallah's dealings with a secret society who for more than two thousand years had sworn to see the Cube destroyed, and of their uncanny ability to know where the artifact resided at all times.

Gabriel and Natasha also warned them of the dark forces that this society was in league with, of the cosmic clock that was ticking as the earth made its way closer and closer to the galactic plane, and of the dark world that would ensue, should they not succeed in fulfilling their mission.

This was to return the Cube to its original resting place at the entrance of the Great Labyrinth of Sarras, and to open the seven seals of gnosis that resided therein.

In short, Gabriel and Natasha told the company of captains everything they knew, along with all the questions that still remained unanswered, leaving out no details so that everything might be open and transparent.

Not one of them doubted what they were being told. The artifact had brought Amir back from the brink of death and left him perfectly healed. This was proof enough.

When they finished speaking Natasha passed the Cube around the table for each man to examine.

"Wherever this labyrinth lies," said Bahaddine, turning the artifact in his hands, "my men and I will see that you arrive there safely."

"As will mine," said another captain solemnly.

"And mine!" said yet another.

From his new place to the right of Gabriel, Scotty was the last to examine the glowing Cube. He held it up before him while the others spoke excitedly, testing its strange density and studying the runes inscribed on its glowing surface.

On the smuggler's face was an expression foreign to all those who knew him. It bore a mixture of purpose and determination, oddly out of character with his normally carefree spirit.

While many discussed how Gabriel and Natasha might be brought safely through the war zone of central Spain and up to the northern coast, Scotty sat silently, weighing the severity of the situation at hand.

"You haven't said anything about the exact location of this labyrinth, mate," he said quietly to Gabriel, giving him back the Cube. "Only that it's on a small lake somewhere in the mountains. I've flown dozens of shipments to Santander. Lots of lakes up in those parts, comrade. Too many to survey in just four days."

Gabriel took the artifact from the smuggler and frowned.

"I know," he said, placing it gently on the table before him. "That's what worries me."

CHAPTER 15

Gibraltar.

Major Richard Roberts stood perched along the battlements at the highest point of the Rock, the earth curving along its horizon in a panoramic, nocturnal view. It was from this point where the extent of the siege was most visible, and a glance through his night vision binoculars confirmed the dozens of Guardia Civil vessels anchored around them on all sides. At the frontier he could see the Spanish troops amassed, a formidable force to be sure, but nothing they could not handle.

"Captain Brown," he said into his radio. "What's the status of the northern fortification?"

"Eighty-five percent complete, sir," came the crackling reply. "It's been fully armed and operational for twenty minutes now, sir."

"Very well," said Roberts, his right eye blinking. "Let me know when it's complete. I'd like to inspect it personally."

"Yes, sir," said Brown. "Anything else, sir?"

"That's all, Captain. Over and out."

Roberts resumed his surveillance of the Bay of Gibraltar below.

What the hell are they doing this for? What could they possibly have to gain?

Roberts' phone rang. It was Anita.

"Richard I'm scared," she said. "I wish I was there with you. The Guardia Civil are everywhere. They call themselves anti-terrorists now, but all they do is terrorize. They take away anyone who talks back to them, accusing them of being terrorist sympathizers. The old villagers are saying that it's even worse than during the times of Franco. I'm scared to get in the car. They've put check points up everywhere."

"Everything will be fine," said Roberts. "Just don't go out unless you absolutely have to, and don't draw any attention to yourself. The last thing we want is for them to find out you're married to a Gibraltarian officer."

"But I am Spanish!" she said. "I have my rights!"

"Listen, cookie," he said in earnest. "Just lay low. Please. Soon this will blow over and they'll open the border again. When that happens I'll come and get you, but until then be invisible."

Roberts knew that Anita was crying on the other end of the line. He waited patiently.

"On the news they're saying that the Muslims are rioting all across Spain," she said at length, "but it's a lie. I was just talking to Blanca in Madrid. She said there have only been a few demonstrations there, and that they've all been peaceful. She says the Muslims are all terrified. The news is making it look like a war's being waged between them and the Christians. Why are they doing this?"

"They want to scare everyone so they can put the army on the streets," said Roberts. "I'm not sure what's going on, but this is bigger than just Spain. The same things are happening all across Europe. Orders are coming from the highest levels of the EU. Something's up, and it doesn't look good. Until I can get you out of there I want you to lay low."

"Is that an order, Major?" asked Anita with a sniffle.

"Yes, it is," said Roberts, smiling tenderly.

"Well then I'll just have to obey my commanding officer," she said quietly. "I miss you."

"I miss you more."

CHAPTER 16

Los Picos de Europa, Northern Spain.

The storm had only just blown past when Isaac and Shackleton made their way into the tiny hamlet. The village sat on the peak of a mountain, and above it the fleeting clouds were already dispersing, leaving behind a clear and star-studded sky.

Isaac had spotted the village through the downpour before sunset, and he had resolved not to stop until they arrived. He approached a stone building that looked to be the village inn, his legs shaking from exhaustion. Its painted sign was well lit.

Pension Santiago. Comidas y Camas.

The door opened before he could reach for the bell, and an ugly, scowling woman appeared on the threshold.

"This village is not on the pilgrimage route!" she snapped.

She was eyeing Isaac suspiciously, taking note of his tattered suit and frayed white collar. They were stained with days of hard travel.

"We are not used to foreigners here!"

"Buenas tardes, señora," said Isaac, dizzily. "Do you have any rooms available for the night?"

The woman continued her surveillance. He and the dog were sopping wet, and she glanced past them in the direction they had come.

"Where are you coming from?" she demanded. "Who else is with you?"

"No one else, madam," said Isaac, a little confused. "It is just myself and my good dog."

Isaac gazed past her into the common room. Through the open door he could see several tables, all empty save one where a group of people sat eating, their dogs lying at their feet gnawing on bones. Behind them a crackling fire burned in a broad hearth. His stomach rumbled audibly.

"We have no rooms available!" barked the woman suddenly. "And there is no food here!"

She slammed the door and Isaac heard the clank of a deadbolt finding home.

"I suppose we'd best keep looking," he said to Shackleton.

The latter was sniffing at the door, as if unable to comprehend the woman's rudeness.

"Aren't you a noble one!" came a friendly voice from behind.

Isaac turned to see a young woman approaching. She bent and ruffled the fur behind Shackleton's ears, smitten by the enraptured expression on his face. She was fashionably dressed, her messy hair dyed blue, and her lips and nose pierced.

"*Buenas tardes*, young lady," said Isaac, with a weary smile.

In the background he could discern the tinny sounds that escaped her headphones, and he realized he had not been heard. Isaac waited patiently until the girl looked up at him and then pointed to his ear.

"My apologies," said the girl, removing her headset.

She stood up, continuing her play with Shackleton. He had clamped his teeth onto the end of her scarf and was engaged in a gentle game of tug of war.

"Do not pay any attention to our innkeeper," she said, squeezing his nose in an effort to get him to loosen his grip. "She is a horrible woman."

Isaac shot a glance at the closed door.

"Yes," he said. "I can see that."

"Are you looking for a place to stay?"

Isaac nodded.

"Then come with me," said the girl happily. "Your dog has won my heart."

They set off at once with Isaac having to make an effort to keep up with the girl's skipping pace.

"There are not many young people left in our village," she said, her Spanish accent becoming more noticeable now. "They have all moved to the cities."

Isaac peered around at the dark and lonely streets as they hiked along. The somber village seemed as old as the mountains, its squat stone buildings ancient among the hollow sounds of their footsteps. There was an indescribably morose atmosphere to the place; as if ghosts of the bygone Spanish Inquisition still haunted the damp gothic arches, and the wrought iron balconies.

They had not been walking long before a pounding rhythm could be heard rising from the ground, and soon the girl led them through an old wooden door and along a gloomy stone corridor. It ended at a spiraling flight of steps that took them into a dungeon of sorts. Isaac was very surprised by what he saw.

Deep in a cellar, the village youth had made a clubhouse, one that seemed more like a Barcelona booze can than anything else. In the blacklight he could see dozens of people huddled together in groups, the smell of hashish and tobacco filling the air. A large screen had been erected amid the dark arches, and a projector was illuminating it with strange images and video clips that mirrored the throbbing electronic music.

The girl entered ahead of them, moving into the space to talk with one of the two young men who appeared to be the creators of the show. While one was mixing the music, the other was using a laptop computer to compile the video sequences that were being projected.

It was with this boy that the girl spoke. Isaac saw him turn his head and look at them, a friendly smile on his face. He motioned Isaac to come closer.

"Welcome to our social club!" he said.

He was bobbing up and down to the music, but still managed to lay a friendly hand on Isaac's shoulder.

"I hear that you met *la bruja.*"

He bent for a moment to ruffle Shackleton's ears. Isaac smiled and nodded.

"She should have been burned at the stake with all the other witches!" said the boy over the music.

And then looking to the girl he added:

"*Nena!* Take our guests to the Chamber of Honour and feed them!"

The girl clapped her hands in delight and wrapped her arms around the boy's neck, giving him a long and passionate kiss. When she had finished, she tousled her blue hair and turned to face Isaac and Shackleton with a bright smile.

"Come along!" she hollered over the electronic throb. "I will show you your room!"

CHAPTER 17

Central Jerusalem, Israel.

Dr. Bennington glanced over at Christian and then down at his watch. They had been driving for almost fifteen minutes now and he had no idea where they were going. Christian was behind the wheel, steering the electric car along a tubular concrete tunnel that stretched off into the distance. Overhead, a steady stream of passing of lights marked their progress.

Bennington swivelled around to check on the young girl sitting in the back seat. She had been introduced to him as Cynthia, Christian's personal assistant, and the seventeen-year-old granddaughter of one of the Vanderhoff Group's oldest directors.

It was clear to Bennington that she had been sedated. He shot Christian a suspicious glance, wondering why he would have brought the girl along in the first place. Something did not feel right.

Where in God's name is he taking us?

Christian responded to his silent question.

"You shall soon see, Doctor."

They drove on in silence until the end of the tunnel came into view. There was a large cargo door there, with a smaller door beside it. Christian pulled the car up, the screech of its tires echoing around them. Leaving the car, he proffered his face to another of the ubiquitous holographic scanners. Bennington watched as the smaller of the two doors slid open.

"Please be so kind as to escort my assistant, Doctor," said Christian over his shoulder.

Bennington obeyed, exiting the vehicle and opening the girl's door.

"Thank you so much," she said through heavy-lidded eyes.

Her words were slurred and drawn out.

Bennington passed through the door ahead of Christian with Cynthia at his side. He was surprised by the masonry within. It lay in stark contrast to the poured concrete that had lined the tunnel, and was comprised of a light brown stone, crudely hewn but incredibly well preserved. He touched its surface.

"Babylonian sandstone," said Christian. "It dates back over two and a half thousand years."

"Where are we?" asked the doctor, studying the heavy arches that supported the ceiling.

"We are precisely ninety-three meters below the Temple Mount, in the centre of old Jerusalem," said Christian, moving off.

They followed a few paces behind.

"And what is this place?" asked Bennington, looking around in amazement.

"This is an exterior hall leading to an interior chamber," said Christian, arriving at a newly constructed concrete wall.

It was equipped with another cargo door, and no sooner had he placed his hand over a scanner than it slid upward to reveal a remarkable chamber within. With a high voltage boom a battery of lights switched on, flooding the space with a warm halogen glow. Bennington's jaw fell open at the sight.

"This is a Babylonian *Apsu*," said Christian, yawning. "It's nothing compared to what's coming."

Bennington stumbled forward in astonishment. The chamber was unlike anything he had ever seen. It formed a large open basin of sorts, as wide as two tennis courts, its domed canopy held aloft without a single supporting column.

Although crude and cave like, it was the room's colour and contents that filled the doctor with awe. Its floor was of the richest crimson imaginable, shining and liquescent, as though it were coated in a glossy film of ruby red blood.

The chamber's walls were made up of a series of arched colonnades and adorned in crystal mosaics of the richest blues, all deep and sensuous. Piled at its centre, as high as two men, were golden treasures of unimaginable worth.

"What place is this?" whispered Bennington, his face lit by the golden glow. "Where have you brought us?"

"This is an ancient storehouse of sacred treasure," said Christian dryly. "One of seven chambers that surround the Inner House."

"The Inner House..." repeated Bennington, glancing over at Christian intently. "Surely you're not referring to the *Holy of Holies?*"

"I am," smiled Christian. "*The Kadosh Hakodashim.* The dwelling place of God."

"*The Most Holy Place...*" whispered the doctor reverently. "But this is impossible. The site was destroyed centuries ago..."

"It was not, Doctor."

"And the Ark of the Covenant?"

"It's there too," said Christian blandly. "Quite tacky, really. Overly ornate."

"But how can this be?" stammered Bennington, taking another step into the space. "The Temple of Solomon was destroyed by the Babylonian's in five hundred BC."

"It was," said Christian. "And a second temple was built on the same site fifty years later. Contrary to popular belief however, the Babylonians did not destroy the Inner House. They built these chambers around it to hold their treasure and then held a public destruction of the outer temple to insure the chamber's secrecy. The secret died with their civilization."

"So how is it that we're here now?"

"Herod the Great discovered the Holy of Holies while renovating the second temple. You can only imagine his delight. He had all his worker's tongues cut out, and when the renovations were complete, he put them to death along with their families. The secret has been passed along by my ancestors ever since."

"But why keep it secret?"

Christian glanced over at Cynthia. Her sleepy eyes were focused on him in silent worship.

"You will soon see, Doctor," he said, looking down at his watch. "Come along."

Christian led them around the perimeter of the chamber to an archway that opened into a wide corridor. Opposite them was another archway revealing a perfect replica of the apsu where they had just been.

A short while later they arrived at a truly enormous hall, circular in shape with a towering ceiling. At its centre was a massive, crudely hewn block of dark stone. It was a perfectly proportioned cube, almost thirty feet in height and bombarded with spotlights. The sight of it reminded Bennington of a museum exhibit.

"The Kadosh Hakodashim," said Christian, pausing for a moment. "A cube not unlike our artifact, but one that is already in my possession."

"My God..." whispered the doctor. "This is unbelievable..."

Bennington followed Christian towards the massive cube with the girl at his side. High above them an expansive domed ceiling spanned the chamber. It was clad in blue mosaic tiles and dotted with countless golden stars, inlaid with astrological precision. Below their feet the ruby red floor gave the illusion of being wet with blood.

Christian motioned to a narrow descending stairwell at the base of the great cube.

"After you, Doctor."

Giving Christian one last look, Bennington proceeded slowly down the passage with Cynthia clinging to his jacket. At the end of a short tunnel a flight of steps appeared. They were bathed in golden light and led up into the interior of the cube.

A practicing Jew himself, Bennington paused for a moment, considering the importance of the place he was about to enter. The smell of ancient antiquity was in the air now, and an indescribable radiance of holiness filled every fiber of his being.

"Dear God," he whispered reverently as he climbed the last steps into the sanctuary.

What he saw within filled him with unbounded awe. The holy space was floored and wainscoted in what he knew from his studies of the Tanakh to be *Cedar of Lebanon*. Its walls and floor were guilt in pure gold, and directly before him stood two massive cherubim, guardians of the highest order. They were beautifully crafted out of what looked to be olivewood, and each stood almost fifteen feet high, their mighty wings spanning the chamber to meet at its centre.

Bennington stopped in his tracks and forced himself to breathe. His eyes had just found that which only legends spoke of.

This cannot be...

At the feet of the towering cherubs lay a gold and jewel encrusted table, upon which sat the Ark of the Covenant in all its glory. At its base was a small platform, not two feet high, and it was covered in purple and crimson linen. This was the chamber considered by the Jews to be the dwelling place of God, and both he and Cynthia fell to their knees instinctively, succumbing to a benign presence that filled their hearts to overflowing.

"Get up, you idiots," said Christian, spitting on the golden floor.

He approached the doctor and the girl and instantly they were brought to their feet by an invisible hand. Christian's eyes were black and reptilian now. A dark power was coursing through him.

"Cynthia," he said dryly. "Go to the platform and do what I told you to do."

She obeyed instantly, walking slowly to the place below the massive, winged angels and turning to take her seat.

Bolted to the dais was a chain, and Bennington watched as she picked it up. There was a sturdy dog collar attached to its end, and Cynthia proceeded to strap it tightly around her neck. Bennington shot a glance over at Christian and saw that he was looking at his watch.

"Why did Cynthia just put on that collar, Christian?" asked Bennington, frowning with confusion. "Why did you bring us here?"

"I wanted you to see what happens at three a.m.," he said, still looking at his watch. "Apparently there's going to be an alignment of planets."

"What are you talking about, Christian?" asked Bennington, only just then noticing Christian's strange, black eyes.

"Satanic superstition, Doctor," he muttered. "We're about to see if there's any truth to it. Here we are. Five, four, three, two, one."

In a clear and emotionless voice Christian called out.

"Cynthia. Use the knife I gave you to pierce your heart."

To the doctor's horror, she did exactly as she was told. Without hesitation she produced a ceremonial dagger from her purse and thrust it forcefully into her chest.

"No!" cried Bennington, trying to rush forward but finding himself held fast by some invisible hand.

He struggled against it, but every attempt sent a surge of excruciating pain through his body. Frozen with terror, he could only watch as Cynthia's lifeless body slumped to the dais. After that, everything began to lose its reality. Bennington felt himself teetering on the edge of madness.

"Don't be so melodramatic, Doctor," said Christian in a bored tone. "You didn't even know her. Don't pretend to be so attached."

Bennington focused his eyes on the dead girl. To his dismay, a transformation was taking place in her body. Similar to the human experiment he had been forced to witness in the secret laboratory, Cynthia's fingers were beginning to twitch. Moments later her cadaver was being gripped by a series of violent seizures. Her hands began to tear at her own flesh and her body twisted and contorted at impossible angles, amid sounds of cracking bone and shattering teeth.

Bennington looked on aghast, his face a mask of revulsion and grief.

"You infected the knife with the virus…" he stammered.

Christian gave a slow nod. He was still looking at his watch. Bennington's eyes darted back to Cynthia. Her body had almost fully reanimated now. Her dead eyes were moving around like a rabid animal's, her freshly lacerated skin hanging in shards the colour of wet ash.

The violent seizures had not only caused her to mutilate herself, they had also dislocated her jaw. It was straining open now, distending from her face on corded sinews and snapping hungrily at the air.

Bennington gagged and coughed. A stench of rotting flesh had suddenly filled the chamber, and over the dais an oily black vitriol was spreading like a black tide. In the blink of an eye it had engulfed the Ark of the Covenant and was already swallowing the two Cherubim that stood behind it. Cynthia's corpse jerked to its feet, straining dumbly against the collar and chain that bound it.

"Quite amazing," said Christian, smiling coldly as he glanced down at his watch yet again. "Kill a virgin on a full moon with the planets aligned and look what happens."

Bennington moved to speak but he was silenced by a hellish sound.

This is a dream… This is not happening…

What began as a single screech was soon joined by other voices, quickly producing a sound more abrasive and dissonant than anything he had ever encountered. Cynthia's corpse was jerking frantically against its bonds now, its gaping jaw snapping viciously with shattered, bloodied teeth.

The sacred chamber had transformed into a living hell, and out of every corner a chorus of demons was shrieking in rage and hatred. Their cries vanquished any hope of survival for Bennington and sent waves of terror through every fiber of his body.

"Dear God," he prayed, gagging from the stench in the air. "Protect me."

"There will be no protection from your Yahweh here!" cried Christian over the rising clamour. "His earthly abode has been desecrated! The virgin has been slain and resurrected! Just look at your god's pathetic Inner Chamber, his *Holy of Holies!*"

Black demonic shapes were whipping through the air all around them now, sending their clothes aflutter. The din was growing louder with every passing second, and Bennington knew that something unspeakable was about to occur. He braced himself instinctively.

"What have you done, Christian?"

Fourteen horrendously disfigured demons were materializing around them now, each as tall as two men, and as dense as iridium. They were in constant motion, their own substance belching out of them like black molten lead, only to be swallowed up as it was replaced by yet more. They were oscillating at an impossible rate as well, and the evil that radiated from them ripped through Bennington like toxic radiation. It was sending every fiber of his being into paralysis.

This is a nightmare! This isn't happening!

Bennington looked over to see Christian standing regally beside him now, his head held high like some dark emperor. It seemed to him that each of the fourteen demons was trying desperately to escape, and that it was only Christian's will that held them fast.

The fetid black shapes were flying faster and faster around them now, circling the chamber at dizzying speeds, and stirring up a scorching wind. At any second everything would explode in annihilation. Bennington was certain of it.

"Hail the Fourteen Emissaries of Lucifer!" sounded Christian's call over the mounting tumult. "They are my captains, and with them I shall command an Army of Darkness!"

The pulsing energy was reaching impossible levels now, yet still it was gaining in intensity. And just then, emerging from a bubbling pool of black vitriol at the centre of the dais, there appeared a lowly demon, twisting and grovelling. Like the fourteen emissaries, it too was comprised of dense matter, and it shot towards Cynthia's corpse, flowing into it like a colony of black maggots.

The change that took place in the cadaver was sudden and horrific, its movements becoming so savage and frantic that Bennington was sure it would break from its bonds.

"I am the Beast upon the Throne of Solomon!" cried Christian, his reptilian eyes fixed on the frenetic corpse. "The prophecy has been fulfilled! From this chamber I shall rule all nations! I will claim what belongs to Lucifer and take back for him what God stole!"

The rising clamour exploded in climax just then, and the Fourteen Emissaries sounded an earthshattering shriek, ripping through the ceiling of the chamber like a swarm of cindery locusts. The flying black shapes followed them, their sickening cries sending Bennington into a violent bout of vomiting.

The stench of death and rot had by now reached outlandish proportions, and what little breath the doctor had was taken by the buffeting gusts. A void had swallowed him, and bowing his head in defeat, Bennington gave up his soul to God. If this were indeed a nightmare, as he suspected it was, there would be no waking from it. Of this he was certain.

CHAPTER 18

The Atlas Mountains, Morocco.

Gabriel entered Natasha's chamber to find her standing on its little stone balcony. She was dressed in a silk nightdress and bathed in moonlight, looking out over a sweeping mountainscape under a star-studded sky. Her room was located above the opium den and sounds of men laughing and singing could be heard filtering up from below. A full moon had just emerged from behind the jagged peaks, and the night air was sharp and chill.

Gabriel approached wordlessly, leaning up against the stone railing behind Natasha and taking her into his arms. She slipped into his embrace with effortless ease, and he was amazed at how perfectly their bodies fit together. It was as if she had always belonged where she was now, and he kissed her neck, taking time to breath in her intoxicating scent.

In a similar way, Natasha could not recall having ever felt so complete. Using the Cube to heal Amir had not only altered her understanding of the artifact, it had altered her understanding of Gabriel, and of herself as well. The event had stripped away the last obstacles that had kept the two of them apart, and shown them, with perfect clarity, that they truly did belong together.

Natasha spun around to face Gabriel, and they fell into a deep kiss. It was like nothing either of them had ever experienced before, and its intensity took them both by surprise. It was as if they were melting into each other, their souls merging into a vibrating field of energy that seemed boundless and intimate at the same time. A desire to fuse further still, filled them both to the quick. It was impossible to resist.

Natasha took Gabriel's hand and pulled him onto the bed. What transpired next would be impossible to describe. The merger that took place between them transcended the parameters of body and mind, opening a way into a mystical reality beyond human comprehension.

* * * * * *

Gabriel awoke to find Natasha sitting up in bed and reading his father's journal.

"Anything interesting?" he asked groggily.

She smiled gently and reached over to run her fingers through his hair.

"You were sleeping so soundly, Gabriel. I didn't want to wake you. I've been studying Gutierrez's third manuscript."

Gabriel sat up beside her and rubbed his face awake.

"What's it say?"

"It talks about *Mithuna.*"

He glanced down at the book.

"What's that?"

Natasha scanned his features.

"It's a way of making love, Gabriel. Have you ever heard of Tantric sex?"

Gabriel raised a curious eyebrow.

"I've heard of it," he said slowly, "but I've got to confess, I don't know much about it. Is that what Mithuna is? Tantric sex?"

Natasha nodded and brought her attention back to the journal.

"Mithuna means *Sexual Union* in Sanskrit. It creates a dreamlike trance when practiced. It looks like we'll have to use it to locate the Book of Khalifah and complete our mission."

Natasha pointed to the page. On it were drawings of figures surrounded by complex structures that depicted energy fields.

"That looks complicated..."

"It's really quite simple," she said, glad that he seemed open to the concept. "Tantra's based on polarity. Men and women are like electrical conduits that join together to make circuits. A bio-energy field runs through us."

Gabriel furrowed his brow and nodded.

"The Chinese call it *Chi*," he said, examining the drawing.

The image was of a sexless figure with lines of energy radiating out from the crown of its head. The fields arched downward, outside the body, only to curve up into the genitals again. From there a twisting concentration of energy spiraled up through the energy centres in the core of the torso and made its way back to the head to begin the cycle again.

"These are the two energy phases," explained Natasha. "Descending and ascending. When Chi gets down to the genitals it usually builds up as tension, until it's finally released through orgasm or ejaculation. The secret to Tantra is that sexual energy is encouraged to be retained in the body, so that it can ascend back to its source in the brain."

"The man doesn't ejaculate?" asked Gabriel.

"It's discouraged," said Natasha apologetically.

Gabriel gave a pained expression and feigned confusion.

"I could see a gasket blowing out down there..."

Natasha laughed and poked an elbow into his side. It was then that Gabriel noticed a smaller drawing that she had not referred to yet. He brought the journal closer to get a better look at it.

"What's this?" he said, pointing.

It was a drawing of a man and a woman standing face to face, encapsulated in energy fields.

"Those are the energy poles," she said. "If you look closely, you'll see that men and women both have positive and negative poles on their bodies, but they're inverted. The woman carries her positive pole at her heart, while her negative pole is at her vagina. The man has the opposite configuration. His positive pole is at his penis, while his negative pole is at his heart."

"And that's what makes the whole thing work," said Gabriel, understanding at last.

Natasha nodded and traced her fingertips over the illustration.

"The *Chi* energy circulates between the poles, creating what Gutierrez calls a *Circle of Light*. Mithuna's based on this. The woman's sexual energy flows out of the positive pole in her breast, and into the negative pole of the man's heart. From there it travels downwards through the man, until it emerges from his penis and enters the woman's vagina. From her vagina it travels upwards through her body and then leaves her breast again to start another cycle."

"I thought we were supposed to be circulating the energy within our own bodies, and not letting it go outside of ourselves."

"We don't want to release the energy," said Natasha, "but we do want to share it. Think of there being two energy circuits happening at the same time. In the end they combine to make a unified flow."

Natasha prepared to turn the page but paused to look over at Gabriel with a sly smile.

"I think you might be interested in this next part."

Rendered on the following leaf, in an ancient Hindu style, were illustrations of the progressive sexual positions they would need to assume in order to achieve Mithuna. Gabriel looked up from the book and gazed deeply into Natasha's eyes.

"You know... I think I'm really beginning to like this mission of ours..."

CHAPTER 19

Tangiers, Morocco.

Nasrallah scanned the luxurious hotel suite. Two blonde-haired Vanderhoff agents were sharing a table with him, and two more stood at the room's only exit. Each was wearing a dark blue suit, their muscles bulging through the cloth.

Having made his escape, Nasrallah had found himself in desperate need of money. It had not been difficult to entice Christian Antov with the promise of a map that pointed to the location of the Book of the Khalifah, but the resulting meeting had not gone as he would have liked. Rather than being given the security deposit he had requested, he had instead been taken prisoner.

"Where is the map?" asked one of the seated agents, his face heavy with malice. "You will surrender it to us at once."

"The scroll is safe," replied Nasrallah, "but its price is one million Euros and as I said, I will need a retainer."

He shot a glance at the other agent at the table. The man had a phone to his ear and Nasrallah knew that he was speaking with Christian Antov.

"No, sir," said the agent. "He does not have it with him but he claims that it is in his possession."

Nasrallah was forced to wait while the agent listened. After a few agonizingly long moments the man placed the phone on the table and activated its speaker setting.

"What lies are you spinning now?" came the voice of Christian.

"No lies, Mr. Antov," said Nasrallah. "I assure you. The scroll is securely hidden in my castle."

"Your castle is currently occupied by your enemies."

"Yes, sir," said Nasrallah, "this is true, but it would be impossible for them to find it. With your retainer I will be able to retrieve it."

There was a pause before Christian spoke.

"Because there is a remote possibility that you might be telling the truth, I am willing to be patient with you. I will most likely kill you, but there is a small chance that I will spare your life if you have pleased me."

"Oh, yes, Mr. Antov," said Nasrallah emphatically. "I wish nothing more than to please you."

"Then tell me where the scroll is hidden," said Christian dryly.

"You must understand, sir," he said, rubbing his hands nervously together. "If I reveal its exact location to you, I will lose my only bargaining chip."

"Would you prefer to be tortured?"

"No, please, I will tell you. It is in a safe, hidden deep in the castle's dungeons. It was my plan to retrieve it as I escaped, but one of my men betrayed me at the last moment."

"We will be executing a missile strike on your castle within the hour," said Christian. "Will this safe withstand a direct strike?"

"Target my castle?" exclaimed Nasrallah. "But why?"

"Will the safe withstand the strike?" repeated Christian menacingly. "I would advise you to be truthful."

"It is deep in the bowels of the castle," said Nasrallah, wiping the sweat from his brow. "It would not be damaged."

"Very well," said Christian. "The strike will be arranged. You will accompany my task force to your castle. When you arrive, you will retrieve the scroll and then I will decide whether or not to kill you."

"You are very generous, Mr. Antov. Thank you."

Nasrallah let out a muted sigh of relief when the agent pocketed his phone. Things had not gone as he had planned, but they could have also gone much worse. His enemies would be eliminated in the missile strike, and he would soon provide Antov with the scroll. For now, that was all that mattered.

CHAPTER 20

The Atlas Mountains, Morocco.

Gabriel awoke from a deep slumber to find Natasha asleep in his arms. Judging by the light entering through the chamber's window, the morning was well advanced.

His gaze passed lazily over the ornately paneled ceiling. A particular pattern had caught his attention and was serving to remind him of one of the night's mysterious revelations. It sent a vivid image of the Book of Khalifah into his mind's eye.

"The Book..." he whispered. "Of course..."

He raised himself on an elbow and passed a hand through his hair.

"Natasha," he said softly, kissing the top of her head. "Natasha. Wake up."

"Gabriel," she said dreamily.

A sweet smile enveloped her face.

"What did you do to me last night?"

Gabriel smiled roguishly and kissed her lips. She was still half asleep.

"We've got to go and get the book, baby," he said softly.

"Yes," she mumbled. "Yes, we do... We must go and find the book..."

"That's why you've got to wake up."

"That's why I've got to wake up..."

Gabriel could feel her tightening her embrace, only to let go suddenly and roll over top of him. In a second she was on her knees and straddling him, her eyes bright with excitement.

"Gabriel!" she exclaimed happily. "Let's go get it!"

She kissed him and jumped out of bed. Gabriel could not help but love her. He watched her patter naked over the cold stone to the safety of a Persian rug. Her skin was glowing in the late morning light, and her tousled chestnut hair was falling over her shoulders and down her back. He remained there unmoving, drunk with love.

"Come on!" she exclaimed, surprised that he was still in bed.

She was giving little jumps as she pulled on her jeans. Gabriel groaned as he sat up a little more.

"I feel like it's Christmas morning."

He threw himself back onto the pillows.

"I think I could use a little more sleep…"

"Shut up!" laughed Natasha, leaping onto the bed and falling into his arms.

"Oh, Gabriel," she said, hugging him tightly. "It was so beautiful last night."

"It really was," he agreed, kissing her neck and taking in a deep breath of her.

It had been something he could never have imagined before experiencing it firsthand. Together with Natasha, Gabriel had entered into a trance that transcended reality as he knew it. He would never be the same man again.

"Come on!" she said, taking his hand and pulling him from the bed. "Get dressed!"

* * * * * *

The bridge of the USS Stalwart looked like the helm of a starship. Like every Arleigh Burke-Class destroyer, it was among the largest and most powerful ever built, more heavily armed than any of its predecessors. Even still, its captain seemed unimpressed.

After decades of service, and countless seminars, the old admiral sitting in its command chair could still not get used to all of its new technology. It was as if the gadgets had suddenly appeared out of nowhere; as though he had woken up one day to find himself in the land of Buck Rogers. He seemed to constantly be studying manuals to keep abreast of the ever-changing technology. It was a task he abhorred.

"Goddamn bloody hell!" he cursed.

It had been a long night for Admiral Chester B. Sterling, and the morning was not proving to be any easier. As of late he had been having problems with his stomach, and he emptied another handful of Tums into his mouth in an attempt to curb the incessant burning.

"I picked a fine time to develop an ulcer," he complained in his southern drawl. "Smack dab in the middle of World War Three."

"Admiral Sterling, sir," said a communications officer seated before a battery of monitors. "We're being ordered to strike a target east of Tangiers."

"What's the target?" asked the admiral routinely.

"A terrorist cell, sir. They appear to be holed up in a castle."

"A castle…?" he asked, minutely interested. "Pull it up for me. Let's have a look."

The sergeant tapped away at his keyboard, instantly producing high-resolution satellite images of the target. The admiral looked at the various monitors spread out before him.

"Well, well, well," he said pensively. "That ain't gonna be an easy one to take out."

"Sir, they're calling for the use of fifteen Tomahawk missiles, sir."

"What?" he said, rising to his feet. "Have they gone mad? Who are those orders coming from, Sergeant?"

"The Commander in Chief, sir," said the sergeant, looking up at the admiral. "They're coming directly from POTUS."

"Well I'll be damned!" said the admiral, returning to his chair. "Wouldn't want to let him down, now would we? Soldiers, let's do a little castle demolition!"

Sterling worked the controls on the arm of his chair, magnifying the image so as to better determine the castle's structure.

"After five missiles, that place is gonna look like a pile of gravel in a Wisconsin prison quarry. After fifteen missiles, the President better get himself a beach towel, cause there ain't gonna be nothing there but silky-smooth sand!"

The communications officer shook his head in disbelief. Whoever it was they were hitting, they would not be leaving things half done, and at a cool five hundred thousand dollars per missile, it was clear the U.S. government was not scared of spending a little money to do the job right.

"Begin the preparation sequences, Sergeant," said the admiral, adjusting his cap. "And make sure you've got a live satellite feed open by detonation time. We've got cameras on every missile, and three up in space. I want to see 'em all. This is gonna to be quite a show!"

* * * * * *

"OK," said Gabriel, shouldering his duffel bag. "I'm ready."

"You're taking your pack?" asked Natasha.

"The Cube goes where we go," he said. "And so does my stuff."

"Do you have my toothbrush in there too?"

"As a matter of fact, I have your entire toiletry kit," he said with a wink.

Natasha moved to the door, shaking her head at Gabriel's over cautiousness. Opening it, she found Suora Angelica standing in the hall, a laden breakfast cart at her side.

"Suora!" exclaimed Natasha, delighted. "Oh, thank you, come in! It smells so good!"

"No, no, dear child," said the old nun, proffering the cart to Natasha. "I do not want to disturb you. I only came to give you this. Young lovers need their sleep, but they also need their breakfast."

Gabriel eyed the cart and was suddenly famished. The smell of coffee and bacon was already filling the room.

"There's no time to eat," he said, scooping some scrambled eggs onto a piece of toast and devouring it as he stood.

"Heavens me," said Suora, noticing that Gabriel had shouldered his pack. "Wherever are you going? And what could possibly be so important that you cannot even sit down to breakfast first?"

"Suora," said Natasha, looking intently at the old nun. "We think we know where the Book of Khalifah is."

"My child!" she gasped. "This is wonderful! Thanks be to the Blessed Virgin!"

"It's as if everything's led us directly to it," said Gabriel, shaking his head in disbelief. "That old gypsy woman didn't want us wasting our time coming here. It turns out it's the best thing we could have done."

"We think it might be hidden in the dungeons," said Natasha excitedly. "Why don't you come along?"

Suora stopped and turned.

"Did you say the dungeons?"

"Yes, Suora," said Gabriel. "Come on, let's go."

"Wait!" she said suddenly. "We must bring all of our things, as though we were going on a long journey."

"Why?" asked Gabriel. "We're just going down to the basement."

"No, my child," she said, her eyes glassy. "Mother Mary came to me in a dream last night, as she has often been doing of late. She said: *When you go to the dungeons, make ready for a long journey.* I did not know what she meant until just now."

"Well in that case, I'll take my backpack too," said Natasha, going to where her things were. "And the BIRIS as well."

"That's really weird, Suora," said Gabriel. "For some reason I felt like I had to take my things along too."

"We must heed our intuitions well in these times," said the old nun. "There are angels at our every side."

They entered into the corridor fully equipped and ready, and as chance would have it, Father Marcus and Fra Bartolomeo arrived there as well, having just finished their daily game of chess.

"Good morning, you two love birds," said the old bishop to Gabriel and Natasha. "I see that Suora is feeding you well."

"Gabriel's eating for both of us," said Natasha, motioning to him as he stuffed a bacon laden mini croissant into his mouth.

The bishop shook his head disapprovingly, as did Fra.

"And where might the three of you be going off to?" asked the old brother, looking curiously at Suora. "I see a pretty nun with a sparkle of excitement in her eyes, and the two of you with your packs on."

They drew closely together at Suora's insistence.

"We are going to look for the Book of Khalifah in the dungeons," she whispered excitedly. "Last night Gabriel and Natasha saw its location while they were…"

Suora stopped short. The bishop had already told her of the amorous way in which the Book would be located.

"While we were meditating," finished Gabriel, smiling slightly.

The old bishop's eyes lit up as he began to understand.

"Ah, yes… Meditating," he said with a wink.

He looked at the others.

"Now who would have thought that old book would be showing up here of all places?" he asked. "Shall we go?"

"We need to find Bahadur first," said Gabriel. "The book's in a safe. We'll need explosives."

"Why, Bahadur is already in the dungeons, my son," said the old bishop. "And I would not be surprised if he had explosives with him."

"What do you mean?" asked Gabriel. "What would he be doing with explosives down there?"

"They are setting up defences," said Fra. "Earlier on we saw a large group of them going down, all of them armed to the teeth. They fear Nasrallah may try to retake the castle."

"But why would they be setting up defences in the dungeons?" asked Natasha.

"Tunnels, my child," said the bishop. "The Moors built them to flank enemies that were laying siege. Nasrallah used one of them to escape."

Gabriel nodded in understanding.

"And he could use them again to stage a surprise attack."

"Exactly, my boy," said the bishop. "But tell me. Why the packs?"

"Suora had a dream last night," said Gabriel. "We're just playing it safe. You'd best bring your gear as well."

* * * * * *

Admiral Sterling stared into the monitor in disbelief. The face of John F. Abbot, President of the United States was looking back at him, a stern expression knotting his brow. What the admiral was being ordered to do was unheard of.

"Mr. President, sir," said Sterling respectfully. "Am I to understand that I am to place this destroyer, along with its entire compliment of three hundred and twenty-three souls under the direct control of a civilian, sir?"

"That's correct, Admiral," said Abbot. "But keep in mind that this is no ordinary civilian. He's the Permanent Secretary of the Vanderhoff Group. I don't expect you to know who he is, but I'll have you know that his organization has aided our country since it was in diapers, and you'll take any of his orders as though they were coming directly from me. Is that understood, Admiral?"

"Understood, Mr. President, sir," he said. "And thank you for the explanation, sir. It was not necessary."

"Admiral," continued Abbot in a more friendly tone. "I want you to know that our country owes a great debt to the Vanderhoff Group. We've got a world war on our hands right now, and our chain of command is stretched too thin to deal with individual terrorist cells, no matter how dangerous they might be. Mr. Antov is privy to all U.S. intelligence. I'm much obliged for his assistance, as I'm sure you can understand."

"Yes sir, Mr. President, sir," said the admiral. "And I will do everything in my power to ensure that his every order is executed with the diligence and bravery that is characteristic of the United States Navy, sir."

"Thank you, Admiral," said the President. "Over and out."

"Over and out, sir."

The admiral swiveled in his command chair as the screen went black, swallowing another handful of Tums and pressing a blue button on his control panel.

"Attention all hands," he said, chewing. "Commence firing sequence Delta Fourteen-Thirty-Two on my mark."

Admiral Sterling paused for the final confirmation from his ballistics officer and then turned back to face his bank of monitors.

"Fire," he ordered sharply, shifting his eyes to an exterior view of the ship.

Like angry hornets exiting a burning hive, the fifteen Tomahawk missiles left the destroyer's gun ports, each one on its way to the same destination.

* * * * * *

Rounding the final bend of their descent, Gabriel and his small entourage were at last able to see the source of the orders they had been hearing. Scotty Roberts was directing a group of six men, and beside him were Bahadur and a fully recovered Amir. Their backs were facing them, and Gabriel was the first to arrive.

"You have no authority to be down here!" he barked in his best foreign accent.

Amir spun around with swinging dreadlocks, but Bahadur did not even flinch.

"Welcome to the dungeons, Dr. Parker," he said, without turning. "No evil tongue could ever deliver a voice so eloquent as yours."

"You're no fun," said Gabriel, putting his arms around both of them. "But I've still got a surprise for you, Captain. I brought you some visitors."

Bahadur turned to see the small group, his smile warming when he noticed that Suora was among them.

"A pleasant surprise indeed," he said nobly, his voice as deep as the dungeon. "And how do I have the honour of this great visit?"

Natasha took hold of Bahadur and Amir and pulled them back into the corridor with the old bishop at her side.

"We need your help," she whispered, and then she proceeded to explain what she and Gabriel had learned of in their trance.

Bahadur seemed astonished.

"I cannot help but recall how you mentioned your need to locate a lost codex in our meeting last night, my lady…"

"That's right," said Natasha.

"Had you said that this codex was the Book of Khalifah, I would have been able to speak of it."

"What do you mean?"

"I have heard tell of this book, Doctor," said Bahadur, glancing aside as the others joined them. "I was among those who unearthed an ancient scroll that spoke of its existence."

Natasha blinked back at the giant wide-eyed.

"A scroll?" asked the bishop, taking hold of Bahadur's forearm. "What scroll, my son?"

"It was found in Ceuta. We were expanding an underground hashish operation there. Nasrallah had built the site years before, in ancient tunnels that ran beneath the city. When production was not meeting his expectations, he ordered me to expand the site by digging new tunnels. It was then that we found the chamber."

"What kind of chamber?" asked Gabriel.

"It was like no other I had ever seen," said Bahadur, his brow furrowing as he remembered. "I was alerted to it by the cries of the workers. They were calling out a name. *Al Tariq! Al Tariq!*"

"The Moorish general," said Gabriel, rubbing the stubble on his jaw.

"It was a treasure house," continued Bahadur. "Built by Al Tariq. I could see the gold in the reflected light before I had even entered the room. There were many treasures there, and on a sole pedestal was a golden scroll, still open and undisturbed for centuries.

"I notified Nasrallah at once. When he arrived, he cried out in victory. '*The Cube and the Book are mine!*' he said. Nasrallah knew much about ancient things. He studied archaeology at the University of Cambridge."

"Did he really?" asked Natasha, surprised. "What a well-bred villain…"

"He is a dog, my lady," said Bahadur, a painful expression coming over his battered face. "Do not be fooled. There were four men digging there that day. They were good men, fathers of families. Nasrallah ordered them to build a door covering the entrance which he later locked. After that he invited us all to a dinner of celebration. We were taken in separate cars. I never saw the men again."

"What happened after that?" asked Gabriel.

"I arrived at Nasrallah's suite to find him with the scroll. He told me many things, just as they had been told to him by his grandfather."

"What did he say?" asked Natasha.

"He told me the legend of the *Cube of Knowledge*, and how it could transform the soul of a man and make him immortal. He then spoke of the Book of Khalifah, and how it had been created by sages from the four corners of the earth, so that the Cube's power could one day be unharnessed.

"He said that the scroll would lead us to both the Book and the Cube. I can still remember how he held it aloft. There was a madness in his eyes."

"What was on the scroll?" asked Gabriel.

"A map," replied Bahadur, frowning. "It showed the Strait of Gibraltar, and Cordoba as it would have been many centuries ago. On it was marked the resting place of the Cube, a burial chamber belonging to the Barghawata ambassador to Córdoba, *Abu Salih Zammur*."

"His tomb was excavated in 1928," said Gabriel.

Bahadur nodded.

"Yes," he said. "And its contents were moved to the Tangiers Museum of Antiquities. Nasrallah told me that the Cube would have appeared to be an unremarkable relic to anyone not familiar with it, and that he believed it still resided in the museum. It was not long before we were planning the robbery."

"So that's how Nasrallah found the Cube," said Natasha, amazed. "His grandfather told him about it."

"Ustadh Darrak was a good elder," said Bahadur. "The most learned in the medina. As a boy I would visit his home every day. He taught me of our Moorish forefathers and infected me with their incessant thirst for knowledge."

"Some people say he was an oracle," said Amir, nodding. "He was blind, but he walked around like he could see. Bahadur would have been a university professor today if old Darrak had had his way."

Bahadur's dark eyes were staring into the past.

"In the end the old man was not so wise," he said deeply. "He did not see the evil that lurked in his grandson's heart. Darrak was the reason why Nasrallah studied archaeology. His tales filled him with wonder. It was a great coincidence that we should have stumbled upon the scroll in those tunnels that night..."

"There are no coincidences, dear Bahadur," said the old bishop. "There is only universal order. Now, what of the Book of Khalifah? Did Nasrallah recover that as well?"

Bahadur shook his head.

"He did not. The map on the scroll showed the existence of a secret tunnel originating in the treasure room, but we could not find it. We spent weeks looking. In the end Nasrallah gave up.

"He seemed content to possess the Cube and all the treasures he had found in the chamber. When everything had been sold, the profits amounted to almost four million Euros. He used the money to purchase this castle."

"Not a bad haul," said Gabriel, shaking his head and looking over at Natasha. "But why did we see the Book of Khalifah in our trance then?"

He turned to Bahadur.

"Nasrallah must have found it. Can you take us to the chamber we told you about?"

"I can," said the giant. "It is next to the chamber where my family was being held."

He turned to look in that direction.

"I know now that Elakhdar did more than just save their lives," he added. "Nasrallah must have tried to get through him to retrieve the Book. If the pigdog does not have it now, it is thanks to Elakhdar. He killed two of his men and sent the rat fleeing into the tunnels."

"Where are they, my son?" asked Suora suddenly. "Where is your family?"

Bahadur smiled tenderly at the old nun.

"They are safe, sweet Sister. They left early this morning. I had two of my men drive them back to Tangiers."

"Let's go," said Gabriel suddenly. "I'm dying to find this book."

They followed Bahadur as he led them through the party of smugglers. As they passed, they spotted Scotty Roberts sending a group of his men off into a tunnel with sandbags and ammunition. Natasha saw him look suddenly over at her. He flashed a smile so charming that she felt herself blushing self-consciously.

* * * * * *

"This is the chamber," said Bahadur. "But I have never seen a strongbox here."

"That's because it's hidden under this masonry," said Gabriel, bending a knee.

By prying his hunting knife into a seam, he was able to lift a stone enough to get his fingers around it. In this way he cleared two other stones of similar size until an iron safe came into view.

"Now we've just got to blow the door off," he said, looking up at Bahadur. "Where do you keep your explosives?"

"I have a sufficient charge here on my belt," said the giant, tossing a fist-sized pouch down to Gabriel.

In a matter of seconds he had laid the charge, and all exited the chamber so that it might be detonated. Gabriel was the first to re-enter after the explosion.

"There's no book," he said through the clearing smoke. "But there's a scroll..."

All moved closer as Gabriel held up a gem encrusted cylinder. Even in the dim light it sparkled magnificently.

"It's beautiful," whispered Natasha, her eyes alight as she took hold of it. "It must be the one from the secret chamber."

No sooner had Natasha finished speaking, however, than they were all thrown to the ground. A barrage of gravel and sand was coming down around them as a series of earthshaking explosions ripped through the castle above.

CHAPTER 21

Central Jerusalem, Israel.

Doctor Bennington awoke to find himself in an enormous bed, in what looked to be the suite of a five-star hotel. Daylight was streaming in through the curtains.

"I dreamed the entire thing..." he muttered sleepily, rising and moving to the window. "I'm not even underground. It's a wonderful day outside..."

He arrived at the window and opened the curtains to find a beautiful view of southern France stretching off into the distance, the sounds of chirping birds and the gentle rustle of leaves filling the air.

"But what is this?" he muttered to himself. "This isn't real..."

Looking more closely, he was able to see that the view was in fact a holographic projection of exceedingly high resolution. He fell back onto the bed, sitting and watching as a group of sparrows swooped off his balcony and disappeared into the lush valley that lay beyond.

"Good morning, Doctor," came the voice of Christian Antov. "I see you are enjoying the view."

Bennington turned to see Christian's face on a monitor above the room's fireplace, and the events of the past days came flooding into his mind. He recalled with horror the terrible experiments he had been forced to witness in the secret research facility, and how Christian had commanded Cynthia to kill herself in the Holy of Holies.

Only then did he remember how he had lost consciousness shortly after that event, and how he had dreamed that Cynthia's corpse had been reanimated and possessed by a demon summoned from hell.

Thank God it was just a dream…

He looked with repulsion at the face that filled the monitor.

"You are a murderous monster," he whispered.

"I am what I am, good Doctor," replied Christian. "Now clean yourself up. You will be escorted to meet me for breakfast in precisely thirty minutes. I hope that leaves you with enough time."

* * * * * *

The breakfast room was as luxurious as Bennington's suite, and every bit as comfortable. He scanned the faces at the tables around him, observing what appeared to be a very normal collection of professionals, each chatting amiably amongst themselves, just as they might have done in any other restaurant setting.

They have no concept of what they are a part of…

Bennington scanned the surroundings, looking up to see a barrel-vaulted ceiling comprised entirely of curved glass panel monitors, each one giving a sectional view of a moving summer sky. The illusion was perfect. To his right, numerous French doors opened onto a terrace shaded in dense grapevines, a holographic view of Provence stretching off into the distance.

Were it not for all that had transpired, Bennington, like the many others who populated the dining room, would have certainly been filled with a sense of peace and relaxation. Even the air was fragrant with the scent of southern France.

"I hope you are enjoying our habitat," said Christian, approaching the table and seating himself opposite the doctor. "We have paid infinite attention to every detail here.

As you can see, today we are in Provence. Next week we will be in Tuscany, and after that on an island in Greece."

Bennington said nothing. He could only think of the cold bloodedness that Christian had exhibited when he had commanded the girl to commit suicide.

"It had to be done," said Christian. "There was no alternative."

"You may be capable of fooling yourself, Christian," said Bennington in the most professional tone he could muster, "but you will never succeed in fooling me. There is always an alternative. You did not have to act on your impulses. You had the strength of mind to resist them."

"Come now, Doctor. You've seen all the movies, haven't you?"

"What are you talking about, Christian?"

"The virgin sacrifice, of course," said Christian, holding up a silencing hand as the waiter approached.

"Eggs Florentine, hot coffee, and extra Hollandaise. My guest will have the same but make his eggs Benedict."

"Very good, sir."

"Now then," continued Christian as the waiter moved off. "Where was I?"

"Why did you kill her?" demanded the doctor.

"So that the captains of my army might be assembled. I also wanted to see how well the virus worked outside the laboratory."

"What the hell are you talking about, Christian?" said Bennington, a little too loudly for Christian's liking.

Bennington leaned forward and whispered.

"You're confusing your delusions with reality."

"Am I, Doctor?" asked Christian. "Perhaps you are doing the same? Did you not also see what happened last night? Why do you deny it?"

Bennington was taken aback by the question. What had occurred after Cynthia had died had clearly happened in his dreams. It could not be real. Christian was simply reading his mind and trying to confuse him.

"But why the girl?" he asked painfully. "She was innocent. She had done you no harm."

At that moment Christian's phone rang.

"Why is the strike behind schedule?" he demanded.

There was a long pause as he listened.

"Are you telling me that you fired fifteen Tomahawk missiles and failed to destroy the target?"

Another pause.

"It is irrelevant that the castle has been demolished. The artifact is still intact!"

Christian's anger was merging with his frustration. His newly acquired powers were telling him that the Cube was in perfect condition. He could sense it, just as he could sense the approximate location of the Two.

"How I know this is not your concern!" he snapped into the phone. "I will inform you when the Cube has been destroyed!"

Christian listened intently, his brow knotting with anger.

"It is most likely below ground, you idiot!" he snapped. "Put Nasrallah on the phone."

There was a pause.

"You escaped the castle by means of a tunnel," said Christian. "Is this not true?"

He listened.

"If you need men, then get men," he said. "My agents will assist you. Search every tunnel. Block every exit. If they are still alive the only place they could possibly be is in the lower levels of the castle. Find them, kill them, and bring me the Cube and the scroll. Is that clear?"

He listened again.

"Go! I want a progress report every hour."

Christian pocketed his phone just as their food arrived.

"Enjoy your breakfast, Doctor," he said standing up. "Unfortunately, I cannot join you. I have pressing matters to attend to."

* * * * * *

Christian sat at a granite desk in an enormous room walled in the same cold stone. He slid a finger over a small, disc-shaped interface before him and watched as a holographic keyboard and monitor materialized. After keying in his instructions, he moved his fingers through the air to activate the necessary node points on the monitor.

"Initiate conference connection," he said, and a moment later the face of Admiral Chester B. Sterling appeared on the monitor.

"Mr. Antov," he said, giving a stiff salute. "An honour to meet you, sir. I've spoken directly with the President and have been ordered to put this ship, and its entire compliment, at your disposal. The missile strike has been executed and the target destroyed. Is there anything else I can help you with today, sir?"

"Yes, Admiral, there is," said Christian. "Am I correct to understand that you have helicopters on board?"

"Yes, sir, Mr. Antov, sir. We have two SH-60 Sea Hawk helicopters on board, sir."

"Very well, Admiral," said Christian. "I would like you to send both of them to the site we have just targeted. It's possible that some of the terrorists have eluded the attack and are escaping on foot. If this is the case, I want helicopters there to eliminate them."

The admiral frowned in consternation.

"Mr. Antov," he said respectfully. "The Tomahawks we fired went in below radar and are not officially traceable to the US navy. Helicopters would be picked up immediately by Moroccan radar. You do understand that deploying any military aircraft into Moroccan air space will be considered a deliberate act of war."

"I am aware of this, Admiral," said Christian dryly. "Please dispatch them as soon as possible, and have your technicians send me live feeds. I want to know what those Sea Hawks are doing. Can you do this for me, Admiral?"

"Yes, sir, Mr. Antov. My men will have your live feeds up and running in the time it takes for the Sea Hawks to arrive at the target."

"Very good, Admiral," said Christian. "I will be waiting."

CHAPTER 22

The Atlas Mountains, Morocco.

Scotty Roberts was the first to get back on his feet after the explosions. He burst into the chamber where the others were to find Bahadur rising from beneath a pile of rubble. Under the shelter of the brown-skinned giant lay the little nun.

"Are you hurt, Sister?" he said to her, his voice deep with concern.

"No," said Suora, a little shaken. "I am fine. Thank you, Bahadur. You saved my life."

She looked around.

"But how are the others?"

Under the dim glow of the emergency lights, their companions could be seen rising slowly in the dusty air. Gabriel had thrown himself over Natasha, and Amir had managed to cover Fra Bartolomeo. It had all happened very quickly, and they were still reeling from the attack.

"Where's Uncle Marcus!" coughed Natasha, spinning to look for him.

At that moment, a heap of rubble near the center of the room began to shift.

"That must be him!" said Scotty, rushing to the mound. "He's the only bloke still missing!"

The smuggler was soon digging through the rubble. The others joined immediately. It did not take long before the good bishop came into view. He sat huddled under an old wooden table, wrapped in his frocks.

"Good of you to dig me out," he said, coughing. "It was getting a trifle close in here."

"Uncle!" exclaimed Natasha. "Are you hurt?"

"I appear to be intact, young lady," he said. "I only hope that our treasure has fared equally well."

And just then the bishop opened his frocks to reveal the glimmering cylinder held safely in his lap.

"You saved it!" said Natasha. "I was sure it was lost."

"Not on your life, child," said the bishop, holding out the cylinder.

Natasha took it while Gabriel helped the old bishop to his feet.

"How'd you act so quickly?"

"Second nature, dear child!" he exclaimed, shaking the dust from his vestments. "As a boy I weathered the London blitzes of World War Two, don't forget! Much more than the bombs, I feared my mother's belt if I'd forgotten to take the china with me under the stairs!"

They all laughed, Scotty Roberts especially. He had never seen people taking to life threatening dangers so easily. He looked at the old nun, amazed. She had fallen into Fra's arms, and they were both laughing merrily.

"Have you all lost your minds?" he said at last, a sudden realization coming over him. "What are we doing laughing? We've got men in the tunnels! And what about all the blokes up top?"

With his words their laughter came instantly to an end. In the joy of their own survival, they had forgotten the severity of the situation.

"Gather the men!" said Bahadur to Amir, his basso voice booming. "See if the way up to the castle is still open! Roberts! Arrange to have the other four tunnels searched! I want to know which ones are still passable! We must move quickly! Nasrallah's men could already be here!"

Bahadur helped the others find their packs in the rubble. It was not long before they were all assembled in the outer chamber, ready for the next move. Amir was the first to arrive back. He was pale with shock.

"The way up's completely blocked..." he muttered. "There were four men in that passage..."

"What?" cried Gabriel. "We've got to dig them out!"

Amir was shaking his head in grief.

"It's impossible, boss. They're gone."

Gabriel kicked a piece of rubble in frustration and looked up at the ceiling.

"What could they have hit us with? I counted five explosions."

"Artillery strikes," said Bahadur, approaching. "There were several explosions in each strike. I was not aware that Nasrallah had such an arsenal."

"That was no artillery strike," said Scotty, appearing with only two of his men. "They were missiles."

"How can you be sure?" asked Gabriel.

"Because we found a way out," he said gravely.

Like Amir, he too was in a state of shock.

"There's nothing left up there, mate. The men in the tunnels have all been lost. We're the only survivors. Everyone else is dead."

"What are you saying?" exclaimed Natasha, waking to the extent of the tragedy. "How can that be? There were almost a hundred people up there!"

Bahadur turned to face Scotty and gripped his shoulders with both hands.

"What did you see, my friend?" he asked gently, his battered features etched with sadness.

"The castle's gone, Captain," said Scotty through tears of anger. "There's just a pile of burning rubble. Everything's been decimated. They're all dead. Bloody hell. Every last one of them."

"What weapons could have done this?" muttered Bahadur, swaying on his feet.

"We counted fifteen hits," said Scotty, stumbling backward and slumping to the ground. "I'm no expert, but by the accuracy of the strikes, and the damage, I'd say they were guided missiles, most likely American or British. They're the only ones with military forces in the area."

"All our friends are dead," muttered Amir, slumping to the ground with head in hands.

There had been almost thirty Gibraltarian men in the castle above, and twice that number of Moroccans.

"How can they all be dead?" said Gabriel. "There's got to be survivors."

"Anyone buried in the rubble won't survive long," said Scotty. "There's no way to get to them. Bloody hell! If you saw it, you'd understand. There's literally nothing left. God damn those bloody bastards!"

"How could the Americans be involved in this?" asked Gabriel. "Was Nasrallah a suspected terrorist?"

"Not to my knowledge," said Amir, bewildered. "But U.S. intelligence has been known to make mistakes before. We can't rule out the Brits either."

"At this moment it is of no concern who did this," said Bahadur suddenly, wiping the tears from his eyes. "Whoever it was who fired those missiles will be on their way here. We must leave this place at once, or we too will be dead. We have some ammunition and supplies, but we are few against such a force. What of the other tunnels?"

"All blocked," said Scotty, rising to his feet. "The only way out is by the front tunnel."

"That would be suicide," said Amir, unfastening the safety strap on his combat knife. "If they're not up there already, they'll be here any second. Even if we could get out in time, they'd just track us down and kill us."

"There might be another way," said Bahadur. "A secret tunnel that leads to the river. We must see if it is still functional."

Gabriel and Amir followed Bahadur out of the chamber. When they returned, they found the others sitting amongst the wreckage. Natasha had removed the scroll from its canister and was studying it intently.

"The tunnel to the river's still good," said Gabriel. "We've got to go now."

"Why, mate?" asked Scotty, dejectedly. "What's the use? We're already dead. The only safe place would be outside Morocco, and unless there's a chopper down there, I can't see what the point of running is. Nasrallah's got agents all over this country."

"I think you should all look at this," said Natasha, peering up from the scroll.

Gabriel went over with the others in tow. Spread out before them, and glimmering in precisely worked gold leaf and silver point, was an ornate map, fashioned in the style of ancient Islam.

"That is the scroll I told you of," said Bahadur deeply.

"Is that Tangiers?" ventured the old bishop, pointing to a coastal city on the Strait of Gibraltar.

"I'd say it was Ceuta," said Gabriel, pushing back his hair as he bent closer.

"And you would be correct, Dr. Parker," said Bahadur.

He pointed to a spot within the city.

"Marked here is the chamber where this scroll was found."

The old bishop produced his spectacles.

"Then this must be Gibraltar on the other side of the strait."

"And what's this?" asked Natasha, running her finger over a meandering golden line that began in the chamber that Bahadur had just pointed out. It stretched across the sea to Gibraltar.

"That, my dear girl," said the bishop, "must certainly be the legendary Tunnel of St. Michael."

"St. Michael's Pass?" said Gabriel. "How could that be? It's just a legend."

"What legend?" asked Natasha, her eyes alternating between the two of them. "What tunnel?"

"The Rock of Gibraltar's a honeycomb of tunnels and underground chambers," said Gabriel. "Some are ancient, others are as recent as the nineteen-forties. There's basically a small city in there."

"And St. Michael's Pass?" asked Natasha.

"There are natural caves under Gibraltar too. They're off limits to the public. If you descend deep enough, you come to an underground lake. I was there once on a military tunnel tour. When you traverse the lake you arrive at Lower St. Michael's Cave. It's basically a bottomless pit."

"It's marked here on the map," said Natasha, pointing to the place. "It's where the tunnel ends."

Gabriel shook his head in amazement.

"There's an old legend in Gibraltar," he said. "It claims the pit descends into a system of caves that traverses the strait, but it's never been confirmed. They've sent dozens of expeditions down over the centuries but the men in them always disappear."

The bishop tapped the spot on the map with an old finger.

"During one of Gibraltar's many sieges, a little boy was lowered down on a rope. He was given a drum and a bag of gold. His instructions were to play the drum continuously so they would know he was still alive. The plan was to use the gold to bring back men and supplies from Africa, but just like all the others, he too disappeared."

"But how could he disappear if he was tied to a rope?" asked Natasha.

The bishop shrugged. Gabriel continued.

"Legend has it that when the drumming stopped, they pulled up the rope to find it severed."

Gabriel turned away from the map and began to pace.

"To all Gibraltarians, Lower St. Michael's Cave has always been an unsolved mystery. It's even rumored that the military once sent an unmanned probe down there but that they lost contact with it as well."

Natasha was amazed.

"Looking at this map," she said, "it would appear that those tunnels really do exist."

She pointed to what looked like a chamber near the halfway point, somewhere deep beneath the Mediterranean Sea.

"And what's this?" she asked.

"That is the Chamber of Khalifah," said Bahadur, frowning. "The place where the Book of Khalifah supposedly resides. But as I said before, we were unable to find an entrance to the tunnel that leads there."

Gabriel looked up from the map, his eyes locking with Natasha's.

"If the tunnel entrance exists, I can find it, but one thing's for sure though. It'll be heavily trapped."

The bishop cleared his throat and readjusted his black vestments.

"Traps would explain why so many people have gone missing over the centuries," he said.

Bahadur rose from his stooped position over the map.

"We will find and take St. Michael's Pass," he said. "Ceuta is thirty kilometres north of here. We will hide in the caves by the river until nightfall, and then follow it to the city under the cover of darkness. I will take you to the treasure chamber, Dr. Parker, and there you will find the tunnel entrance. The Pass will lead us to safety. We must leave at once."

He tossed Scotty a packet of explosives.

"Plant them in the short tunnel. Time them to detonate in fifteen minutes. I want that passage completely sealed so they cannot follow us. We leave now!"

CHAPTER 23

They were still descending when the explosives detonated. There would be no going back now. Bahadur had made sure of that. To eliminate any risk of pursuit, he had insisted on blowing the entrance to the tunnel they were in as well. The only way to go now was down, and they all hoped that the path would be open.

They proceeded in single file, each member of the party of ten clinging to the rough walls. The tunnel descended steeply, its perilous steps carrying them to the valley floor. Here a wide and fast-moving river stretched out before them, flanked by towering cliffs. Although swollen from heavy rains, there was just enough space to walk along its edge. The sun had yet to rise above the chasm and all was still in shadow.

"We must move north as quickly as possible," said Bahadur, breathing in the cool river air. "Nasrallah must not see us. If he does, there will be no hope of escape."

At that very moment the ground at their feet began to explode under a rain of bullets. Looking up they could see a cluster of men on the clifftops. They were shooting down at them.

"Get back against the wall!" bellowed Bahadur.

Everyone obeyed instantly, taking shelter beneath the outcroppings of rock. Two of the men that were with them, Miller and Stephenson, jumped out into the open to return fire. They were armed with assault rifles and the deafening rattle left Suora and Natasha bringing their hands to their ears.

"Get back in here, God damn it!" bellowed Scotty. "You're wasting ammunition!"

The two men did as they were told and the group remained pinned where they were, desperately thinking of a way out.

"How could Nasrallah have known we were down here?" asked Natasha. "And that we were even still alive..."

"The answer is obvious, my child," said the bishop. "He must be in communication with the Nautonnier."

"The who?" asked Gabriel as another barrage of bullets struck the rocks above them.

"The Nautonnier is the leader of a powerful organization, my son. I will tell you more of him later."

Amir shuffled over to Gabriel's side.

"Are you thinking what I'm thinking?" he asked, tying back his dreadlocks with a bandana.

"I've been thinking it the whole way down."

Natasha joined them.

"What are you two conspiring about?"

"Feel like getting to Ceuta really fast?" asked Gabriel.

Natasha nodded.

"As long as it doesn't involve getting shot."

Gabriel reached over and tapped Bahadur.

"I think there's a way out of here."

The giant frowned.

"There is very little time, Dr. Parker," he said. "Thirty minutes at most."

"That's more than enough to get to the raft."

Bahadur was confused.

"What raft?" asked Natasha.

Gabriel and Amir exchanged a glance.

"If it's still there," said Amir, producing a hot cinnamon toothpick from his pocket and slipping it into his mouth.

"What raft?" asked Natasha again. "What are you guys talking about?"

Another hailstorm of bullets commenced, this time sending blasts of sand and stone fragments down upon them. Gabriel took hold of Natasha and sheltered her with his body.

"When Amir and I came to steal the Cube, we used a river raft to escape," he said. "We took it down stream to where we had our truck parked, but we didn't have time to deflate it and take it with us."

"We hid it in the bushes instead," added Amir over his shoulder. "It might still be there."

"But Gabriel, my son," said the old bishop. "There are ten of us, and all of our equipment as well."

Gabriel nodded, shielding his face from yet another barrage of flying sand and grit. The bullets were coming down with increased ferocity now. Gabriel had to raise his voice to be heard over the maelstrom of bullets.

"When we tried to buy an inflatable raft, we couldn't find one anywhere!" he cried. "The only place around was an Australian white-water rafting company just upriver. They didn't have any small rafts, just those big round ones that hold eight people. We bought one anyway. I think it would hold us all if we squeezed in."

"And you think we could escape on it?" asked Natasha. "How could we possibly paddle that quickly?"

Gabriel shook his head and pushed back his hair. They did not understand.

"We're on the banks of a river that people from all over the world come to for white-water rafting," he said. "It flows fast; *really* fast. It goes through the mountains and empties into the sea right around Ceuta."

"Where is this raft?" asked Bahadur, frowning in disbelief.

"It's on this side of the river," said Amir. "Only about twenty minutes from here if it's still there."

"It might even be closer than that," said Gabriel. "It's hard to say."

"Then we must go at once," said Bahadur. "Already the firing has stopped. They will be moving away from us. South to the only place where they can descend into the gorge. They will come quickly."

He turned to the others.

"We go now!" he said. "Stay close to the rockface!"

They had only begun to move when the shots began again, but this time from a single sharpshooter that had been left behind. They jumped back under the cover of the rocks, but Gabriel was holding his shoulder. Natasha gasped when she saw blood soaking through his shirt.

"I'm all right," he said, wincing in pain. "It's just a graze. Let's go. We haven't got time."

They made their way downstream as quickly as possible, hugging the wall until they were confident that they were out of the sniper's range. The swollen river was already beginning to look dangerously turbulent.

"And will it be safe in this raft?" asked the old bishop, looking out over the swelling torrents.

"Safer than bullets, priest," said Scotty, squinting up at the cliffs.

Amir kept track of the time as they made their way along. They had already been walking for fifteen minutes with no sign of the raft. He frowned and chewed worriedly on his toothpick.

It had been dark that night, and their speed hard to measure. The distance that had only taken them minutes to cover in the raft was proving to be much greater than he had expected.

"They will soon be upon us," said Bahadur. "Are you certain that we have not already passed the site?"

"Not a chance," said Gabriel. "I'd recognize it in a second. It's in a little cul-de-sac. There was a lot of vegetation around it. I'm sure we're almost there."

Just then the blast of a rifle sounded behind them, and the rocks to the right of Gabriel's head exploded under the impact of a bullet.

"Stay close to the rockface!" bellowed Bahadur. "We must continue to move downstream at all costs!"

"We'll cover you!" said Scotty, slapping the backs of Miller and Stephenson. "Come on gents, let's do this!"

The three Gibraltarians tucked in as close to the rocks as possible, sending controlled bursts of bullets into the enemy. Bahadur and Amir joined them, their assault rifles singing. They could see at least fifty men running for cover, not three hundred yards upstream. They had come hard and fast.

"Keep moving!" cried Bahadur. "We must make it to that raft!"

They shot as they went, two of them stopping in turn to return fire while the others advanced. Alternating in this way, they managed to cover their flight with a continual spray of bullets.

The enemy was finding it very difficult to gain any ground on them. Already the only two marksmen who had attempted to emerge from their cover lay wounded on the sand. The twist of the river was working against them, allowing their prey to continue downstream while they remained pinned to the rocks and unable to advance.

In this way Gabriel led the party ahead, arriving at last at the cul-de-sac they had been looking for. He pulled the circular raft from the undergrowth and sighed with relief. It was in perfect condition. With the help of Natasha and Fra they moved it into the water and began loading it with equipment. Thanks to the rock formations, the shallow cul-de-sac offered decent cover from the incessant barrage of bullets.

"We're good to go!" bellowed Gabriel over the clatter.

Their guns rang out in unison as they jumped into the raft. Suora, Fra, the bishop and Natasha huddled in the middle, with Gabriel and Amir manning the paddles in front. In this way the four gunners were able to climb into the rear of the raft and cover their backs with a spray of bullets. It worked perfectly, forcing the enemy to take cover and return only sporadic fire.

"We are pulling out of range!" cried Bahadur. "Drop your guns and take up the paddles!"

Within seconds they had navigated the raft into the centre of the river where stronger currents accelerated them out of harm's way. Behind them in the distance they could see a large group of men, perhaps a hundred strong, emerging from their cover. They stood at the base of the towering cliff face, watching as their prey slipped away.

"We did it!" cried Natasha happily.

"So far so good," said Gabriel, "but we've saved the best for last."

In a matter of seconds, they were learning why the river was one of the most sought-after white-water rafting destinations in the world.

"Steer left!" bellowed Gabriel, the raft lurching over a massive boulder. "We need to get to the right of those rocks!"

Back at the rafting outfitters, Amir had casually studied a map of the river while Gabriel had arranged their purchase. He knew that the worst was yet to come. Before opening into a smooth flowing waterway, the river would first pass through a very tight gorge dubbed *The Eye of the Needle.* Here the ride would take on its most challenging aspects. It was an extremely dangerous run and not for the novice rafter.

"Have you ever done this before, boss?" hollered Amir to Gabriel over the roaring water.

"Only once when I was a kid!"

The raft was already dangerously low in the water and Amir swallowed hard, tightening his grip on his paddle and getting ready for the fight of his life.

"To the right!" yelled Gabriel, a sudden explosion of river water dousing them all from head to foot. "Hard! Now!"

The group responded instantly, each of them paddling with all their might. Up ahead Amir could see the Eye of the Needle approaching rapidly. It was still a ways off, but at the speed they were moving, he knew it would not be long before they were in the worst of the rapids. From that point of entry, they would travel over two kilometres before finally being ejected into the open river beyond. If they could get through the narrow gorge without capsizing, the rest of the way would be smooth sailing.

* * * * * *

Christian sat at his desk. The expansive holographic monitor before him held a dozen different windows, each containing a live video feed from helicopter cockpits, helmets cams, and satellite images. It was in several of these that he could see the river raft making its way towards the mountain gorge.

"Estimated time of arrival to target location, three minutes and counting," came the voice of one of the pilots.

Christian spotted the two Sea Hawks approaching the river on a satellite image.

"Fire on the target as soon as you see them," he ordered dryly.

"Roger that, Mr. Antov, sir," said a pilot. "Terrorist target will be destroyed at first visual."

Christian moved uneasily in his chair. He could see that the raft was rapidly approaching the narrowing of the gorge and knew that the helicopters would not be able to pursue them into it. He shifted his gaze between the various satellite feeds on his monitor and passed a hand through his hair anxiously.

* * * * * *

"Helicopters!" cried Fra, his keen hearing picking up the beating blades of the Sea Hawks before anyone else.

Gabriel turned to see the two military choppers descending to within an arm's length of the river's surface, not three hundred meters behind them. They were gaining quickly, their massive guns poised and ready to fire the moment they came into range.

Before them the Eye of the Needle was approaching rapidly as well. If they could make it there before the helicopters commenced their firing they would live a little while longer. Ultimately, however, Gabriel knew they had little hope. When their raft emerged on the other side of the gorge there would be no cover to be had. They would be sitting ducks.

At that instant the river behind them began to boil with a spray of high calibre rounds. They were just at the edge of the gorge now and the shadows of the towering cliffs were falling over them.

"Go! Go!" cried Gabriel, paddling frantically. "We're going to make it!"

They moved as one, paddling with every ounce of their strength. As of yet, no bullet had found them, and with every passing second they plunged deeper and deeper into the gorge. If they could make it a little further the helicopters would be forced to let off their chase and fly to the north side to await them there.

"We're in!" cried Amir just as two missiles slammed into the rockfaces directly to their left and right.

The fiery explosions were deafening, and the blasts sent large sections of cliff sliding into the river. A shower of boulders was raining down around them, and Gabriel could see dangerous rock fragments flying past on all sides. It seemed impossible that not a single projectile struck them.

He shook his head in disbelief and shifted his attention to where the river was leading them. Its surface was churning treacherously, and it seemed preposterous that any vessel could be expected to pass through such a furious mass of water without being utterly destroyed.

"Bloody hell!" screamed Scotty, paddling for his life. "Out of the frying pan and into the bleeding fire!"

The river was exploding beneath them, the raft lurching and bending as the angry countercurrents tried to suck them under. It was all Gabriel could do to pick a path through the chaos and hope for the best. With his lack of experience, it was more a guessing game than anything else.

"We must stop the raft somewhere in this gorge!" cried Bahadur amid powerful strokes. "They will be waiting for us on the other side!"

Gabriel scanned their surroundings and knew the order would be impossible to obey. The current had them in its grip. Merely staying above it without capsizing would be a feat in itself. Stopping was not even a possibility.

* * * * * *

"Take up positions on the other side of the gorge," said Christian calmly.

He had watched the raft disappearing into the dark chasm from the helicopter cameras, but he was not worried. Even if his prey managed to survive the rapids, there would be no escape for them on the other side. This time he had them. There was not a doubt in his mind.

"No," muttered Christian in disbelief.

He had just noticed ten objects on the long-range radar feed. They were approaching rapidly, and he knew by their speed that they could only be one thing: Moroccan fighter jets.

Christian cursed as he watched them converging on the helicopters. The two Sea Hawks would be no match against ten Mirage F1 fighters. Even still, there was a good chance that the Sea Hawks would be able to destroy their target before the fighter jets arrived.

In that moment he saw the helicopters beginning to move away.

"What's happening?" he screamed. "Where are you going?"

"Enemy fighter jets approaching, sir," came the voice of the admiral. "This is standard procedure."

"Return to your positions immediately!" bellowed Christian in fury. "Destroy the enemy target!"

Christian saw the admiral's face appear on his monitor.

"Mr. Antov!" he said. "The pilots will be lost! They must retreat to international airspace!"

"They will accomplish their mission!" snapped Christian.

"Then they will die," said the admiral.

Christian watched the helicopters return to their positions, and just then the voice of a Moroccan captain sounded over the radio feed.

"You are in Moroccan air space. Leave immediately or you will be shot down."

Christian peered at the opening of the cliffs on his monitor, his eyes darting back and forth between the helicopter view and the satellite image of the rapidly approaching fighter jets.

"Prepare for evasive action!" ordered the admiral.

"Belay that order!" commanded Christian. "You will hold your positions!"

* * * * * *

Gabriel looked ahead. A vertical sliver of light had only just appeared out of the shadows. Against all odds they had made it through, but he felt no elation. Along the entire run there had been no opportunity to dock the raft, let alone even slow it down. They now found themselves barreling to their doom at top speed. It would take a miracle to save them now.

As if in slow motion, Natasha spotted the two Sea Hawks hovering over the surface of the river. Their rotor blades were chopping the air, their missiles and guns on the verge of firing. She turned to face Gabriel. He had since stopped paddling and the others followed suit. The end had come, and they all made ready to be taken into the great unknown.

Natasha fell into Gabriel's arms as the missiles left the helicopters. Their raft had been ejected into open water now, and above them black clouds were amassing.

"It is a good day to die," said Bahadur with a grim smile.

"Maybe not!" cried Amir, suddenly noticing the trajectory the missiles were taking.

In seconds their raft was lurching in the turbulent air as the rockets flew past, missing them by a metre on each side and exploding onto the bluffs behind them.

A rain of gunfire had suddenly enveloped the helicopters, the deafening roar of jet engines clapping against the echoing cliffs.

The hovering Sea Hawks exploded in great fireballs a moment later, crashing to the surface of the lake amid chopping blades and burning hulls. They disappeared from sight almost instantly, and just then the fighter jets swept past in a chest-rattling pass, roaring upwards and away in tight formation.

By the swiftness of the attack, it appeared as though their small raft had gone completely unnoticed. Everyone let sound a cheer of relief and joy, unable to believe their eyes.

"Thanks be to Allah!" cried Bahadur.

"And long live the Moroccan air force!" exclaimed Amir.

Natasha hugged Gabriel as tightly as she could, unable to contain her joy. Beneath her she could feel the fast-flowing river pulsing under the raft's rubbery bottom. It would soon carry them northward to Ceuta, and to the mysterious tunnels of St. Michael's Pass.

* * * * * *

Christian sat at his desk, his face twisted with anger and frustration. On the satellite feed he could see the raft speeding its way towards the Mediterranean Sea. With both helicopters destroyed, he would be forced to pursue his prey on land before he could acquire more aircraft. All would have to be done according to military protocol. He cursed bitterly. He was the most powerful man on the planet, yet even he was a victim of bureaucracy.

CHAPTER 24

Los Picos de Europa, Northern Spain.

Isaac looked away from the computer monitor, his eyes burning as he struggled to make sense of everything he had just learned. He scanned the room, still amazed by its uniqueness. Comprised entirely of abandoned furniture, the decor resembled that of a nineteenth century boudoir, complete with hanging veils, glowing oil lamps, and a blazing silver candelabra. At his feet he could see Shackleton lying fast asleep on the tattered rug.

After having bathed and eaten, Isaac had settled happily into his new accommodations, dressed in the warm flannel pyjamas he had been given. It was the first bit of civilization he had seen in weeks, and the fact that their strange suite resided in a medieval dungeon made no difference whatsoever. The bath had been heavenly, and the hearty food rejuvenating. To his delight he had found a computer in the room, complete with an internet connection.

After informing himself of the dreadful events occurring around the world, Isaac had managed to gain access to the church orphanage database, his old password surprisingly still active.

"Incredible," he whispered, his eyes scanning the text.

There now remained no doubt that Gabriel and Natasha had been born on the same day and hour as his own son, and like his son, they too had both been in rare coma vigils at the time. Further investigation confirmed that one month after their births, Gabriel and Natasha had both awoken in a state of demonic possession. Accounts of their adoptive parents were mentioned as well. Professor Agardi Metrovich was named as Gabriel's adoptive father, and Father Franco as Natasha's legal guardian.

Isaac produced the old priest's diary. There was one more question he needed answered. He flipped through the book until he found an entry that spoke of the *Rex Angelus Monastery.*

Metrovich and Father Franco had planned to visit the place after the burial of his son, and it appeared to be a destination of great importance. Acting on an impulse, Isaac did an internet search on the name. The articles that came up left him perplexed.

In one of them, Rex Angelus was being referred to as a secret aristocratic bloodline, comprised of powerful leaders and nobility, both living and dead. The name appeared to be woven into the very fabric of European history.

Isaac had always been a loyal Roman Catholic, but if the information he had unearthed was true, it would forever change the way he viewed the church.

According to one of the articles, the Rex Angelus bloodline had descended directly from Jesus Christ. They were supposedly the keepers of what was being referred to as the *Original Teachings of the Kristos*; a body of knowledge that the Vatican had purportedly gone to great pains to wipe from existence.

Isaac bent closer to the monitor, his brow furrowed in confusion as he re-read the text.

The Rex Angelus families had allegedly kept the heretical teachings a secret, privately practicing the initiatory rights handed down to them from their ancestors, while maintaining an outward appearance of religious conformity.

Scrolling down, Isaac came upon an embedded video and clicked it despite his misgivings. In it a distinguished British historian was being interviewed, his elbow propped casually on a cluttered bookshelf as he spoke.

"Rex Angelus had become fully established in the European aristocracy by the early fourth century," he said. "By the Middle Ages they had not only assimilated themselves into the highest courts and parliaments, but infiltrated the innermost chambers of the Vatican. Their secret mission was a simple one: To overthrow the blasphemous Church and reveal to humanity the true initiatory teachings of Jesus Christ. This they would do through their newly formed Cathar religion."

Isaac had to force his jaw shut.

The blasphemous Church?

The video played on.

"The political sway of Rex Angelus reached a critical point at the beginning of the eleventh century, with the formation of over sixty-eight Cistercian houses, one of which was known as *The Poor Militia of Christ*, an organization later to be officially recognized by the Church as *The Knighthood of the Temple of Solomon*, or *The Templar Knights*, as they are more commonly known.

"It was this organization that provided the greatest impetus to the Rex Angelus bloodline, but one that would also, over the span of one hundred and eighty years, be responsible for the family's eventual fracturing.

"Notwithstanding, the Knights Templar would become the equivalent of history's first multi-national corporation, and their rise to power would be swift and radical."

Isaac gave a long sigh and shut down the computer. He needed sleep desperately and would finish watching the video the following morning. He rubbed his face and glanced down at the slumbering Shackleton.

"A bloodline of Christ..." he said to the sleeping dog. "A church of lies and deception.... How can any of this possibly be true?"

Swiveling in his chair, Isaac reached over and took hold of the topographical map he had only just printed. It showed the exact location of the Rex Angelus Monastery, the very same one that Father Franco and Professor Metrovich had been planning to visit. Considering its elevation, Isaac estimated it would take Shackleton and himself approximately twelve hours to reach it on foot. His mind went over the incredible story he had just read on the internet. It told of those who had built the monastery, and the incredible events that had led to its construction.

After obtaining enormous wealth, power, and an unhindered influence within the Vatican, the *Knights Templar* had become divided. On one side were those who still held to the strictures of the original teachings of Jesus. These knights worked diligently to support the ever-growing Cathar church.

On the other side, however, were the knights who had forsaken their Rex Angelus bloodline. They had aligned themselves with a secret society of corrupt power mongers who had been operating within the Vatican since its inception.

The new society they established would be called *The Illuminati*, named after Lucifer, who bore the Latin name *The Illuminated One*. In less than a year the *Illuminati* would take full control of the Vatican, crowning the first of a series of puppet popes and ordering a papal bull issuing the arrest of all nonconforming Templar Knights, and the immediate destruction of the Cathar church.

This would mark the beginnings of the Inquisition, and the subsequent massacre of hundreds of thousands of peace loving Christian Cathars in what would later be known as the Albigensian Crusades.

The monastery Isaac would soon be visiting had been built by a renegade group of these Templar Knights. They had eluded the papal bull centuries before and allegedly preserved the original teachings of Jesus Christ to this day.

Isaac climbed into the canopied bed and gave a great yawn.

"Tomorrow we shall see..." he murmured, and just then a deep slumber took him.

CHAPTER 25

Northern Morocco.

It had been over three hours since they had left the rapids behind, and as of yet they had seen no sign of Nasrallah's mercenaries. Bahadur and his men sat at the ready as they were carried downstream, their assault rifles propped on the hull of the raft, prepared to return any fire that might come at them.

Having weighed the options, they had decided that staying on the river would be the best course of action, even if it offered them little protection. An attack was inevitable, but at least in this way they would remain moving targets, as opposed to being surrounded and trapped.

Around them the chiseled gorge had now been replaced with a softer terrain, the swollen river coursing through a broad valley dotted with abandoned tier farms and the occasional empty village. Even as the waters had calmed, the weather had grown dark and ominous, and the small group found themselves under a tumultuous sky, its boiling clouds blotting out the sun. Amir had his radio on.

"Good evening," said the commentator. "You are listening to GNN's European radio broadcast. This hour: Violent storms sweeping across Spain and Italy, moving northward into France, Austria, and Switzerland. We have reports of massive devastation occurring in many points across the Iberian Peninsula, as well as severe flooding in Southern Italy. One hundred and fifty kilometre an hour winds have been reported in Paris, and violent electrical storms are blanketing most of Europe.

"What is happening to the environment? With us now is Dr. Walter Fischer of the European Meteorological Society. Dr Fischer, could you tell us exactly what's happening?"

"We cannot say we know exactly what is going on," he said in a Swedish accent. "These weather patterns are completely foreign to our climes. What is truly remarkable, however, is that these anomalies are occurring on every continent."

The commentator paused for effect.

"Are you saying that the latest earthquakes in California are a part of this same weather pattern?"

"Yes, I am," came the grave reply. "All these anomalies are most definitely linked."

The commentator spoke urgently.

"In California we've seen over a dozen very brief, very intense tectonic shifts along the San Andreas Fault. Some geologists feel that the plates will soon give way to a major earthquake. Could this be the Big One?"

"It could very well be," said the climatologist. "There have also been earthquakes registered over many parts of China and Russia. As we speak, violent storms are raging over South America, and massive volcanic activity is occurring in the Indian Ocean, as well as in Japan and Hawaii.

"Only one hour ago, I was speaking with a colleague at the Royal Society of London. He was telling me of the unprecedented activity being recorded along the entire mid-Atlantic ridge."

"So, what, in your opinion, is the cause of this, Doctor?"

"I believe that much of the weather we are experiencing is a direct result of climate change, but the severe variances that are occurring in the movement of tectonic plates is still a mystery."

"Will we see it getting any better soon?"

"We should be prepared to witness these patterns worsening before they eventually improve."

"What can families do to survive this crisis?"

The climatologist paused before answering.

"Stay indoors," he said slowly. "Get underground if you can, and never forget that storms always pass."

"Thank you, Doctor."

"You are very welcome."

"That was Dr. Walter Fischer of the European Meteorological Society. Coming up next in our broadcast: Citizens of the United States reel under the iron grip of its new police state."

Gabriel switched off the radio and looked up at the sky.

"We're getting closer and closer to that Dark Rift," he said, glancing over at Natasha. "This is precisely what the old gypsy woman said would happen."

Bahadur turned to speak, his voice deep with concern.

"What will occur if the earth enters into the Dark Rift before we find the labyrinth?"

Gabriel shrugged.

"The gypsy woman said something about perpetual darkness for all mankind. It didn't sound very promising."

Amir gave a grunt and spat out his masticated toothpick. The weather was getting worse. When the tempest struck, it would do so mercilessly. Already the wind was blowing in buffeting gusts, pushing their raft around as though it had been equipped with a sail.

"Bloody hell," cursed Scotty Roberts under a pummelling squall. "It feels like the bloody end of the world…"

Bahadur had to raise his voice to be heard.

"What is our distance from Ceuta, Dr. Parker?"

The sky had suddenly become as black as pitch. It was churning like a witch's cauldron. Gabriel pulled out his phone and checked their position.

"We're getting close," he said. "We're only twenty kilometres from the city centre."

"Take up the paddles!" cried Bahadur, rising suddenly to his knees. "We will bring the raft to shore here!"

"Why?" cried Natasha.

Bahadur grimaced.

"Nasrallah and his men have not yet attacked us," he said. "This can only mean they will be waiting for us outside Ceuta. We will visit a friend of mine here on the river. He will take us into the city by land."

They picked up their paddles and made their way to the banks of the river amid a deafening series of thunderclaps. With the widening of the gorge the current had become much more manageable, and it was not long before they were feeling the bottom of the raft scraping along the gravel at the river's edge.

It was at that very moment that the stormfront arrived, and the sky unleashed its fury. Grape-sized balls of hail were suddenly falling all around them, and the lightning strikes were blinding.

"Up there!" bellowed Bahadur over the rolling thunder.

He was pointing high and to the right, and Gabriel peered up to see what looked to be the abandoned ruins of a village, not a hundred meters away.

"Pick up the raft!" he hollered. "We can use it to shelter us!"

In this way the group made its way up the rocky terrain to the village, the inverted raft acting as a shield against the onslaught.

Like many other villages in the region, the hamlet lay abandoned after a decades-long drought. Bahadur squinted up at the ruins, remembering a time when it had been a happy, populated place. He was certain that one man still resided here however; an eccentric Sufi hermit whom he knew would assist them.

It was not long before Bahadur steered his company into the shelter of a small cave-like home carved directly into the mountain.

"Miller and Stephenson!" he ordered, pointing to a crude hearth in the corner of the chamber. "The temperature is dropping. Gather wood and light a fire. Amir and Scotty. Come with me. Bring your weapons!"

Natasha watched as they disappeared into the hailstorm, using their packs as shields. It was only early evening, but it was as dark as night. Along with the storm had come a strange, frigid wind.

"It's a good thing we found this village," she said, shivering. "I've never seen a storm like this before."

She smiled in thanks when Gabriel wrapped her in a blanket, a sudden clap of thunder making her jump.

"Neither have I," he said. "One thing's certain, though. If it hadn't been for this turn in the weather, I'm sure we would have seen more helicopters. We've been lucky."

"Luck has nothing to do with it, my children," came the old bishop's voice from behind. "We have been receiving special assistance."

Natasha turned to face him.

"I was thinking the same thing. They fired four missiles at us in the gorge and not even a splinter of rock touched us. What's happening? In the professor's journal it says that spirits can't interfere in the physical world, but it seems to me that's exactly what they're doing."

"They can interfere only according to divine law," said the old bishop, nodding. "With the coming of the hermaphrodite, many demonic entities have entered into our world. Universal law dictates that for every number of evil spirits that arrive on the earth sphere, a certain number of spirits from the world of God can come as well. Gutierrez claims that the ratio is approximately twenty to one."

"Twenty demons to one angel," said Gabriel, looking out into the storm. "That doesn't seem very fair."

"On the contrary, my dear boy," said the old bishop. "Angels are much more powerful than demons."

"And why's that?" asked Gabriel.

"Because one good act is far more powerful than many bad acts combined."

"Then why not bring in a whole bunch of angels and end this thing right now?"

"Because the battle between good and evil must be fought and won fairly," said the bishop. "In this way, Lucifer will be unable to make any excuses when he has lost. He will have no choice but to surrender to God's will. This is why it is so important that the playing field always be kept level. The universal laws ensure that this is always the case."

With that the bishop turned and went to join Suora and Fra. They had managed to find a few chairs and a table to sit at. In the light of the fire that Miller and Stephenson had just lit, Natasha could see the brother and the nun preparing some sandwiches. The bishop was soon pulling a bottle of wine from his pack, his eyes twinkling mischievously.

Natasha shook her head and smiled. Even under the direst of circumstances some things never changed.

"Come on," she said to Gabriel. "Now's a good time to try and locate that labyrinth."

They sat next to the fire and began their studies of both the professor's journal and the map they had found, but nowhere could they find any clues as to where the mysterious island might be.

"It's pretty clear that neither the Moors or Gutierrez wanted any written record of the island's location," said Gabriel, rolling up the map in frustration. "They couldn't risk it. I just can't figure out how both our dads knew where it was…"

"The father of the hermaphrodite must have told them," said Natasha.

Gabriel sat up, his eyes alight with hope.

"Well then all we've got to do is find him."

Natasha was shaking her head as she flipped through the old journal.

"Uncle Marcus already tried," she said. "His name is Isaac Rodchenko. He's gone missing. Even the police can't find him."

Gabriel slumped back against the wall in defeat. Natasha finished reading an entry she had found and looked up from the book.

"Gutierrez says that the Labyrinth of Sarras is constructed of cubes within cubes," she said. "The cubes are separated by seals, and passing through each seal takes you further into the labyrinth until you arrive at a central chamber.

"He says that each seal holds a riddle that needs to be solved before it can be passed through, but that ultimately, the only way to gain entry into the central chamber is by transcending duality."

Gabriel cocked an eyebrow.

"Is that all?" he asked sarcastically.

Natasha shot him a sidelong glance.

"He refers to this central chamber as *Ostium Sanctus.*"

"*The Sacred Gate,*" translated Gabriel. "Osiris and Isis were looking for a similar portal in the myth, weren't they?"

He paused for a moment to consider the implications.

"If the parallel is consistent," he said slowly, "and reality really does mirror the myth, then the central chamber of the labyrinth must be some kind of a gateway to—"

He stopped himself short. The idea was preposterous.

"A gateway to heaven," finished Natasha, her eyes wide with wonder.

"One that would apparently mirror the Portal of Ahreimanius," cautioned Gabriel. "Which is basically a gateway to hell."

Natasha shuddered at the thought.

"Gutierrez says that gaining access to the inner chamber will be the most difficult task imaginable. He says that no one has ever done it before."

Gabriel was going to say something but the roar of a loud engine stopped him. They looked over to see an old school bus pulling up.

"Get all your things together, mates!" ordered Scotty Roberts, rushing in.

To everyone's surprise he was carrying a portable anti-aircraft missile launcher, its stout barrel pointing to the ceiling. Outside the storm had grown into a raging tempest. It was nothing short of apocalyptic.

"Bahadur's friend is dead!" he cried over the thunderclaps. "We found two of Nasrallah's men downstream! We took their Stingers, but they got off a distress call before we could take them down! Nasrallah's men will be here any second, mates! We've really got to move!"

In a moment all was in chaos. Bahadur left the bus idling and came in to help the others gather the equipment. The incessant pounding of hail on the bus's metal roof sounded like battle drums, driving them all to quicken their pace.

"Their plan was to ambush us at the next village where the river is at its slowest!" boomed Bahadur.

He was carrying a huge load of packs and ammunition.

"They know we are here! They are on their way! Perhaps a hundred strong!"

"Bad timing…" said the bishop to Fra, taking a final bite from his sandwich before stuffing it into one of his vestment pockets. "We'll have to make this take-away, old friend."

In a matter of seconds they were boarding the bus, with Amir and Bahadur bringing in the last of the supplies. The door had not even closed before Gabriel gunned the old engine and sent the vehicle roaring out into the deluge.

"Hold on to your hats!" he cried over the pounding hail.

"Make for the south of the square!" bellowed Bahadur.

The smuggler captain looked enormous at the front of the bus, his battered head bleeding from where a chunk of ice had hit him.

"Miller! Stephenson!" he ordered. "Grab your guns and get to the back! Get ready to return fire! Amir! Roberts! Prepare the Stingers!"

Gabriel shot a glance over to see Bahadur use a fire extinguisher to punch out windows on either side of the bus. Amir and Scotty rushed up with the missile launchers they had taken from the enemy.

Gabriel cursed aloud. He was having a very difficult time seeing the road ahead. He squinted into the blur of lashing rain and hail, the windshield cracking more and more with every passing second.

"What the hell is that?" he cried, and only then was he able to make out the extent of their predicament.

The square they found themselves in had once served as a kind of village roundabout, and to Gabriel's horror, he could see that a huge procession of military trucks was converging on it, some from the left, and others from the right. Their escape route was closing before his eyes.

"Make for the exit!" bellowed Bahadur.

"I can't!" cried Gabriel. "They just blocked it off!"

"Make for the exit!" repeated Bahadur louder still, and just then Gabriel saw Scotty and Amir in each of the side-view mirrors. They were leaning outside, braving the hailstorm to point the Stingers directly ahead.

"Aim for the middle transport!" cried Bahadur. "Fire!"

Gabriel swallowed hard when he saw the missiles leave the launchers and converge on the truck that was blocking their way.

"This had better work!" he bellowed, shifting into a higher gear and slamming the accelerator to the floor.

The bus lurched forward, taking a path directly through the centre of the roundabout. A second later the missiles met their target.

"Get down!" he cried, grabbing the wheel with both hands and preparing for impact just as the Stingers detonated in unison.

The ensuing explosion had a far greater effect than they ever could have hoped for. In order to deny their prey any means of escape, the convoy had stopped bumper to bumper. As it was, many of the transports were carrying caches of ammunition, and in a matter of seconds the explosions were having a domino effect, ripping through the convoy in both directions.

With the momentum of a runaway train, the vintage bus crashed through the burning wreckage, sending what was left of the transport careening out of the way. Gabriel slammed his foot to the floor again, using the acceleration to bring the skidding tail of the bus back under control. The explosions were deafening.

"When you get to the main road, head north!" roared Bahadur, but Gabriel had already made the call.

Battered and broken, the old bus made its way through the icy deluge, its undercarriage lit by the flickering flames of the burning debris that still clung to it. Behind them, the chain reaction of detonating ammunitions continued, lighting up the stormy sky with flashes that rivaled the lightning itself.

CHAPTER 26

Central Jerusalem, Israel.

Christian stood in his new command centre, a glowing hologram of planet Earth hovering before him as tall as a man. Within the desecrated sanctity of the Kadosh Hakodashim, the globe could be seen. It was a high-resolution replica of the fragile planet, and its surface was rippling with activity. Ribbon-shaped sections of reconnaissance were wrapping themselves around the sphere in a constant state of update.

Covering its surface were hundreds of interactive icons, each one providing access to the thousands of real-time events occurring around the world. Demonstrations, terrorist bombings, troop movements, missile attacks, stormfronts, natural disasters, and staggering regional death tolls.

Amidst the clutter of electronic equipment, Christian worked the holographic interface like a conductor before an orchestra, rotating the globe effortlessly with one hand while circling areas on its surface with the other and directing them to monitors on the periphery.

Snaking over the golden floor were the countless cables that connected the equipment to the massive servers that had been assembled in the refrigerated chamber outside. From there, a dozen technicians monitored and maintained live feeds from NORAD, SIGINT, GCHQ, NSA, and the CIA, to name only a few.

Dr. Bennington left his armed escorts at the tunnel entrance and entered the holy chamber alone. The shock of what he saw there made him clutch the wall as he climbed the final step, his knees threatening to give way.

There could now be no doubt that the events of the previous night had not been a dream. The walls were still coated in the black vitriol that had desecrated chamber, and in the air still hung the fetid stench of rot and decay.

Before him, under the shadow of the two blackened Cherubim, Bennington could see Christian silhouetted against the giant hologram of the Earth, but it was not he that commanded his attention.

Chained to the defiled Arc of the Covenant was Cynthia's undead, demon-possessed corpse. She was hunched over, and in the act of devouring the gory contents of a bucket at her feet, her dead eyes radiating cold malevolence. Her movements were frenetic, and the guttural sounds that escaped her mouth echoed through the chamber as she fed.

Bennington shuddered when those fiendish eyes shot up to meet his own. Her distended jaw was snapping and tugging at a rubbery length of pig intestine held fast in her hand. The stench of the offal made him gag and cough.

"Thank you for joining me, Doctor," said Christian without turning. "I wanted you to be a part of this."

Bennington noticed something in Christian's voice immediately. It was very subtle and would have been undetectable to anyone other than an experienced psychiatrist. Even still, observing it was all the doctor needed to pull himself together. His patient needed help.

With a decisive effort Bennington shifted his attention away from the strange, paranormal events, and directed it at Christian. The relief he felt was substantial, even if a part of him knew that it was only temporary.

Bennington scanned the back of Christian's form. There was an unsteadiness in his body language, and something in his demeanor was amiss. In order to ascertain what it was, he would need to get him talking.

"What have you done to this sacred chamber, Christian?" he asked, gathering himself.

"I have transformed it into what it was destined to become," said Christian, turning momentarily to face him. "My throne room."

Bennington stepped over the cables to arrive at Christian's side.

"Why did you call me here?"

"I have called you here to witness the beginning of the end," said Christian. "Today, the Coalition will attack China in response to their recent occupation of Taiwan, and in so doing spark a tactical nuclear war that will eventually spread to the Middle East and Africa. From there it will graduate into a full-blown nuclear holocaust."

"Have you lost your mind?" said Bennington, forgetting his professionalism. "Christian, this is madness! You do not have to do this."

"Of course I do not have to do this," said Christian dryly. "But I *want* to do this. There are far too many souls incarnating in China and Africa. The populations in these places must be culled.

"Besides, the Asian and African Unions must begin to become more than fanciful ideas on these continents. They will soon become a necessity, established out of the ruin of the People's Republic of China.

"As the years pass, and the losses are compounded, all nations will at last concede and merge into a fully unified world government."

"This is madness," began Bennington, but Christian held up a hand to silence him.

A communication was coming in. Christian brought a finger to his earpiece.

"You what?" he said, beginning to grow angry.

Bennington strained to hear the tinny voice.

"They have escaped, Mr. Antov," it said. "They have killed seventeen of our men."

"Are you telling me that a group of archaeologists and senior citizens have defeated your entire battalion?"

"The weather here is severe, sir. We have lost them."

"Wait," ordered Christian.

Bennington watched as Christian closed his eyes in concentration.

"They are approaching Ceuta," he said. "Find them and kill them, or I will annihilate the entire coastal region and you along with it. Where is the scroll?"

"We are still digging, sir," came the shaky reply. "We are making good progress."

"I want those artifacts!" snapped Christian. "My patience is wearing thin."

"The Compostela Cube?" asked Bennington, seeing that Christian had severed the line.

"A thorn in my side, Doctor. But one that will soon be extracted and destroyed."

Turning suddenly, Christian made his way down the steps of the dais, past Cynthia's feeding corpse, and towards a bank of eleven monitors that were grouped on a nearby table. Bennington followed, observing Christian as he brought the monitors online.

Each one contained a video feed of a particular steering committee member. There was fear and anxiety in their faces, and it became clear to Bennington that they were no longer even tenuously in control.

"Well, my esteemed colleagues," said Christian, sitting down in a chair. "It would appear the time has come to officially start World War Three."

"The coalition governments have all been notified," said one of the old men in a grim tone.

"Our media infrastructure as well," said another.

"All military levels have ratified the action," said yet another. "Tactical missiles are ready and waiting to launch on your command, sir."

Dr. Bennington shuddered.

What could Christian have done to these men to break their wills so?

He thought of young Cynthia dying by Christian's hand.

How many of the committee's family members has he put to death to achieve this subservience?

Bennington watched Christian leave his chair and suddenly felt as though he were in a dream. An encompassing feeling of twisted *wrongness* was seeping into the ancient chamber now, permeating the air around him. He thought he could hear an echo of the demonic chorus that had assaulted him the previous night. It was faint, but nevertheless present. The supernatural quality of it sent an evil chill up his spine.

My God in heaven, can you not prevent this?

Banks of lights had been installed throughout the cube-shaped chamber. They sent a dimmed glow up onto the ceiling, with the blackened wings of the cherubim casting ominous shadows.

"Launch phase one!" cried Christian suddenly, and Bennington gasped in horror.

On the holographic globe, twelve missiles had emerged from the central Pacific Ocean. Christian magnified them with the wave of a hand, their tails glowing as they made their way to a dozen different targets.

Bennington swallowed hard. The projected planet seemed almost alive to him; as though it were trembling in anticipation of the blow it was about to receive.

"Witness the birth of a new era," said Christian.

A computer-generated voice of a woman spoke out.

"First impact in nineteen minutes and counting."

Bennington staggered backwards. He could see Christian standing before the glowing planet, a distinct climate of psychological uncertainty about him. The head of the most powerful organization in the world was doubting himself. Bennington was sure of it.

Looking to the globe, he could see the twelve ICBMs making their way ever closer to their targets. He brought his hands to his face as the grim realization set in. The world he had always known and loved would soon cease to exist.

"Dear God in heaven," he whispered, aghast. "Save the children."

CHAPTER 27

Ceuta, Spanish Morocco.

Natasha followed the others as they moved through a derelict tunnel beneath the ancient city of Ceuta. Around her was the clutter of what had once been a busy underground hashish factory, the overturned tables and dried out piles of marijuana stalks giving testament to the tunnel's former purpose. Having been tipped off by Vanderhoff operatives, the Spanish Civil Guard had raided the site a week ago, stripping Nasrallah of yet another operation, and driving him one step closer to complete Vanderhoff subservience.

Just ahead, Natasha could see that Bahadur had stopped before a metal door set in a wall of newly laid brick. The door looked to have been forced open during the raid.

"We are here," he said deeply, his bear-like hands on his hips. "This is the treasure room, the chamber where we found the scroll."

Bahadur entered first. He tripped a breaker that the smugglers had installed and the room was instantly flooded with light, revealing a golden interior.

"We searched extensively," he said as the party shuffled in behind him. "We could not find the secret entrance depicted on the map, nor any other entrance for that matter. There is only the hole we came in through."

Gabriel scanned the room. It was circular in shape, and relatively large for an underground chamber, measuring approximately thirty feet in diameter. Above him, some ten feet aloft, was a shallow domed ceiling of intricate geometric design, its abundant use of gold leaf and mosaic confirming the chamber's importance.

"This place is like a mini-Alhambra," he said, moving towards one of the many intricate niches adorning its walls. "Outstanding…"

Natasha and the others could not help but be amazed as well. Everything was shimmering magically under the bright lights.

"This must have been wonderful to see when it was full of treasure…" said Natasha, moving to the centre of the chamber and spinning slowly to take in the space.

What Bahadur had said was true. Apart from the haphazard hole the excavators had made when they had discovered the room, the chamber had no doors or exits.

"How could anyone have entered this place?" she said, looking over at Gabriel. "There's no entrance."

Gabriel pulled the bejeweled cylinder from his pack and spread the scroll out on the floor. Natasha knelt down next to him.

"What are you thinking?"

Gabriel pointed out a geometric pattern that was incorporated into the map's design.

"There are two entrances in this chamber," he said. "One of them is up there."

He used his thumb to point at the centre of the ceiling. Natasha looked up and saw the map's pattern duplicated in the carvings there.

"And the other entrance?"

Gabriel rose to his feet and moved to stand beneath the pattern. He bent down and ran his hands over a section of floor just as Bahadur was approaching. There was an expression of curiosity on the giant's face.

"We did not check the floor," he said deeply, raising a crooked eyebrow. "We were searching for doors."

"No doors in this kind of chamber," said Gabriel.

He brushed away some sandy gravel to reveal a large hexagonal stone depicting the map's pattern again. Natasha and Bahadur watched as he cleared away its edges with his fingers, and then peered up at the ceiling. He appeared to be counting.

"What are you doing?" asked Natasha.

He patted the hexagonal stone with the flat of his palm, thinking.

"This is the entrance to St. Michael's Pass," he said. "I'm sure of it."

He glanced over his shoulder at a section of the chamber's wall.

"The Moors were trading partners with Carthage," he said, rubbing the stubble on his jaw. "If this mechanism is what I think it is, they must have also traded engineering tips..."

Gabriel rose and walked over to the section of wall he had been looking at. Natasha and Bahadur followed close behind. It was covered in a three-dimensional honeycomb structure that mirrored the map's pattern perfectly. Gabriel frowned.

"What's wrong?" asked Natasha.

He pointed at a section of the design.

"Someone's been here already," he said, perplexed. "Look at that actuating stone."

"I see nothing," said Bahadur, bending closer.

"It's the only one not covered in dust," said Amir, coming up behind Bahadur. "Whoever it was knew exactly which stone to press."

Natasha chewed her lip.

"Maybe Nasrallah figured it out. Maybe he already has the Book of Khalifah..."

Bahadur frowned in confusion.

"There is no other man alive who knows of this chamber. Who else could it be?"

"There's only one way to find out," said Gabriel.

He looked over his shoulder and saw that the old nun was dawdling in the centre of the room.

"You might not want to stand there, Suora," he said.

"Oh dear me, child," she stammered, looking down to see the hexagonal stone that Gabriel had only just brushed off. "Do excuse me. Good heavens."

When Suora had moved aside, Gabriel gave the honeycomb structure one last look and then placed his palm on the stone that had been cleared of dust. All watched as it slipped effortlessly into the wall. Almost immediately a low rumbling could be felt reverberating beneath their feet.

"Is that normal?" asked Natasha, stepping back.

"As normal as ancient counterweights slipping along cast bronze tracks can be," said Gabriel.

"Gotta love Phoenician engineering," added Amir, biting down on a toothpick.

Amazingly, the section of stone where Suora had been standing dropped and slid aside, clearing the way for an elaborately carved spiralling wooden staircase to rise slowly from the floor.

At the same time, from a cleverly hidden section in the ceiling, there descended another staircase of the same design. Within seconds the two had met with a solid thump, forming a perfectly proportioned stairway that led up into the ceiling and down into the floor.

"Good work, Gabriel!" cried the old bishop, clapping his hands in delight. "Well done, man!"

Gabriel approached the staircase with hands on hips. He was looking up into the ceiling.

"Everybody wait here," he said. "And for God's sake, don't touch anything."

They all watched as Gabriel ascended in measured steps, the wandering beam of his flashlight remaining temporarily visible after he had vanished. Everyone waited expectantly.

"Where has he gone to now?" said Natasha, more to herself than anyone else.

"Have patience, child," said Fra.

He was standing beside her and could sense her concern.

"Gabriel has done things like this many times before."

As if in response to the brother's words, Gabriel emerged from the dark opening and began his descent in a carefree trot. Oddly enough, tucked under his arm were two floral bouquets, fresh and blooming.

"For the two loveliest ladies in the entire Moorish empire," he said with a bow, handing the flowers to Natasha and Suora.

"You're crazy!" said Natasha, smiling with delight.

"Wherever did you get these, my child?"

"It would appear the Caliph's primary residence has over the centuries become Ceuta's flower market," said Gabriel. "The passage led to a concealed door right behind the main steps."

Bahadur moved to the stairs and looked up, frowning with concern.

"We must seal this entrance immediately."

"You're absolutely right," said Gabriel, "We'd best get downstairs. With any luck we'll find a mechanism that'll do just that."

Gabriel went first, with Natasha close behind. Immediately the earthy smell of an underground chamber filled their olfactory, a cool and damp air engulfing them as they descended. By the echoing sounds of their footsteps, they knew they had entered a large chamber, but the walls could still not be seen. Only an inky blackness surrounded them, swallowing the beams of their flashlights.

"You'd all best come along," said Gabriel, glancing up at the others. "There's plenty of room down here. This chamber's massive."

They followed the spiralling steps down to what appeared to be a round platform, surrounded by a stone railing. Bahadur was last to descend, and he lit a flare when he had reached the bottom. In that instant their surroundings burst to life, revealing a scene that none of them had been expecting.

"Good God!" exclaimed the bishop. "This is outstanding!"

The other's gasped in surprise. Under the light of the flare, they could see that the secret staircase had descended onto a terrace of sorts. It was perched on the peak of a great rock formation, one that rose from the base of an enormous underground cavern.

Stretching out in all directions was a jagged sea of stalagmites and stalactites, clinging like teeth to the oddly shaped cave. In the light of the flare, glossy surfaces of rock glowed as though illuminated from within, with sporadic groupings of quartz crystals at the extremities of the chamber, shining like stars in a night sky.

"It's so beautiful," whispered Natasha in awe. "I've never seen anything like it."

However captivated by the sight, the party's attention soon turned to something far more pressing. The spiral staircase they had just descended was sinking into the ground, and above them, two slabs of stone were sliding into place over the opening they had come down through. A resounding boom echoed through the cavern as the heavy stones met.

"Well, Captain," said Gabriel to the giant. "Problem solved. The entrance to the treasure room is now shut."

"You were expecting this to happen?" asked Bahadur, his voice sounding even deeper than usual in the echoing gallery.

"Not exactly," said Gabriel, rubbing his chin, "but by the design of that mechanism, both exits will have closed, and that's what we wanted, right? Just don't ask me to open them again."

"Look at this, boss," said Amir suddenly.

He had moved to the side of the platform and found a section of intricately worked mosaic tiles.

"It's a map of the caves," said Natasha, coming up beside him.

Gabriel bent closer to read.

"You're absolutely right," he said, "but there's also a warning here. Under no circumstance is anyone to enter into the tunnels without royal escorts."

He read on and then turned to face the others.

"Well guys, it looks like we found it. Welcome to the legendary Pass of St. Michael."

"And which way is Gibraltar, my son?" asked the old bishop, barely able to contain his excitement.

Gabriel pointed at two ornate pedestals. They were waist high, and they marked where a flight of steps descended to the cavern floor.

"The pedestals are markers," he said, "All we need to do is follow them. They should take us directly there. The only thing we've got to worry about is bumping into Nasrallah."

Scotty Roberts tightened his hold on the assault rifle.

"And you're sure he came down, mate?"

Gabriel nodded slowly, pointing to the mosaic map that Amir had discovered. The dust that covered it had been recently wiped clean.

"And there was only one set of tracks on the stairs," he said to Scotty. "If they didn't belong to Nasrallah then who?"

Bahadur rubbed his colossal chin.

"It's not like Nasrallah to go anywhere alone," he said deeply.

He looked over at Miller and Stephenson.

"Follow up the rear and be on your guard. We go now."

CHAPTER 28

Central Jerusalem, Israel.

Christian awoke with a start. He was seated at a table in the desecrated Holy of Holies, his head still resting in his folded arms. He had been dreaming of his brother Isaac's death again. It was a repeating nightmare, brought on by what the Zurvanites had revealed to him only days before.

Through their eyes he had seen Isaac butcher the corpse of his son and open the Portal of Ahreimanius. Christian knew that no man could have survived the fires that ensued, and something in his heart cried out in pain. His brother had been the only person who had ever shown him kindness and love. He stifled his emotions at once and forced himself to sit up.

Christian glanced at the holographic earth suspended above him. It was glowing and rippling with life, as though it were a living organism. To his right a blinking bank of monitors offered views of a nuclear war that was rapidly engulfing the planet.

His eyes focused on one of the screens. A drone was flying a low surveillance route over a decimated city. There were countless dead littering the streets, their corpses like blackened logs in a burnt-out fire pit. Christian felt a spasm of grief despite himself. He denied it at once.

I don't give a shit. Let them all die.

His words did little to squelch the guilt that was welling up in him. For the first time since his childhood, Christian was experiencing traces of compassion, and its presence sent a deep wave of fear and uncertainty through him. He grew angry with himself.

I'll have none of this bullshit! Humanity is a scourge! They're rats needing to be exterminated!

He sprang to his feet, the room spinning as the blood rushed to his head. Compassion was weakness. It was his enemy, and he reacted to it as though his very life were at stake.

In a matter of seconds his dark self had surfaced in response, a reptilian shadow that claimed with unquestionable authority to be his true identity. It came on a wave of fear and hatred and exploded into fury.

Christian jerked his head around with murderous intent. The oscillating forms of the four Zurvanites had just materialized behind him, and his hatred of them merged with his wrath to produce a surge of unbridled dark power. Instantly he felt nothing for the dead that lay strewn in the streets. He cared not that tens of thousands lay trapped and dying in the rubble. They were a blight. They deserved to die. He pushed himself away from the table, drunk with rage.

"Kill them!" hissed the Zurvanites wickedly. *"Kill them all and you will be God!"*

Christian could see Cynthia's undead corpse as it squatted in the shadows. There was a cruel, demonic light in the cadaver's eyes, and it fueled his hatred and fury like gasoline to a flame. He was the one in charge, and now he would show everyone just how powerful he had become.

"Computer," he said with cold malice. "Prepare to execute the Lazarus Sequence."

Even within the Vanderhoff Group, the Lazarus Sequence was a covert and highly classified operation. Only the Nautonnier and Christian's father had been fully aware of its sinister, occult objectives.

By annihilating the populations in the mountainous regions surrounding the Portal of Ahreimanius, their new biological weapon would supply tens of thousands of reanimated corpses to an army of demons waiting to possess them.

Christian trembled with dark anticipation. Ever since he had seen how swiftly Cynthia's corpse had been taken, he had been filled with an irrepressible urge to set the Lazarus Sequence in motion.

"Viral components activated," said the computer in its seductive female voice. "Bringing drones online."

Christian waited. The sequence would utilize four unmanned drones stationed at a US airbase in Torrejon, Spain. Having given the orders to transport the virus from the Jerusalem complex the previous day, Christian knew that the drones would by now be fully armed. It was just a matter of deploying them.

"Drones will be fully functional in three minutes and counting," said the computer.

The bank of screens came to life next to Christian just then. Several of them were filled with the faces of steering committee members.

"Nautonnier!" cried one of them. "Please! You must not do this!"

Christian looked over his shoulder to see the mortified faces of his colleagues. He gave a dry chuckle. They only knew of the contagion, and the rampant undead that the virus would bring. They had no clue as to the throngs of demonic entities that would soon be taking possession of the newly made cadavers. He smiled coldly.

The dead shall walk.

"Your Eminence!" said another. "This is not part of our agenda. These drones must not be launched. Please reconsider!"

Christian muted their displays with the wave of a hand and continued to wait impatiently.

"All drones armed and ready to execute Viral Sequence Lazarus," said the computer. "Awaiting your order, Mr. Antov."

Christian could see that the entire muted Steering Committee was online now, speaking and gesticulating frantically. He dismissed them with a hateful scowl.

Weak and compassionate fools. They make me sick to my stomach.

Christian's mind was made up. He would not stop the killing until the prophecy had been fulfilled and two-thirds of the world's population was either dead or undead. He was the one in control now, and he would prove just how indifferent he was to the suffering of others.

"Computer," he said coldly. "Deploy the drones."

CHAPTER 29

Northern Morocco.

They had been descending for a little over an hour when Bahadur at last called for a halt. The path they followed had spiraled down from the platform where they had first entered into the caves, a series of markers guiding them through a landscape of fractured rock and tangled stalagmites. Although constantly on the lookout, they had as of yet been unable to find any tracks belonging to the mysterious person who had gone before them.

From where she stood, Natasha could see Bahadur squatting low with Gabriel at his side. The two were studying a marker and talking quietly amongst themselves.

"We're in good hands," said Amir, coming up beside her. "They're the two smartest people I know."

Natasha watched Bahadur lift a powerful arm to point at something. Gabriel looked and nodded in agreement.

"He isn't like the other smugglers," said Natasha. "Why didn't he become a university professor?"

Amir was looking at them as well.

"My cousin grew up in a family of pirates," he said, pushing aside his dreadlocks to look at her. "His father was a smuggler captain. Bahadur was expected to follow in his footsteps."

"He should have refused."

Amir smiled slightly.

"He did. He had already passed his university entrance exams when his father was arrested. Bahadur took a seven-year wrap for him."

Natasha turned to look at Amir in disbelief.

"Why would he do that?"

Amir slipped a cinnamon toothpick into his mouth and shrugged.

"He did it for the family. Things were at a point where everything would have been lost if his father got put away, but Bahadur was—"

"Bahadur was expendable," said Natasha, shaking her head. "What a waste of a good mind."

"He studied all the time he was in jail," said Amir. "Bahadur is obsessed with knowledge. He's like a caliph from the Golden Age. He believes knowledge can transform a person. That's why he got that tattoo on his neck while he was in jail. So that he would never forget his destiny."

Natasha shook her head again, but this time in amazement.

"A moth," she said softly. "The universal symbol of transformation…"

Amir looked back at his cousin.

"Bahadur is honoured to be on this quest, Doctor. The Cube stands for everything he holds sacred. It's funny, but we couldn't have found a better man to assist us. He's helping to finish something that our Moorish ancestors started a thousand years ago."

Natasha's eyes were wide with admiration now. Their battered and bruised captain was not only selfless and brave, he was also spiritually inspired. She was going to say something when Bahadur rose and turned to face the party.

"We will stay here for the night," he said in his deep basso. "It has been a long day, and we have made good progress."

Natasha looked around to see that he could not have chosen a better spot to make camp. There was even a trickling stream of sweet water here, and the floor of the cavern was smooth and warm to the touch.

It was not long before the party settled down to eat the sandwiches that Fra had prepared back at the village. They chatted excitedly while they dined, revisiting the many events that had transpired over the past few days, and trying to figure out what their best course of action would be once they reached Gibraltar.

Only Scotty Roberts remained silent and lost in thought. He was sitting next to Amir, quietly watching him pack his ancient chillum and stoke it to life.

Amir exhaled a billowing cloud of the fragrant smoke and pointed to Natasha's equipment case with the stem of the pipe. He had seen her carrying it since they had first met in Estepona.

"What have you got in there, Doc?" he asked, passing the chillum to Scotty.

"It's a BIRIS," she said, reaching for it. "A portable 3-D imagining scanner. We brought it to scan the Cube, but we haven't had a chance to do it yet."

"How does it work?"

"It uses lasers to image an object at varying depths."

Gabriel popped the last bite of his sandwich into his mouth.

"That thing runs on batteries, doesn't it?"

Natasha nodded.

"Let's scan the Cube right now then," he said, rising to his feet with a weary groan. "Maybe we can get an idea of what makes it tick."

Having finished eating, the others seemed less interested in the Cube and more interested in getting some sleep. Scotty in particular. He was not used to the potency of Amir's special blend and had soon returned the pipe to him with a bewildered expression on his face.

One by one they curled up in the blankets that Miller and Stephenson had salvaged from the village, leaving Gabriel, Natasha, and Amir to pursue their investigations alone.

It was not long before the three had set the Cube spinning on a platform in the BIRIS, watching as the computer began to render a three-dimensional scan of it. They were amazed by what they saw.

"That's really strange," said Natasha, frowning. "This artifact is comprised of thousands of layers. There seems to be no end to them..."

They watched as one image replaced the next, each comprised of chaotic patterns similar to that of snow on a television screen. To the bottom right of the computer's monitor, they could see the counter clicking forward as each new layer was detected. It was already nearing three thousand and showed no signs of stopping. Just then, an error window appeared in the centre of the monitor.

"What's the problem?" asked Amir over Natasha's shoulder.

"We're out of RAM," she said. "The file's too big, even though I've been scanning at low res."

Gabriel rubbed his chin. The monitor was showing that the BIRIS had penetrated less than a millimeter into the artifact.

"Would it be possible to dump all these files and just get a single, high-res scan of the first interior layer?"

"Sure," said Natasha, liking the idea. "But it'll take about an hour to do it."

"We've got nothing but time," said Gabriel, leaning back against the smooth cave wall and closing his eyes.

Natasha initiated the scan and then took up one of the blankets, curling up next to him. It was not long before they had both fallen asleep.

"Baby, wake up. I think it's done."

It was Gabriel who spoke, and Natasha opened her eyes to see Amir bent over the computer, encased in a cloud of smoke.

"It's covered in markings," he said, looking over at them through his dreadlocks.

Natasha rose to her feet, keeping the blanket wrapped around her. She was amazed by what she saw on the screen.

"They look like symbols..." she said, studying the rotating cube. "Thousands of them, and all lined up in perfect grids."

"They're too small to make out," said Gabriel, pushing back his messy hair. "Could we zoom in and isolate just one of the sides?"

Natasha manipulated the scan until the screen was filled with hundreds of triangular symbols.

"Look familiar?" asked Gabriel, peering over at Natasha.

"It's cuneiform," she said. "I saw something similar to this in your father's journal."

Gabriel brought out the diary, removing it from the watertight freezer bag he was using to store it in now. There, on the left side of two opposing pages, could be seen a square grid containing symbols similar to those on the screen. On the facing page was a grid comprised of standard numerals. Gabriel shook his head.

"Cuneiform numerals on the left, and their conversions on the right... I don't know where my father could have dug this up, but it matches the layout of our scan perfectly. I wouldn't be surprised if every layer of the Cube is structured the same way."

"But why Sumerian cuneiform?" asked Natasha.

Gabriel shrugged.

"Whatever the reason, these numbers are definitely based on the Sumerian sexagesimal system."

"Sexagesimal," repeated Amir. "What's that?"

"It's still around today," said Gabriel. "It's a numerical system based in sixty. We use it to measure time and degrees.

Sixty seconds in a minute, sixty minutes in an hour, three hundred and sixty degrees in a circle.

"The ancient Sumerians and Babylonians used it to solve complex astronomical calculations. Sixty is an HCN, or a Highly Composite Number. It allows for calculations that would be impractical with the standard Arabic numerals we use today."

"But what do these numbers mean?" asked Natasha, her brown eyes wide with concern.

"They look to me to be matrices, my child," came the unexpected voice of the old nun.

"Suora," said Natasha, noting how drained she looked. "I thought you were asleep."

"I was, dear girl," she said weakly, "but nature calls the old more often than the young. I was only going off to have a pee when I saw you all gathered here."

"You're sure these are matrices, Suora?" asked Gabriel.

He passed her the journal, along with a flashlight so that she could have a better look.

"Most definitely, my child," she said, nodding. "They appear to be representing linear transformations. Do not forget. I taught mathematics for most of my life. I know linear algebra when I see it."

The old nun produced her glasses and squinted at the numbers.

"This is very complex," she said quietly, shaking her head. "It would appear to be a type of algorithm, but what it is expounding I could not even begin to say."

She rubbed her chin and took a closer look.

"It could very well be emulating a quantum mechanical model... It reminds me of Dirac and Heisenberg's work back in my university days..."

Gabriel and Natasha looked at each other amazed. They would never have suspected that Suora would have known such things, but doing the math, Gabriel realized that most of the quantum mechanics used today had been discovered around the time of Suora's birth. Her generation would have been the first to study these models.

"What else can you tell us about these matrices, Suora?" he asked.

"Not much without further study, my child," she said. "Only that they appear to be using different dimensional vector spaces at the same time... Solving this would be a challenge even for Albert Einstein. It would take a very powerful computer to make sense of these coefficients; much, much bigger than this little one you have."

Suora had no sooner said these words than Gabriel and Amir exchanged a glance, the same name popping into their heads simultaneously.

"Peralta," they said in unison.

"Who?" asked Natasha.

Gabriel scratched his head.

"He's a crazy Gibraltarian. A hacker and a smuggler. If he can't decipher these numbers, then nobody can."

"There's only one problem, boss," said Amir. "He's been AWOL for months now. Word was that he partnered up with Nasrallah last spring. Nobody's seen him since."

"Really?" said Gabriel, perplexed. "But Peralta hates Nasrallah. Why would he be doing business with him?"

Amir shrugged and pocketed his pipe.

"Nobody can figure it out. Not even Bahadur."

"I hope he's all right," said Gabriel.

"He's smart, boss," said Amir in his even tone. "I'm sure he's fine. I just wish there was a way we could contact him. I'll start asking around when we get back to Gib."

Gabriel nodded and passed a hand through his hair. He looked over at the old nun.

"Suora," he said, holding the journal out to her in its plastic bag. "You might as well hang on to this. If you get a chance tomorrow, it would be great if you could take a closer look at those numbers. The more we know about them the better."

"I most certainly will, my child," she said, taking the journal and shuffling off.

The three of them turned to see her disappearing into the shadows.

"Go to sleep, all of you," she said over her shoulder. "It has been a long day, and we can talk more about this in the morning. I am off to pee now. No peeking!"

CHAPTER 30

Gibraltar.

It was well past sundown by the time Major Roberts returned to the Governor's House. His day had been spent playing political ping pong with what seemed to be a divided and entirely dysfunctional European Union.

With the global climate in the state it was, it seemed there were no delegates available to help resolve the dispute that had erupted between Gibraltar and the Spanish Civil Guard. On the one side, he was being told to comply with their mandate, while on the other, that he should in no way do so.

With half of Europe now under martial law, it was becoming more and more obvious that regional authorities were disregarding statutes in order to accomplish objectives that would have normally been impossible.

"The Guardia Civil is accusing Gibraltar of harbouring terrorists," Roberts had told one of the officials at the European Commission in Brussels. "And the Spanish government is doing nothing to stop their aggressive behavior. There are no grounds for their claim. It's a fabrication created to validate what is nothing other than an aggressive act of war against Gibraltar.

"At this very moment our city is besieged by radical Spanish militia posing as EU anti-terrorist police. I would like it to go on record that Gibraltar will defend herself. She will not fall prey to Spain's new inquisition."

Passing through the main chambers, Roberts thought back on what he had said. Perhaps dubbing the incident as Spain's new inquisition had been a bit much, but he had been tired and frustrated with the EU's lack of coherence on the matter.

I'll phrase things differently in the letter.

He made his way through the convent, his footsteps echoing in the empty hallways. It was late now, and everyone had gone home, leaving him with an odd sense of foreboding. He was not looking forward to telling the governor the latest news.

He arrived at the old knight's door only to find it slightly ajar. Within he could hear the voice of a woman speaking in hushed tones. He knocked quietly.

"Come in," said the woman, and entering, Roberts recognized the pretty nurse at once.

"Hello, Clara," he said. "How's our governor feeling this evening?"

The nurse shot him a sad smile.

"Alas, Major," said the old man, summoning the little strength he had left. "The governor is feeling heartbroken if the truth must be told. I have asked young Clara if she would like to go out dancing with me this evening and she has regretfully declined."

Roberts smiled.

"She knows she could never keep up with you, sir."

The governor did his best to return the smile, and then seeing the major's face said:

"Ah, but I see you are troubled, my faithful Aide du Camp. Clara, be a lovely thing and do leave us alone for a moment. I fear the major has some important matters he wishes to discuss."

The young nurse made a quick alteration to the governor's blankets and then left the room, closing the door softly behind her.

"I could never have imagined I would have fallen in love again," said the governor between coughs, "but that pretty little thing has truly softened my brittle old heart."

"She's lovely, sir," said Roberts, smiling. "An angel, to be sure."

"Come and sit down, son," said the old man. "Tell me what has happened."

Roberts did as he was told, a deep concern furrowing his brow as he spoke.

"The United Coalition has responded to China's invasion of Taiwan, sir," he said solemnly, his right eye giving a few quick blinks. "There's been an exchange of tactical nuclear strikes in the region. Millions are dead."

The old governor gazed into Roberts' eyes without saying a word. He was digesting the news as best he could.

"We also had a small nuclear device go off in the Madrid airport," added Roberts solemnly. "It was similar to the one that went off in Atlanta last week."

"It has begun," said the governor at length. "It will not be long before the entire world is drawn into the conflagration."

Roberts held the governor's eyes.

"You warned me many times that this would happen, sir," he said. "And I always doubted you. I'll never doubt you again. What would you have me do, sir?"

"The time has come to prepare the people of Gibraltar for the worst," said the old duke. "As you know, the purpose for this war is to destroy the free world. The controlling elite want to build a global police state, run by a centralized world government. This has always been their plan."

The governor broke into a fit of coughing, and only after regaining his composure did he continue to speak.

"The destruction will happen on many levels," he said. "We are already experiencing one such level. Gibraltar is besieged by the enemies of freedom. Do not call them Spanish, for the Spaniards are a noble people. These are the pawns of those in higher positions. We must never overlook this fact and be fooled by what the media says. Should these forces enter onto the Rock, Gibraltar will never again be the same."

"They will not enter," said Roberts unfalteringly. "Gibraltar has never fallen to any siege, and thanks to your foresight we are well prepared, sir. Gibraltar will hold."

The governor smiled weakly. These were the words he wanted to hear from his Aide du Camp. He patted Roberts' hand and continued to speak.

"It is time that the people began growing accustomed to the possibility of having to retreat to the underground city," he said, even weaker now. "The nuclear war will soon spread to the Middle East and Africa. It will not be long before contaminated air makes its way here. Biological weapons will also be used. Viruses will be propagated to cull populations. They will find their way here as well. It has all been planned."

"But, sir," whispered Roberts. "How can this be? How could something so monstrous be on our very doorstep?"

"Gibraltar's population will eventually have to go inside," strained the governor. "There is no other way. It will only be for a certain time, perhaps for a year, perhaps two."

"And what shall become of my wife?" said Roberts, more to himself than to the governor.

"There is still time to bring her over," whispered the old knight.

"But how, sir?" said Roberts, his heart sinking. "The border's closed and there's a blockade in the sea all around us. They'll shoot down any aircraft that attempts to leave our airport, sir. There's no way."

"Be patient," said the governor, patting his arm reassuringly. "A way will be made."

Roberts looked up at him. For some inexplicable reason he believed the old man.

"I'll contact the chief minister in the morning, sir," he said, composing himself again.

"Have them all underground as soon as possible," said the governor, slipping slowly into unconsciousness. "Give them time to make the necessary preparations, but don't let them dally. You know what needs to be done, Major. We have drilled this many times before."

* * * * * *

Major Roberts stood upon Princess Anne's Battery, overlooking the Bay of Gibraltar. The night was bright with the light of a full moon, and the heavy rains had left the sky clear and star-studded. Stretched out below him he could see the many ship lights of the blockade scattered across the water, and in that moment his thoughts went to his wife and the unborn child in her womb.

Roberts made the calculations in his head. Anita was not thirty-five kilometres away as the crow flies, but the distance could have been a hundred times that and it would have made no difference.

He turned himself in her direction, trying to feel her presence over the space between them. In that moment, he promised himself that he would get her back, despite the fact that he had no clue as to how he might do so. In the silence of the night, he could still hear the governor's encouraging words as if they had only just been spoken.

"A way will be made," Roberts said to the night. "A way will be made."

CHAPTER 31

Under the Mediterranean Sea.

They had been travelling for the better part of the morning, their path leading them deep into the entrails of the earth. By each of the directional markers they had found stockpiles of torches, and it was under their flickering light that they made their way through expansive caverns and along tight chasms.

The subterranean geography of the place had proven to be so diverse and breathtaking that the group spent much of their time in silent contemplation as they walked. It was in a particularly unique cavern that Bahadur called for a stop. They had come upon a new marker, and it would need to be consulted before they could proceed.

Bahadur bent over the stone to read its surface. The network of low pedestals had proven to be invaluable, guiding them faithfully past many deadly traps designed to prohibit southward passage, and through what would have otherwise been an unnavigable maze.

At present they found themselves in a steeply angled chasm, the massive rock shelf before them fragmenting into four possible directions. Gabriel squinted into the narrow spaces around them, feeling much like an insect in danger of being squashed should the planet so much as hiccup.

Turning to look in the direction they had come, it appeared to Gabriel as though a massive rock formation had been wrenched apart by tremendous forces, leaving between its two severed halves the meter-wide gap that the group had only just made its way along. Natasha was looking back as well.

"What do you think?" asked Gabriel, using the sleeve of his shirt to wipe the sweat from his brow.

The temperature had been growing progressively hotter as they descended.

"It's as though I could feel the weight of the entire Mediterranean Sea over my head."

Natasha touched the perspiring rock and then tasted the tips of her fingers.

"It's not salty."

"Not this far down," said Gabriel. "All the salt's been filtered out of it."

Natasha chewed her lip and looked around.

"Shouldn't we have found the Chamber of Khalifah by now?"

"I've been thinking the same thing," said Gabriel. "We've got to be really close. I'd wager we're at the halfway point to Gibraltar, and down at least a couple of kilometres, judging by this heat."

He glanced over at Suora and Fra, a look of concern coming over his features. They were both sitting on the chamber floor, their faces white from exhaustion. Out of the two, the old nun looked the worse. Her breathing was strained and irregular.

"I'm worried too," said Natasha, guessing Gabriel's thoughts.

"Uncle Marcus is doing great," he whispered, so as not to be heard. "He's like a giddy schoolboy, but Fra looks like hell, and Suora even worse. Maybe we should call it quits for the day."

At that moment Bahadur rose to his feet, his flaming torch held high. The rest of the party had dropped to the chamber floor, and the only one still standing was Scotty Roberts. He was perched on a rock, smoking a cigarillo, and silent as usual. Too many good men had been lost back at the castle, and the smuggler was still coming to grips with the tragedy.

"Dr. Parker," said Bahadur deeply, directing his gaze at Gabriel. "Perhaps you could assist me with this marker."

Gabriel and Natasha approached the brown giant. Following his lead, they squatted down beside the stone, the Islamic text merging with complex geometric patterns in the gold and alabaster.

"Of the four possible routes," said Bahadur, running a thick finger over the stone to tap a particular section, "there are only two that will serve us, and those barely so. I am gravely concerned for the elders. They will not endure this heat very much longer."

Gabriel nodded sombrely and bent to study the text. It did not take him long to decipher their limited options.

"This doesn't look good," he muttered, rubbing the back of his neck as he read.

"What is it, Gabriel," whispered Natasha. "What does it say?"

He replied in a hushed tone so as not to be overheard.

"By the looks of it, this igneous formation's the weakest point in the whole cave system. It's prone to seismic activity. The marker says that up ahead we're going to see the chasm we're in fall off into some kind of fissure, and that it's not uncommon for torrents of water to empty into it from the sea above. It warns of a great danger to travellers should this happen when they're in the vicinity."

Gabriel turned his gaze away from the stone marker and towards Natasha. Bahadur did the same.

"There are four ways to go," said Gabriel. "Two of them lead to galleries located east and west of here. They're basically dead ends unless you want to crawl on your belly for a kilometre in sweltering heat. The other two passages cross the fissure above us and below us."

He pointed at a heavy bronze door set into the cavernous wall behind Natasha.

"All four passages are behind that water lock."

Natasha glanced at the door and then looked back at Gabriel and Bahadur.

"So what's the problem?"

Bahadur frowned and spoke, his voice deep with apprehension.

"The marker warns that the lower passage is very treacherous. It is exceptionally hot and can often become flooded with seawater."

"No one is advised to take it," added Gabriel. "The one above us is the one they recommend. Apparently, there's a bridge that crosses the chasm there."

"So why not take that one?" asked Natasha.

"The Moors made the bridge retractable."

"And?"

"And it takes a guide to operate it. A guide who would, at that point, turn back to Morocco."

"I don't understand," said Natasha.

Gabriel frowned and pushed back his hair.

"Back when we first entered the caves," he said. "There was a caution that forbade anyone to proceed without royal escorts. All these markers along the way have basically been for their use. It would appear that at least two escorts accompanied each expedition. This marker's saying that one escort will stay behind in order to operate the bridge."

"Why would they do that?" asked Natasha angrily.

Gabriel shook his head.

"The Moors didn't want enemies using the pass to sneak into their palaces," he said. "My guess is that there's some kind of barrier in the lower passage as well."

"So what are we going to do?"

"We cannot take the lower route," whispered Bahadur, turning his massive head in the direction of the old nun. "It is utterly out of the question. Not just because the elders would never survive the heat, but also because the Chamber of Khalifah could easily reside on this side of the bridge."

Gabriel nodded.

"I was thinking the same thing. If the lower route's prone to flooding, the upper passage would be the place to build the secret chamber."

"Then what can we do?" asked Natasha. "One of us can't just stay behind…"

"We have no choice but to take the higher path," said Bahadur. "I will carry Suora. You and the others can help Fra and Bishop Marcus along. If anything, gaining altitude will offer them a break from this heat. If we cannot all pass the chasm, I will activate the bridge from this side and then proceed to the lower path. We will reunite at the first junction point on the other side."

Gabriel and Natasha nodded in agreement and rose to their feet. There were no other alternatives if they wanted to keep Suora and Fra alive and avoid the risk of accidentally skirting around the Chamber of Khalifah.

Gabriel checked the bronze door for traps and then worked the heavy iron wheel set into the wall next to it. Soon the door was rising noisily into the ceiling, a cool draft of air pouring in from the passage beyond.

"We go up!" announced Bahadur, turning to the others. "We will soon leave this heat behind."

When they had all passed through the door, Gabriel released the holding mechanism and the heavy barrier came down with a rattling crash. He turned to peer up the dark passage, holding up a flickering torch to dispel the gloom.

"All right," he said with a grimace. "Let's see where this goes."

CHAPTER 32

Los Picos de Europa, Northern Spain.

Isaac awoke to a violent pounding and opened his eyes in time to see the blue-haired girl burst into his room. Her boyfriend was clinging to her side, pale, frightened, and wounded. There was an open gash on his left shoulder.

"Something terrible has happened!" she blurted through her tears. "My Pedro has been hurt. Help us. Please!"

Isaac watched her lay the boy down on the floor and then turn to lock the door behind her. There was a frantic urgency to everything she was doing, one that Isaac could not understand.

"There is no need to panic," he said kindly, rising from his bed and beginning to dress. "I have some medical experience. The wound does not look life threatening. All will be well, young lady."

"You do not understand!" she cried, frantically sliding the room's armoire to block the door. "They've gotten inside!"

Isaac buttoned his shirt and watched as Shackleton approached the boy. The dog sniffed him suspiciously and then shot him an intense glare. Isaac frowned in confusion. They were obviously in danger, but from whom?

"My dear child," he said, putting on his shoes. "What are you saying? Who has gotten inside? What is happening?"

"The people of the village," stammered the girl. "All those poor people…"

The boy was only semi-conscious now, perched lifelessly against the wall. She turned from him to face Isaac, her expression grave.

"They walk around as though they were asleep, but they are not. They are dead. I am sure of it. They are dead yet they still walk!"

Isaac donned his ragged suit jacket and approached her.

"They're killing everyone!" she cried, clinging to him and bursting into tears. "Those they don't eat rise up again and join in the killing."

Isaac pulled away enough to see her face. As gently as he could he lifted her chin until he could look into her eyes.

"Start from the beginning, child," he said, his brow furrowed. "Tell me exactly what has happened."

The girl swallowed hard and brushed aside her frazzled blue hair.

"I was sleeping with Pedro in the room above here when we heard the screaming. Right after that my phone rang. It was my mother. She told me not to go outside. She said that early this morning a strange plane had flown by. She said that after it passed people started to fall dead in the streets; that it was spraying some kind of poison. Then I heard her screaming…"

The girl pressed her head into Isaac's chest and sobbed uncontrollably.

"They killed her! They killed my mama!"

Isaac's eyes scanned the room as the girl wept. He could hear movement outside the door. Something appeared to be scratching at its surface. Shackleton was sniffing the crack under the threshold. He growled suspiciously and then shot a glance back at Isaac, his amber eyes intense.

"What happened after that, my child?"

"When I told Pedro, he got up right away and left our room. I was so scared. I didn't want him to leave me alone. My mother had said not to go outside, but he didn't listen. Why didn't he listen?"

The girl pushed away from Isaac and bent to tend to her boyfriend again. He had fully lost consciousness now. Before Isaac could do anything, he saw the boy's body go into seizure and then fall suddenly still.

"No!" cried the girl. "No Pedro! Don't die! I love you!"

Shackleton turned and began to bark at the boy. Isaac did not understand what was happening. He searched for a pulse but found nothing. Although deep, the wound in the boy's shoulder had severed no arteries.

How could he have died so quickly?

Isaac moved away. If the boy had been infected with some kind of virus, it would be best if they kept their distance.

"I am so sorry, my child," he said, taking the girl by the arm. "He is gone. Come over to the bed. You must rest now."

In that instant, several things happened at once. No sooner had the girl risen to her feet than the armoire began to shake violently under a barrage of forceful blows. The door behind it had already come off its hinges, and the tips of bloodied fingers came into view, probing the crack that separated the armoire from the wall.

"It's too late," whispered the girl, her eyes wide with fear. "They've found us."

Isaac looked down in time to see the dead boy's eyes jerk open, his hand darting out to take hold of the girl's leg.

Merciful Father in heaven!

Isaac could not understand. In the space of a moment the boy's body had somehow reanimated, and in his mind there came a vivid recollection of the corpse of his son.

"No," he gasped, shaking his head from side to side. "This cannot be…"

The boy was jerking spasmodically now, his mouth snapping at the girl like a rabid dog. Isaac watched as Shackleton came suddenly to the rescue, taking the dead boy by the throat, and dragging him away from her.

The girl, who had only just loosed herself from the clutching hand, now struggled to free herself from Isaac's embrace, desperately wanting to stop Shackleton's attack. Isaac held her fast, looking over to see that the armoire was already sliding away from the wall.

The probing fingers had now been replaced by grey and bloodied arms. There were at least four victims prying their way into the room and it was utterly obvious that just like the boy, they too had transformed.

"Let me go! Can't you see he's killing him?" screamed the girl, but just then Shackleton finished his grisly work, tearing the head from the jerking torso.

The girl was in hysterics now, fixated on the corpse of her boyfriend and screaming incessantly.

"Is there another way out of this chamber?" cried Isaac, turning her away from the source of her panic. "Listen to me!"

The effect was almost instantaneous.

"The service stairs to the laundry room," she whispered, wide eyed.

"Show me where it is!" said Isaac, releasing her and taking up his belongings.

They made their way to a sliding door in the corner of the chamber. Opening it they found a narrow flight of stone steps winding upward. Shackleton bounded up first, followed by the girl, and then by Isaac, who managed to slide the door shut behind him just as the armoire came crashing to the floor.

Moments later they had gained access to a laundry room with a single door and window. They were on the ground floor now, and outside, laundry could be seen hanging from a clothesline.

"We've got to get out of here!" cried the girl.

She rushed to the door and took hold of the knob.

"Wait!" cried Isaac, but he knew it was too late.

The girl turned to face him just as the door splintered behind her. A dozen groping arms took hold of her instantly, dragging her back into a mob of at least twenty undead. A loud bark sounded, and Isaac spun to see Shackleton looking back at him from the other side of the window, his amber eyes insistent.

"Dear Father in heaven," he sobbed, climbing over the sill. "Save their souls..."

CHAPTER 33

Central Jerusalem, Israel.

Christian looked blankly at the video images. The sweeping devastation caused by the viral weapon was like nothing he could have imagined. This was not death, but rather a desecration of life, and something in him was appalled that he could have instigated such a monstrous act of destruction. He found himself repeatedly confirming the reality of the events to himself, as though he were somehow unable to accept them.

These are live feeds. This is actually happening.

Through the enhanced satellite imagery, Christian could see the macabre spectacle unfolding before his eyes. A plethora of high-resolution videos were offering him every grim detail. Four drones had flown along precise aerial routes, spreading the virus in a fine spray of specially engineered bio-gel. By taking advantage of wind currents in the mountainous landscape, they had managed to spread the virus along the entire northern coastline, and about twenty kilometres inland.

Christian's eyes scanned the affected region on the hologram. The virus itself would not affect everyone, only those caught outdoors, and only during a short window of time. In open air the genetically engineered pathogen could only survive an hour at most, but once absorbed into a host it would sustain itself indefinitely.

After terminating all brain functions, the virus would proceed to alter the host's DNA, and in this way attain the unsettling reanimation that gave the virus its horrific characteristics. Endowed only with the primordial instinct to feed, the infected corpses would then spread the virus via the bite wounds they inflicted. Christian knew this would soon become a plague of biblical proportions. He recalled what he had learned from the Zurvanites.

The demons will soon take possession of these corpses...

Writhing masses of humanity stretched out before Christian in real time. Some were in the process of being taken by the virus. Others had already reanimated and were feeding. He could see hordes of cadavers filling the streets like walking zombies, but it was the undead children who affected him the most.

Christian passed his hands over his face, pushing his fingers into his eyes as he rubbed them. He was struggling to regain his apathy but there were too many children among the infected. Their faces were horrific.

I don't give a shit. I don't give a shit!

He turned away from the hologram to spot the thick-necked admiral Chester B. Sterling appearing on one of his communications banks. In the shadows behind the monitor, he could see Cynthia's ragged grey corpse devouring a glistening mound of pig offal. His eyes lingered on her for a long moment.

I don't give a fucking shit.

"We've searched the entire strait, Mr. Antov, sir," said the admiral. "There's no sign of them."

Christian's eyes returned to the monitor and scanned the admiral's ruddy face, his mind starting as it remembered the temporarily forgotten Cube. This was his priority. What had he been thinking? The artifact had to be either recovered or destroyed. He turned away from the monitor to clear his mind, just as his father's insistent hiss exploded in his brain like a bursting tumour.

"All power is based in fear! Fear must be maintained at all costs!"

Christian cringed visibly as the ghost of his father wormed into him yet again, violating his personal boundaries and filling him with an uncontainable urgency to destroy the Cube. He began to tremble uncontrollably, and looking down at his hand, saw that his body was shifting and jerking in and out of solidity. For fleeting moments his skin was reptilian.

"Mr. Antov, sir," said the admiral. "Is everything all right, sir?"

"Everything is fine," said Christian, keeping his back to the monitor. "Did you complete the underwater search?"

"Affirmative. If they were under there, our sonar would have picked them up. They've vanished, sir."

Christian closed his eyes in concentration. His ability to determine the exact position of the Two was lessening as the spiritual separation between them disappeared. He ground his teeth in frustration. Everything was falling apart. He jerked around to face the monitor.

"Look again!" he barked, his eyes cold and reptilian. "Report back to me in sixty minutes!"

"Aye-aye, sir," said the admiral, his monitor going black.

It was at that moment that a video communication from Nasrallah arrived. He was in Ceuta, and his countenance resembled that of a greasy rat. Behind him could be seen the upper torsos of two Vanderhoff operatives, their burly arms crossed over their chests.

"What news do you have for me?" asked Christian in disgust.

"We located the safe where the treasure was kept, Master. The scroll is missing."

"Missing?" asked Christian, a deep rage beginning to boil in him. "You are an incompetent fool! I have no more need of you!"

"Please, Master," pleaded Nasrallah, knowing that his death would come swiftly. "Perhaps I can still be of use. Parker will go to Ceuta. I have many connections there. I can aid you in your hunt. He will not escape that city."

"He has left Ceuta!" bellowed Christian in frustration, "They have all disappeared somewhere in the Strait of Gibraltar!"

"They are in a boat, sir?"

"No they are not in a boat!" cried Christian. "They are not in a plane, or in a submarine! They have disappeared you useless fool! And with them the Compostela Cube. I have no further need of you. Now you will die."

"Wait, please!" cried Nasrallah, cringing in pain as one of his captors clamped a hand onto his shoulder. "I believe I know where they are."

"You lie!"

"On the scroll was a map," stammered Nasrallah hurriedly. "A map of the strait! It showed a passage beneath the waters; a passage that began in Ceuta and that led to Gibraltar!"

Christian bent close to the monitor, his face filling the screen and sending waves of fear through Nasrallah. Christian Antov did not appear human anymore. Perhaps he was losing his mind, but for fleeting instances it seemed to Nasrallah that he was looking at a reptile; a lizard-man…

"What did you see on that map?" asked Christian slowly, his fury on the verge of explosion.

"I do not know exactly," lied Nasrallah. "I did not have an opportunity to study it in detail."

"What kind of map was it?"

"I do not know, Master," pleaded Nasrallah. "Please have pity on me. I only know that I saw a passageway. I can be in Ceuta in a few hours, Master. I can find the entrance of the tunnel for you."

Christian could sense that Nasrallah knew more than he was saying. The roach of a man was planning something, but it mattered not. He would be accompanied by an entire task force. He had nowhere to run.

"You *will* find the entrance to that passage," said Christian menacingly.

"Yes, Master," said Nasrallah, nodding emphatically. "Immediately, Master. Thank you, Master!"

CHAPTER 34

Ceuta, Spanish Morocco.

Nasrallah made his way through the familiar underground tunnels, the sight of his ravaged hashish operation intensifying his hatred of Christian Antov. Over the past few days, he had learned from his taunting captors that Christian had been the one responsible for his ruin, having given the orders to inform Interpol of his numerous drug operations.

Nasrallah smiled wickedly as he passed the ransacked debris. He would have his revenge shortly. Having led his captors to a place where he knew it would be easy to disappear, he had slipped away unnoticed, and left them searching for him in the upper tunnels. Accompanying him now were the six hired men he had secretly arranged to meet; filthy cutthroats who would have gladly turned him over to his captors for a reward, were it not for the promise of riches that Nasrallah had made them.

"The treasure chamber is just ahead," he said. "There we will find the entrance to the tunnels I spoke of."

The plan was simple. Ambush the unsuspecting group in the tunnels and take the Cube and the scroll. With any luck they would have already recovered the Book of Khalifah, and they would take that too. Christian Antov had made it very clear how much he valued these artifacts. Now he would pay dearly for them.

Nasrallah opened the door to the treasure chamber to find the lights still on.

They have been here recently. It is just as I suspected...

Like a rat following a scent, he made his way to the wall where the actuating device was located. He could see that one of the stones was free of dust. The swarthy cutthroats gathered around him.

"Where did you hide the treasures that filled this room?" said one of them, his lips drawn back in a snarl.

"Those treasures are gone!" snapped Nasrallah, but he calmed down immediately. "Nevertheless, still greater ones await us."

He laid a filthy hand on the stone and gave it a push. It sunk inwards effortlessly, and within moments, a deep rumbling could be felt at their feet.

* * * * * *

"So what you are telling me is that the existence of an underground passage is theoretically possible."

It was Christian who spoke. He was seated in the Holy of Holies, his face showing signs of a fatigue that was taking everything in his power to hold at bay.

"Yes sir, Mr. Antov, that is correct," said the admiral over the monitor. "We've consulted with our geologists, and they have confirmed that there is a divergent tectonic plate boundary located directly beneath the strait. It is at the point where the African and European plates meet, sir."

"And what does that mean?"

"Well, sir," said the admiral, looking down at a report on his desk. "It would appear that about six million years ago there was a tectonic shift in these plates and the Strait of Gibraltar closed up tight, effectively locking out the Atlantic Ocean.

"Over a period of about seven hundred thousand years, the Mediterranean Sea repeatedly evaporated and flooded, sir, the result of which created extensive sedimentary formations to a depth of several kilometres, sir.

"About five million years ago there was another tectonic shift and the strait opened up again, this time permanently filling the Mediterranean with seawater from the Atlantic. Our geologists believe it's very likely that there are pockets within the sedimentary rock that could have produced underground caves. They would be highly unstable, but they could nevertheless exist, sir."

"What do you mean by highly unstable?"

"Well, sir, there's always been a history of seismic activity in the area, but most of it's minor. Even still, with all that pressure from the sea above, it wouldn't take much for those caves to flood. Many of them have probably done so already, sir."

Christian sat back in his chair, an idea forming in his mind.

"Admiral," he said. "I remember hearing about newly developed weapons capable of penetrating bunkers. Do you know of these?"

"Yes, sir," said the admiral. "They are nuclear devices designed to target underground installations."

"Could these missiles be used to target the sea floor?"

"I can't see why not, sir," said the admiral, raising an eyebrow. "I'm sure they would need to be modified slightly, but I know for a fact that they can be launched from submarine installations. It would simply mean reprogramming their guidance systems."

"Very well, Admiral," said Christian. "I want you to consult your geologists again. This time I want to know where the weakest point in that fault line is. We will detonate one of these weapons there and see if we cannot create an earthquake to collapse the underground caves."

"Very good, sir," said the admiral. "I will update you the moment I have this information."

"Thank you, Admiral," said Christian wearily. "Our target must be destroyed at all costs."

* * * * * *

Having descended the spiralling staircase, Nasrallah bent over the mosaic panel at the cave's entrance. The six dark characters gathered in close behind.

"The way will be marked clearly for us as we proceed," he said, passing his fingers over the stone as he read it. "It will not be long before we find them. There will soon be riches for us all."

Having said this, there sounded a deep rumbling, and they turned to see the staircase vanish into the floor. A deep and inky void encapsulated them, and Nasrallah shuddered unintentionally.

The thump of the stair's closing mechanism had sounded to him like the sealing of a tomb.

CHAPTER 35

Gibraltar.

Major Richard Roberts watched as the ranks of chattering civilians filed into the tunnels, each with their allotted piece of luggage in hand. The recent detonation of a nuclear device in a Madrid airport, coupled with reports of biological weapons being used in Northern Spain, had proved to be sufficient motivation for the majority of Gibraltar's population to wish to take shelter.

"Private Henderson here, sir," came the crackling voice over Roberts' radio. "The governor wishes to see you, Major."

"Very well, Private," replied Roberts. "Tell him I'm on my way."

From his perch atop an old fortification, the major made his way down a narrow flight of stone steps, emerging into a crowded area by the tunnel mouth. Much to his satisfaction, he had earlier that morning seen the governor installed into his private apartments within the complex. Knowing the old duke would now be in close proximity to Gibraltar's best military doctors gave him one less thing to worry about.

With a light step he slipped past the entry checkpoint and hopped onto an electric golf cart waiting for him inside.

"Take me to the governor's lodgings, Private."

"Yes sir, Major Roberts," said the soldier at the wheel, jerking the cart into motion.

Even under the grim circumstances, there was a palpable excitement in the air as they drove into the underground city.

The hustle and bustle of the entering populace made the gallery appear more like a busy hotel lobby than a bomb shelter. The people of Gibraltar were a close-knit society, and under the crisis they were becoming even more so.

Groups of them milled about peacefully and chatted amongst themselves, their preparations appearing more like a holiday excursion than an emergency retreat. Roberts looked around in satisfaction. His cart was moving along the central tunnel now, passing lines of pedestrians as they made their way towards their new lodgings.

The majority of the spaces they would be inhabiting had been excavated by Canadian miners during the Second World War. What had before been damp and musty chambers in the rock, had recently been transformed into warm and comfortable abodes, with thousands of cubic meters of freshly scrubbed air being pumped through the complex every minute.

"Good work, men," said Roberts as his cart slowed to pass through a check point. "We're making excellent progress."

The soldiers saluted proudly as the Aid-du-Camp's cart sped off again. The operation was running smoothly, and all were pleased, on both civilian and military sides. In just a few more hours the sanctuary would be fully locked down, its main doors secured, and the bio-support systems activated. When this had been accomplished, the underground city would be able to provide food and shelter for its occupants almost indefinitely.

The governor's apartments were located directly below the Central Command Centre. Wanting a status report, Roberts decided to take a quick detour up to the facility before visiting the old governor.

Leaving the golf cart behind, he entered a broad cargo lift and soon found himself immersed in the command centre's lively environment. It was an expansive, semi-circular chamber, excavated high within the northern face of the Rock, and fully renovated. Dozens of personnel bustled around here, surrounded by batteries of surveillance monitors, communications arrays, and defence system terminals. In control of power generation, life support, and sanitation, this room constituted the central brain of the underground city.

"Corporal," said Roberts, stopping a supervisor as she passed. "How are we making out with the hydrogen generators?"

"Steady as she goes, Major, sir," came her enthusiastic response. "They should be online in twenty minutes."

"Any hiccups I should know about?"

"Smooth sailing, sir."

"Excellent," said Roberts, his right eye twitching. "Keep up the good work, Corporal."

Roberts circled the facility and returned to the main lift when he was satisfied that all was well. Within seconds he was back in the golf cart and passing through the maze of tunnels and chambers that comprised the military residences. Complete with a hospital, a restaurant, a pub, and even a cinema, the military sector boasted all the amenities of the civilian complex.

After whisking past a group of doctors and nurses, Roberts' cart arrived at a set of dark oaken doors, flanked on either side by the Gibraltar coat of arms, and those of the Gibraltar regiment.

"Thank you, Private," said Roberts to the driver. "Please wait here. I shan't be long."

Roberts made his way through the heavy doors, entering into an oak-paneled chamber. He was greeted by the governor's secretary.

"Good morning, Major," she said with a smile. "Welcome to the New Governor's House."

"Thank you, Silvia," said Roberts with a smile. "It certainly looks familiar."

Silvia returned the smile, knowing that Roberts had been referring to the fact that all the furnishings had simply been moved here from the original Governor's House. The effect was quite agreeable, lending a familiarity to the apartments that would have been otherwise impossible to obtain.

"He's particularly weak this morning, sir," she added quietly as Roberts passed. "The doctors have only just left."

Roberts knocked softly and entered slowly. Were it not for the lower ceilings, it would have been impossible to tell that the governor's abode had changed, so similar was it in size and layout. In the dimmed lights, Roberts could make out the old duke in his bed. He seemed to be sleeping.

"Are you awake, sir?" he asked quietly.

"Indeed I am, my son," said the old man, opening his eyes.

"You called for me, sir?"

"Sit down, Major," he said, waiting until Roberts had seated himself next to the bed before continuing. "What is the condition of our defences?"

"Fully operational, sir," said Roberts, bending closer. "We've left a contingent of men arming the exterior posts, but everything is prepared so as to continue our defence from within, should the need arise, sir."

"And the civilians?"

"Almost all have been relocated, sir," said Roberts proudly. "Those remaining outside are either foreigners who have decided to remain in Gibraltar, or citizens either not willing to enter the sanctuary, or wishing to wait until the danger is more imminent."

"And the siege?"

"Still fully in effect, sir. There's been an increase in patrol ships and a slight decrease in troops at the frontier. It would appear they're planning to lock us in until we run out of supplies, sir."

"Good," said the governor weakly. "This tells us that they are unaware of our resources. Geothermal hydrogen generators and hydroponic gardens are the last thing they think we have."

"That's correct, sir," said Roberts, nodding. "They think we're still burning coal over here."

CHAPTER 36

Somewhere under the Mediterranean Sea.

Gabriel reached out just in time to stop Fra from falling. The old brother had insisted on making his own way, but it was becoming more and more obvious that he was in no condition to do so. Both he and Suora had been severely affected by the heat of the lower passages, and though the air was slightly cooler now, the strain of their earlier endeavors was weighing heavily on them.

"Thank you, my son," said the old brother, his face pale and drawn. "It would appear that this old body of mine is giving me some trouble."

"You're doing great, Fra," said Gabriel. "I'm feeling half dead myself. The heat down there was crazy."

Gabriel looked up from his place at the rear of the procession to see Suora riding weakly on Bahadur's back. Their captain was leading them up a narrow tunnel, his flaming torch casting flickering shadows as they passed.

Behind Bahadur, were Miller and Stephenson, followed by Scotty Roberts and Amir. Directly in front of him, Gabriel could see Natasha sticking close to the old bishop.

In this way they continued their slow ascent until the tunnel leveled off and then dipped into a small, open area. Just above them, a fracture in the rock was giving vent to a steady gust of cool air being channeled down from above. In an instant everyone had thrown themselves onto the cavern floor, lying flat on their backs with smiles of relief lighting up their faces.

After some time, Natasha sat up to find that Suora and Fra were talking quietly among themselves, seated with their backs against the cavernous wall. The fresh air was helping them tremendously, but their faces still seemed dangerously pale to Natasha, and this concerned her greatly. She tilted her head in their direction to hear what they were saying.

"We have lived a wonderful life together, my love," said Fra, smiling peacefully. "We have been blessed."

"E vero, il mio tesoro," said Suora, resting her head on Fra's shoulder.

Natasha's eyes welled with tears, and seeing this, Gabriel put a hand on her shoulder.

"What's wrong?"

"Suora and Fra are talking as though they're going to die down here," she whispered.

Gabriel frowned.

"They're just being silly," he said. "They're going to be fine."

* * * * * *

Nasrallah and his men were making fast progress now, navigating the passageways at a brisk trot. Unlike the group they pursued, his men were young and unencumbered, driven by a lust for riches that served well to fuel their pace. The sooner they could kill their prey, the sooner they would receive payment.

Knowing their greed, Nasrallah pushed them harder still. He was anxious to get his hands on the artifact, and in so doing win back the life that had been taken from him.

"They have three elders with them," he said as they ran. "They will not have gone far."

Already Nasrallah had covered the distance it had taken the others an entire day to complete. At this pace they would be on them within the hour.

* * * * * *

Not fifteen minutes had passed before Bahadur ordered the party to rise again, stating that with the cooler air, the way would now be much easier for them all. What he did not relate to them was that his smuggler's intuition was warning him of an impending danger, urging him to press onward despite the fatigued state of his company.

"We will all rest in Gibraltar," he said in his deep basso, hoisting Suora gently onto his back. "Let us press on. We are very close now."

They had not been walking long before Bahadur's fears were confirmed.

"Stop!" came a hoarse whisper, and turning, Bahadur saw that all eyes were fixed on Fra.

Both of the brother's hands were held up in an urgent plea for silence. He turned his old head to face the tunnel behind them and listened intently for a moment longer.

"There is someone there, my friends," he whispered. "They have opened that metal door that we passed through."

All listened but could hear nothing. Knowing well of the brother's uncommonly keen sense of hearing, Bishop Marcus was the first to take heed of the warning. He turned to Bahadur, a look of consternation on his old face.

"But how can that be?" asked Bahadur, frowning. "The door is too far away to be heard."

Gabriel put a hand on Fra's shoulder.

"You're absolutely sure?"

Fra nodded confidently.

"These old ears have never lied."

Scotty was already moving off with Miller and Stephenson at his side.

"We're going to check it out, mates," he said, patting his assault rifle. "I've got a little something I want to give to that rat."

Bahadur was perplexed. He looked over at Gabriel.

"Dr. Parker. Is it possible that we could have passed Nasrallah somewhere along the way, if it is indeed him?"

Gabriel looked back at him, thinking.

"He must have taken a wrong turn down one of the passages, and then found his way back."

Bahadur nodded and turned to Scotty.

"Go with great care, my friend," he said. "A cornered rat can be very dangerous. We will continue forward."

Scotty gave them a wink.

"We won't be long, mates."

It was only a short while later that the group finally came upon what they had been longing to find. Hewn directly into the granite was a low archway leading into a widened area of tunnel, the complexity of its architecture showing its obvious importance.

"The Chamber of Khalifah!" exclaimed Natasha. "We found it!"

She was going to rush in but Gabriel took hold of her shoulders and held her back.

"Careful," he said. "Let's do this slowly."

He took a cautious step forward and aimed his flashlight into the space. Within was a natural formation, measuring a dozen feet in diameter. The granite was particularly fractured here, with deep crevices and fissures all around. A soft rumbling sound was emanating from the walls.

"There's a gallery behind this portico," he said, looking back over his shoulder. "The chamber's got to be close by."

"What's that sound?" asked Natasha.

"Seawater," said Gabriel, looking around suspiciously. "It's coming down from above. We must be at some kind of fault line."

With practiced stealth, Gabriel made his way forward. He was scanning every surface for traps but paid particular attention to a horizontal crevice high and to the left. He hoisted himself carefully upwards so that he could aim his flashlight into the space, and then turned to survey the gallery. He was amazed by what he saw.

Much of the stone had been very carefully worked here, and the floor was perfectly level. Across from him was an elaborate stone wall covered in ornately designed fist-sized symbols, each set into a grid that stretched from floor to ceiling. Positioned at its centre was what looked to be two peepholes, complete with an indentation to accommodate a viewer's face. It resembled the backside of a mask. He hopped down and waved the others forward.

"It's all right," he said. "Come in and take a look at this."

As they entered, he brought their attention to the mysterious wall of stone carvings. Its textured surface danced under the flickering light of their torches. Gabriel began to examine the friezes in more detail.

"It looks like the Chamber of Khalifah could be directly behind this wall," he said, "but for God's sake, don't touch any of these stones. They might have been designed to trigger some kind of mechanism. I've never seen anything like this before."

CHAPTER 37

Central Jerusalem, Israel.

Christian could see the admiral's face in the monitor before him, but his voice was almost inaudible over the icy whispering that filled his mind. The desecrated Kadosh Hakodashim loomed around him, and Cynthia's possessed corpse was particularly agitated.

The demonic voices were feverishly insisting that the Cube be destroyed at once. They infected Christian's psyche with a frenzied urge to act immediately; to obliterate anyone or anything that stood in his way.

"Mr. Antov. Is everything all right, sir?"

Christian heard the admiral's voice at last and clung to it desperately.

"Yes, yes," he managed to say. "I'm fine. Continue."

"Our geologists inform us that there's an igneous formation one kilometre south of Gibraltar that appears to be the weakest point along the tectonic rift, sir. There's only one problem."

Christian battled to regain control of himself. He made a concerted effort and at last managed to lower the volume of the voices in his head.

"I don't like problems, Admiral," he said with a final shudder. "What is the issue?"

"Well, sir," said Sterling, "on the positive side, our geologists all agree that if a nuclear device were to be detonated on this fault line, the chances are almost one hundred percent that any underground cave systems would begin to collapse immediately. The only problem is that the explosion would also create widespread damage in other areas."

Christian nodded. Dr. Bennington had just appeared at the entrance of the chamber.

"Yes," said Christian. "Please continue."

"First of all, sir, an undersea explosion of this size, at this depth, would create significant disturbances in the water, sir. A good example would be the WIGWAM test that was carried out in the South Pacific in 1955.

"A nuclear device was detonated at a depth of two thousand feet, sir. It created three high-velocity shockwaves before surfacing as a nine-hundred-foot spray dome. In the strait we would be detonating at three thousand feet, sir. We could most likely count on generating four to five shockwaves."

"And?"

"Well, sir, they stir up the water something awful. The WIGWAM test created massive waves, sir. Something similar to a tsunami. We're dealing with some enormous forces here. The device you want to explode is about ten times the size of the device used at the WIGWAM test, and it would be detonated at an even greater depth.

"The waves generated from a blast such as this would basically take out all the coastal regions in the vicinity, and severely damage coastlines as far away as Malta and Greece."

"Is there anything else?"

"Well, sir," continued the admiral, swallowing hard, "there's also the question of the radiation that would be released. The spray dome would be well over twelve hundred feet high. It would scatter millions of tons of radioactive water into the atmosphere, sir. It would be an ecological disaster."

"Is that all?"

"Well sir, no it isn't," said the admiral. "What I've just described to you is the damage we are guaranteed to obtain. There is another effect this detonation could possibly have that would make this other stuff look like a walk in the park, sir."

Christian bent closer to the monitor; his eyebrow raised ever so slightly.

"And that is…?"

"Ground zero would basically be right on the active fault line between the African and European plates, sir. The Strait of Gibraltar registers low-level earthquakes almost monthly. Our geologists warn of the possibility of a massive earthquake being unleashed if this detonation were to occur; an earthquake that could rival the one that measured 8.8 back in 1755. Back then, the number of casualties amounted to one hundred thousand, sir, but our geologists estimate that a similar quake would take out ten to fifteen times that amount of people in the present day."

"Good work, Admiral," said Christian with a nod. "Notify all military installations in the affected areas to be on high alert should the worst-case scenario come to pass. I want that missile fired within the next thirty minutes."

"But Mr. Antov, sir," said the admiral, a shocked look of dismay overriding his normally hardened features. "There are coalition boats in the Strait of Gibraltar that would need several hours to move out of range, sir. Perhaps by tomorrow…"

"You have my orders, Admiral," said Christian coldly. "Proceed immediately."

"Yes, sir, Mr. Antov, sir," stammered the admiral. "Immediately, sir."

Christian ended the call. His face had become pale and damp with sweat, as though he had just awoken from a nightmare. He rose to his feet, swaying dizzily before the glowing holographic planet. He reached up and turned it, pinpointing the area of the Mediterranean that would soon be decimated.

Let them all die. I don't give a shit.

He could see Dr. Bennington approaching out of the corner of his eye. The atmosphere was warping around Christian now, a tremendous pressure mounting in his head. He battled to silence the voices as they began their litany once again but failed hopelessly. Everything was in turmoil. He feared for his sanity.

"Destroy the Cube! Destroy it now!"

"Christian," came the doctor's sober voice. "You asked to see me."

Christian turned to face him but said nothing. Bennington could see that he was crying out for help. Christian's defences were collapsing. For better or worse, the time had come for Bennington to intervene.

"Dear, Christian," he said. "Can you not see what you are doing?"

He put a calming hand on his patient's shoulder.

"Let's talk for a moment. It's important you understand something, my friend."

The four Zurvanites appeared to Christian just then, jerking and shifting, and filling his mind with even more madness. They were insisting that the doctor's life be terminated at once. Christian reeled under their attack. He pushed Bennington away viciously.

"Kill the doctor!" they hissed. *"Kill him now!"*

Bennington fell and struck his head. He looked up from the floor to see Christian's eyes filled with murder. He could feel a trickle of blood running down his face. He dabbed it with a handkerchief and struggled to lift himself into a chair.

"More killing will not make the pain go away, Christian," he said dizzily. "You are trapped in a vicious circle. You must extract yourself from it."

Christian was hunched over in rage.

"What are you talking about!" he bellowed, the veins on his neck bulging.

An encompassing confusion had taken him. He was reacting like a cornered animal.

"What the fuck are you talking about?!"

The dark reptilian beast in Christian had surfaced once again, and this time it wanted nothing more than to strangle the doctor where he sat. Christian battled with himself. The doctor was all he had. He was his only friend. Even still, Christian found himself moving slowly towards the old man, the urge to exterminate him too great to resist.

"I am talking about *numbness*, Christian," said Bennington, his eyes widening at the impending danger. "I am talking about your only defence against the pain."

Christian stopped in his tracks and dropped into a chair, kneading the armrests with clenched hands. He was looking straight ahead, his eyes glazed from the tempest of his inner conflict. He wanted blood, but Bennington's words had struck a chord in him. Numbness was what he most yearned for. It was the one thing he desperately needed to regain.

Even still, the murderous urges continued to engulf him nonetheless. They were impossible to resist. He shot his head around to see Cynthia's corpse jerking in the shadows behind him. His rage was on the verge of exploding. It needed to be vented.

"Give me another injection!" he snapped, then he pulled open his desk drawer and produced a large calibre handgun, complete with silencer.

Bennington rummaged through his bag hastily, watching as Christian staggered over to where Cynthia crouched. The first bullet struck her in the chest with a dull thud, but she continued with her feeding as though nothing had happened.

Christian ground his teeth. His face was spattered with her coagulated blood, but he had garnered no satisfaction. The next shot severed Cynthia's hand at the wrist, and the third left her jaw hanging by a tendril of flesh, but still there was no reaction in her; no cries of pain; no suffering.

Instead of being quenched, Christian's rage was only growing. He stepped forward, his eyes gaping. With shaking hands, he unscrewed the silencer and proceeded to empty the remaining fifteen rounds point blank into her skull.

Deafening reports filled the chamber, and though Christian's face and body were soon painted with blood and gore, his rage was still undiminished. He dropped the heavy gun to the floor and turned to face the stunned doctor, drawing up his bloodied sleeve with a trembling hand.

"Give it to me now or I swear I will murder you!"

Bennington tore his eyes from the pulpy mass that had once been Cynthia's head. There was no time to waste. He got up and administered the sedative at once. Christian slumped into a chair; the lids of his eyes heavy. Seeing this, Bennington took a deep breath and returned to his seat.

"I want you to try very hard to understand what I am going to tell you, Christian," he said, sitting forward. "As a boy, your only defence against all of the cruelty you suffered was to become numb to it. Is that not correct?"

Christian nodded.

"It's true," he said quietly. "I never let myself give a shit."

"Precisely," said Bennington. "And you found that the best way to be apathetic to your own pain was to be apathetic to the pain of others. If you could witness somebody else suffering, and be unaffected by it, that meant you could also be unaffected by your own pain. Is that not also correct?"

Christian looked up at the doctor. He had never thought of it that way, but it was true. To this day, seeing someone suffer pain or humiliation was always a pleasurable experience for him. It proved to him that he truly did not care. It validated his sense of numbness. It made him feel strong and secure.

"And for this reason," continued Bennington, "as a child you were sometimes driven to be cruel to others, perhaps to animals, just so that you might demonstrate your numbness."

Christian nodded.

"As a boy I used to catch field mice and dissect them alive. I never knew why I was doing it. It was just something I did..."

Bennington smiled gently with understanding. It was important that Christian did not feel judged. Cruelty to animals was a typical compulsion in abused children.

"The trouble with this kind of validation is that it always creates the same problems, Christian," he said. "It makes us feel guilty, and the pain from this guilt gets added to the original pain, so that we have to become even more numb to deal with it."

"What are you talking about?" asked Christian, sitting up in his chair.

He had hoped the doctor would assist him in regaining his numbness, but he suspected that Bennington was moving in a very different direction.

"I feel no guilt whatsoever," he lied. "You're wrong."

"You know that's not true, Christian," said Bennington firmly. "You are caught in a vicious circle. Each time you lash out at the world, you do so to prove to yourself that you are numb to the suffering of others, and thus to your own suffering, but it is not working anymore. You only find that your pain increases. So you lash out again, thinking that more of the same remedy is all that is needed."

"Shut up!" said Christian, rising to his feet. "Shut your mouth!"

"The solution you used as a child will no longer work for you, Christian," said Bennington, rising to his feet as well. "You are in an emotional crisis, my friend. Your numbness has broken down, as it was always destined to do. Such defences cannot last indefinitely. They are based in denial."

"That's not true," said Christian, beginning to tremble.

His reptilian self was returning more forcefully than ever now. He could resist it no longer. Bennington's words were a direct assault on his last remaining subterfuge; they were awakening in him a primordial urge to defend himself.

Christian approached the doctor with clenched fists. He would not accept what he was being told. Without numbness he was lost. He needed to regain it immediately. What did he care if this pathetic old man lived or died? He would throttle him now with his own hands and prove to himself how numb he really was.

Bennington backed away from Christian in fear. His patient's face was blood-spattered and dripping with gore. There was murderous intent in his eyes.

"The only solution available to you is to confront the guilt you're feeling, Christian," he said unsteadily. "You must accept what you have done and allow yourself to grieve over it. More killing will not alleviate your suffering. It will only make the pain worse."

Christian said nothing in response. He had not even heard the doctor's words. His eyes had become like those of a snake, and Bennington knew in that moment that he had failed. He could see Christian shapeshifting before his eyes, his body jerking and oscillating violently from side to side as his reptilian self battled for dominance.

"You must not identify with the entity that controls you at this moment, my friend," he said, feeling Christian's trembling fingers wrapping around his neck. "It is just a fragment of your personality, a culmination of all the pain and fear that you have repressed throughout your life. It is a shadow, Christian. It does not really exist."

Bennington was struggling to breathe but he made no effort to free himself from Christian's stranglehold. When he felt the strength leaving his legs, he let himself fall back into his chair, his eyes bulging from the mounting pressure.

"You are not wicked, Christian," he strained to say as consciousness left him. "In your heart you are good."

* * * * * *

Christian looked down at the cold corpse of the doctor, his eyes glazed over with glorious numbness. He could see the repugnant Zurvanites oscillating around him, but he paid them no heed. A gaping void had opened in Christian's heart, and he cared not.

Before him lay the lifeless body of his only friend, and he felt no pain. A part of Christian knew that he himself had died in this murderous act, and that it was through his own self-destruction that he had come to obtain the numbness he had so longed for.

There remained only the reptile in him now. Christian Antov was dead. He recalled Oppenheimer's famous quote from the *Bhagavad Gita*, uttered shortly after the world's first atomic bomb had been detonated.

"Now, I am become death," whispered Christian, as all went black. "The destroyer of worlds."

CHAPTER 38

Under the Mediterranean Sea.

Natasha examined the little clay bottle that Gabriel had given to her. Its neck was sealed in wax.

"What is it?" she asked.

"It's lamp oil," said Gabriel, still studying the slot in the wall where he had found it.

"But I see no lamp," said the old bishop, surveying the area. "Are you certain, my son?"

Gabriel nodded and pointed the beam of his flashlight at two oval niches to the left and right of the peepholes.

"The lamps are on the other side of the wall."

A reflection came from within the niches as Gabriel's beam of light passed over them. Natasha moved to get a closer look.

Within each niche could be seen the wick of a lamp, and a small reservoir for oil. It was what lay behind the wicks that caught her attention however; hundreds of crystal lenses comprising what appeared to be optical instruments. They reminded Natasha of the astrolabe they had found in the Chamber of the Sphere.

"Have you seen this?" she asked, turning to face Gabriel.

He was shining his flashlight into one of the peepholes and looking intently through the other. He pulled away and turned to her.

"Take a look in there."

Natasha peered inside. Shining back out of the darkness were dozens of tiny reflections, delineating a sizable chamber within. She looked back at Gabriel.

"They're mirrors," he said. "Just like the ones that were inlaid in the dome back in the Chamber of the Sphere. It's the same optical technology. These lamps are projectors."

Gabriel was stepping back to examine the wall in its entirety when the faint rattle of gunfire could be heard.

"They must have found Nasrallah," said Amir, pricking his ears.

Bahadur frowned and moved to the chamber's entrance, readying his assault rifle.

"Be on your guards," he said over his shoulder.

Gabriel nodded and returned his attention to the wall.

"This is definitely a trap," he said with hands on hips.

He looked up to study the ceiling and then returned his gaze to the wall.

"I really don't think the Book of Khalifah's in there."

Amir held back his dreadlocks and peered through the peephole.

"What if it's not a trap, boss?" he asked. "What if we need to light those lamps to see where the book is?"

Gabriel shook his head and pointed to his feet.

"This floor isn't carved into the rock," he said. "It's a slab, and my guess is that it's hinged somewhere."

He turned to study the facing wall and was about to say something when a loud explosion sounded. Seconds later Scotty burst into the gallery with Miller at his side. The two smugglers were shaken and clearly out of breath.

"We're in trouble, mates," said Scotty, his face grave.

Bahadur put a hand on his shoulder.

"Where's Stephenson?"

Scotty grimaced and shook his head.

"He's dead. Nasrallah's back there with six ugly blokes and they're armed to the bloody teeth. We're totally out gunned. We've got to get the hell out of here fast! We set off a grenade, but it won't hold them back long. They'll be on us in a minute."

"But there was only one set of tracks on the stairs when we entered the caves," said the old bishop. "I do not understand."

"There's no time to understand," said Gabriel. "But I'm thinking this could work to our advantage."

He hurried over to Suora and Fra and brought their attention to the horizontal crevice he had examined earlier on.

"Do you think you guys could make it up there if we helped you?"

"Most certainly, my child," said Suora.

"We still have some life left in us yet, young man," added Fra.

Gabriel gave a half-smile and nodded, moving to where the crevice was.

"There's plenty of room up there for all of us," he said to the others. "I say we let Nasrallah figure the hologram thing out for us. He can show us what not to do."

Bahadur took charge immediately, ordering Miller and Scotty to go up first so that they might help the others as he hoisted them up. In a short while they had all hidden themselves away in the crevice. Gabriel and Natasha were the last to ascend, and they took up lookout positions, lying side by side on their bellies and peering down into the chamber below.

A minute had not passed before the patter of trotting feet could be heard. Moments later Nasrallah burst into the gallery, his six cutthroats filing in behind him with rifles poised and torches ablaze.

"Wait!" barked Nasrallah. "Guard both exits and touch nothing!"

Gabriel and Natasha watched as Nasrallah examined the wall, his experience in archaeology leading him to the discovery of the niches and lamps almost immediately. He took hold of the little clay bottle that Gabriel had replaced in its slot and pried open the lid. The rogues gathered around.

"What is that?" grunted one of them.

Nasrallah dipped his finger into the bottle and tasted its contents.

"Lamp oil," he said, spitting on the floor. "Just as I thought."

He directed his attention to the peepholes, producing a flashlight and shining it into one of them while looking through the other.

"What do you see?" asked one of the mercenaries. "Is there treasure?"

Nasrallah said nothing, but instead moved the beam of his flashlight to the niches and examined each one of them in turn.

"What do you see?" repeated the cutthroat impatiently.

Nasrallah turned.

"Nothing yet, but we will light these lamps and find out."

Taking great care, Nasrallah poured oil into both of the lamp reservoirs and proceeded to light each of their wicks. He stepped back and addressed the man nearest him.

"The honour shall be yours," he said. "See with your own eyes what lies beyond this barrier."

With a mixture of distrust and excitement the swarthy character made his way to the wall. No sooner had he brought his face to the peepholes than he gasped in surprise.

"Great Allah!" he cried. "What heavenly place is this?"

"What do you see?" demanded Nasrallah, and noting that there was no danger, he attempted to squeeze his way in. "Stand aside!"

"There is much treasure here!" said the rogue, remaining where he was. "How it shimmers and glows!"

Gabriel exchanged a glance with Natasha. This was precisely what he had wanted to happen, and he looked on with great curiosity to see how things would unfold.

Nasrallah had by now pushed the man aside and was staring covetously into the chamber.

"I have never seen its like…" he whispered in awe.

He turned to the others; their sodden faces consumed with greed.

"The Book of Khalifah lies within," he said. "It sits upon a podium surrounded by a mountain of treasure. We must gain entry to this chamber at once."

"And why have the others not done so?" asked one of the mercenaries. "They were just here. The smoke from their torches still lingers in the air."

Gabriel and Natasha pulled back into the shadows as the band of thugs began to scan the room.

"We have them on the run, idiot!" snapped Nasrallah. "We arrived before they had a chance. We will take this treasure, and then we will hunt them down and take the Cube as well!"

Gabriel and Natasha exchanged another glance, and then resumed their surveillance. Nasrallah was running his hands over the wall now, studying each of its many carvings.

"There is an assortment of images here," he said at last. "But only one is of any relevance to the Book of Khalifah."

He pointed to a carving that depicted an apple with its peel arranged around it in a coil.

"This is the image that resides on the Cube of Knowledge, and as the Cube and the Book are linked, it can be the only image that is of any importance here."

With arrogant confidence Nasrallah pushed the carving, jerking back his hand as the surrounding stones sank unexpectedly into the wall along with it. The movement was accompanied by the loud rumbling of coursing water and a split second later the floor fell suddenly away.

In the blink of an eye Nasrallah's men were tumbling into a chamber below, their surprised cries cut short as they were impaled upon the many spikes that lined its bottom. Only

Nasrallah and two others were able to escape death, grabbing hold of the walls and clinging to the edge of the precipice.

"Where have you led us!" sneered one of them. "You will die for this!"

A curved dagger flashed into view and went straight for Nasrallah's throat. The latter reacted instinctively, pushing himself off the man next to him to avoid the blade, and sending him careening into the pit. A second later he had scampered up the angled floor and disappeared into the tunnel. His attacker did the same and vanished as well.

Gabriel and Natasha watched as the floor returned to its original position, sealing itself with a resounding boom. It was followed shortly after by a light clinking sound as another bottle of lamp oil was dispensed into the slot.

"Ingenious," said Gabriel, rubbing the stubble on his jaw. "The trap just reset itself..."

He looked over at Natasha in relief.

"If we hadn't seen that holographic tech in the Chamber of the Sphere, I probably would have fallen for it too..."

When the rumbling sound of rushing water stopped, Gabriel turned to face the others at the back of the cave.

"We're good to go," he said. "Nasrallah figured out the booby trap for us."

"Are they all dead?" asked Bahadur from his crouched position.

Gabriel shook his head.

"Just five of them. Nasrallah got away and one of his thugs went after him. He chased him back in the direction they came."

Gabriel hopped from the sill and helped Natasha down.

"I think that rat will be more concerned with saving his own hide than killing any of us right now," he continued. "We should be safe for the time being at least."

"Seawater-powered, you say…" pondered the old bishop when they had exited the hiding place. "Remarkable. But where is the Book of Khalifah?"

"Right behind this wall," said Gabriel, bringing their attention to an inconspicuous part of the gallery.

Partially hidden behind an outcropping of rock, six square-shaped stones had been inlaid into the cavernous wall. They were arranged in the form of a cross, and each was crudely carved with runes.

"Why, they look identical to the carvings on the Cube," said the bishop in surprise.

"I noticed them just before Scotty and Miller got back," said Gabriel, examining them closely. "They're very similar to the runes on the Cube, but if I'm not mistaken, only one of them will be identical."

He produced the glowing artifact and handed it to Natasha.

"Why don't you do the honours."

While Natasha compared the carvings with those on the Cube, Gabriel studied the rock wall itself. Unlike its counterpart on the opposite side of the chamber, this one had been made to resemble a natural formation.

"I found it," said Natasha. "You were right. Only one of the carvings is identical."

Gabriel returned to her side.

"Give it a little push."

Natasha bit her lip and looked at the others, following their eyes to the floor beneath them.

"Don't worry," said Gabriel. "It won't move an inch. I promise."

Natasha took a deep breath and pushed on the stone. Moments later, a section of the rock face before them pivoted silently away, revealing a humble circular chamber, with a single book podium at its centre. In that instant they all saw their worst fears confirmed.

"It's missing!" gasped Natasha. "The Book of Khalifah's gone!"

CHAPTER 39

Los Picos de Europa, Northern Spain.

Isaac Rodchenko looked up from the map. The light was fading rapidly and at some point Shackleton had gone off, leaving him alone atop a rocky perch. A cold mass of dead air was settling down around him, and the mild shivering he had been experiencing up to then was growing more intense.

They had been travelling all that day, and even though Isaac should have been thinking of setting up camp, a voice in him was insisting that he not stop. The monastery could not be far now, and something around him did not feel right. It was only after a few minutes of observation that he was able to pinpoint what was wrong.

An unnatural silence had fallen over the land. Not a single bird or insect could be heard anywhere. Overhead, the daunting sky hung heavy and immobile, an impenetrable blanket of somber cloud. Isaac scanned his surroundings in the dying light. A dense fog was forming in the hollows.

"Where is that dog?" he muttered to himself, frowning with worry.

At that moment he saw Shackleton trotting up the path towards him, a sense of uneasiness expressed in his movements.

"What's the matter, boy?"

Shackleton did not stop to greet him; instead, he moved briskly past, climbing to the place where the path continued upward. Only then did he turn to look at Isaac, a deep urgency filling his amber eyes.

He is trying to tell me something, but what?

Turning on an impulse, Isaac peered down the path that Shackleton had just come from. There was a group of shadowy figures approaching, numbering a dozen or so. It was difficult to see them through the failing light and fog, but they appeared to be stumbling up the mountain towards them, their movements slow and clumsy.

"Dear God in heaven," gasped Isaac, straining his eyes. "How can this be?"

They had not encountered any of the undead since they had made their escape from the village, and Isaac had begun to believe that the anomaly had been localized to that particular place.

Looking down at the approaching horde, he could see that this was not the case. He turned back to Shackleton and found that the dog had once again vanished, only this time the disappearance caused him great concern.

"Shackleton!" he called out in a sharp whisper. "This is no time to be disappearing!"

Isaac hurriedly collected his things and moved to follow, turning one last time to look down, but seeing nothing in the fog. It was creeping upwards in waves now, each crest followed by another, and advancing quickly.

Moving around a rocky bend, Isaac found Shackleton again. The dog was up ahead of him, a grey silhouette against a darkening sky. He moved off the moment their eyes met, and in that instant, it became clear to Isaac that Shackleton had been telling him to make haste. Now he knew why.

Isaac scrambled his way up the twisting path and Shackleton only returned to his side when he was convinced that Isaac was moving as quickly as he could. Even still, there was a continued urgency in the dog's demeanor; a ridged body language that communicated the grave danger they were in.

Isaac hurried along, and below them they heard the muted and strangled cries of a small animal rising from the fog, only to go suddenly silent. Shackleton's eyes opened wide at the sound, and Isaac swallowed hard as he stumbled forward. The undead behind them were drawing closer with every passing second. They desperately needed to find somewhere to hide.

Rounded stones were lining the path now, and the irregular gravel was soon giving way to the occasional step or section of cobblestone. The cold fog was rising ever quicker, curling over Isaac's feet and in some areas wading up to his knees. He moved forward with haste. An inky shadow of fear had engulfed him, carrying with it flashes of his ordeal at the Portal of Ahreimanius.

Isaac looked around with haunted eyes. Ancient stone structures were materializing out of the mist now, their forms dark and dripping with moisture. They had come into a solemn village and were moving along a cobbled lane flanked by low buildings. Not a soul could be seen anywhere, not a single light in any window. Isaac made the connection at once. This was the village from which the mob had come.

He could see Shackleton just ahead, turning nervously and continuing to communicate haste. It was only then that Isaac spotted a throng of figures emerging from the fog behind them. They were twisted and stumbling and numbered fifty at least. To make matters worse, vague shadows of yet more undead lurked in the mists to their left and right. Isaac peered into the gloom and realised they were surrounded.

It was only then that a potent demonic force came upon him, paralyzing him with a coursing fear that drove the breath from his lungs. A full recollection of the time he had spent possessed pushed itself into Isaac's mind just then, filling his eyes with flashing images of the gore and carnage he had endured as he was made to butcher the corpse of his son.

Isaac's breath was coming in short pants now. The mob was approaching swiftly, and he dared not budge, fearing that the slightest movement would send him plummeting into insanity. He could only watch dumbly as the space that separated him from the shadowy horde diminished.

Shackleton darted to his side and nudged him hard with his muzzle, and just then Isaac broke from the spell. He watched the brown dog dart off and followed him at an awkward gait, the closest thing to running his panic-seized body would allow him to do. His flight ended at an old monastery, its ancient wooden doors crouching under a mist-enshrouded portal of gothic masonry.

Isaac's throat was too constricted with fear to shout, so he pounded on the heavy wood instead. Try as he might, the reports he made were weak and muted, and the thick fog swallowed them instantly. It was only when Shackleton let sound three barks that he dared hope again. They were loud and sharp, and they cut through the fog.

Isaac turned and pushed his back hard into the doors, trying in vain to force them open. A full moon had just appeared from behind the cover of an overhead cloud, its cold light shining down like a graveyard lamp.

Dear God in heaven...

The walking cadavers were almost upon them. It was only then that a small hatch slid open in the door behind him. He jerked around to see a shadowy face appear on the other side.

"Melchizedek?" it said in a loud whisper. "Is that you?"

Shackleton barked in confirmation, but Isaac was sure it was too late. Looking over his shoulder he could see that the shadowy figures had arrived, their arms outstretched, their jaws snapping hungrily. A second later he felt them tugging at his pack. He struggled frantically against their clawing hands. Their bodies were grey and festering, their eyes bereft of life.

"For the love of God!" he cried in desperation. "Let us in!"

Isaac squirmed out of his backpack, using it to push away the undead who had already taken hold of it. In that instant he heard the scraping friction of an iron deadbolt, followed by the clank of an ancient latch.

Within seconds a pair of strong arms had pulled him into a dark, medieval courtyard, and slammed the door behind him. Almost instantly the inhuman sound of clawing and scratching filled the air. Isaac turned instinctively, peering through the door's open hatch to see the throngs of undead gesticulating outside. He threw his body against the door and turned to face his rescuer.

"I am Isaac Rodchenko," he panted, his eyes wide with fear. "I owe you my life."

"You owe me nothing, my son." said the man, ruffling the fur atop Shackleton's head.

He had a large build and was bearded and dressed as a monk, with an ample belly and a bald, chiseled head. His height, combined with his strong jaw, gave him a powerful appearance, but it was tempered by a pair of gentle, patient eyes.

"If you owe your life to anyone," said the monk in a thick Spanish accent, "you owe it to Melchizedek. Were it not for his bark, I would never have heard your call. This evil fog swallows all sounds."

"But how is it that you know this dog?" asked Isaac, still breathing heavily. "Who are you?"

"I am Brother Bernardo," he said. "You are now in the care of *The Order of St. James the Just*. Melchizedek is an old friend of ours. He comes and goes, but he is always welcome."

"He saved my life," said Isaac, patting Shackleton's rump.

The fat monk looked up at him urgently.

"Have you been touched by the dead?"

"I have not," said Isaac. "I was speaking of this dog's miraculous appearance not three days ago. After my plane crashed, I came to be in a lake. He appeared out of nowhere and saved me from drowning."

The monk raised his eyebrows in wonder.

"It would appear you have been through much, my friend," he said. "Were there many others on the plane with you?"

"Only three," said Isaac, still catching his breath. "All of them perished. One of those killed was Father Franco Rossi. I found his journal amongst the wreckage. He was planning to come here."

"Father Franco?" asked the monk urgently, taking Isaac suddenly by the shoulders. "You say he is dead?"

Isaac nodded solemnly. By the expression of loss in the monk's eyes, he could see immediately that the two had been good friends.

"Are you Rex Angelus?" asked Isaac.

"Yes," said the monk sadly. "I am. But there are few outside the walls of this monastery who would know that, apart from Father Franco and Professor Metrovich, that is. Was the professor on the plane as well?"

Isaac nodded solemnly.

"I do not know why I am here, Brother," he said. "I was guided by powers greater than my own. Like you I am a man of faith, and I say to you that something of unparalleled importance is occurring; something that is for the most part a mystery to me. It would seem to revolve around an artifact known as the Compostela Cube."

At the mention of the Cube, the monk's knotted brow seemed to relax, an air of perfect understanding engulfing him as he looked at Isaac. He reached past him and slammed home a second deadbolt in the gate.

"There is much to talk about, my good Isaac," he said. "But first you must come with me."

The monk laid a gentle hand on Isaac's shoulder, glancing back at the heavy door. Outside, the undead had retreated into the night fog, but he knew they would return.

"You and Melchizedek will need food and rest," he said. "You have both been through a great ordeal."

CHAPTER 40

Under the Mediterranean Sea.

Bahadur led the group in a single file, their treacherous path hugging a narrow ledge that clung to the side of a deeply fractured fissure. With all hopes of finding the Book of Khalifah gone, the giant had no choice but to push the company forward.

His priority was to get them out of St Michael's Pass and deliver Fra and Suora to the Gibraltar hospital as soon as possible. The tunnel expedition had proven to be too much for the octogenarian couple, and it was clear that they were both suffering from severe exhaustion.

"Unbelievable," muttered Gabriel, holding out his flaming torch. "Who would have thought that all this could be hidden beneath the Mediterranean?"

To their left, the fractured wall of rock had fallen suddenly away, exposing a black void. The stone here was dark and slippery with dampness. Gabriel cast a small stone into the divide, counting to five before hearing it strike something far below. For all intents and purposes, the chasm was bottomless, just as the marker said it would be.

"We made it!" cried Amir suddenly. "The pass is just up ahead!"

Within moments, all realized he was not mistaken. After arriving at an open ledge, they discovered their path had come to an abrupt end. A dark shadow on the opposite side of the chasm showed where the tunnel continued on.

In the centre of this open area, they found a marker, but unlike the others before it, this one was flush with the cavern floor. In it were set two shoe-sized depressions, each of them oval in shape and adorned with the familiar Islamic text.

"This is the actuating device for the drawbridge," said Gabriel, moving his torch closer to the marker so that he could read its carvings. "As long as one of these ovals are depressed, the bridge will remain open."

"Let's just push one down with a rock," suggested Natasha. "That way we can all cross."

Gabriel shook his head and frowned.

"There's a catch," he said. "After one has been depressed, the other will need to be depressed while the first returns to its original position. To keep the bridge open, the ovals need to be stepped on in alternating cycles, kind of like an exercise machine. Rocks wouldn't do it."

Natasha looked over to see Bahadur standing fearlessly on the edge of the precipice.

"I was hoping we might have been able to jump across," he said, gauging the distance. "But this would be an impossible leap. Even if we had a rope, there would be nowhere to secure it."

Natasha looked around and saw that it was true. The walls in the chamber were utterly smooth. The Moors had gone to great lengths to ensure that the chasm could not be crossed by any means other than the bridge.

"Let's give this a try," said Gabriel, taking Natasha's hand. "Would you like to do the honours?"

Natasha nodded and stepped into one of the two ovals.

No sooner had she done so than it dropped several inches.

"Now switch," said Gabriel.

She stepped into the other oval and found that it lowered just as the former returned to its original position. With each alternation, it became easier to depress the steps, and a slow rumbling could soon be felt at their feet. Below them, a hidden flywheel began to pick up speed.

After alternating her steps a few more times, the sound of rushing water sounded beneath them, and in the space of a minute, a narrow wooden catwalk emerged from a concealed opening in the cliff's edge. It shot suddenly across the chasm and found home in a slot on the other side, forming a bridge.

The catwalk remained extended while Natasha continued to shift her weight from oval to oval, but it retracted immediately when she discontinued her work.

"Well," said Gabriel, "so much for stepping on these stones and then trying to make a run for it. This mechanism uses water pressure to pull the bridge back the moment the pumping stops."

Natasha frowned.

"We wouldn't make it to the middle of the gorge before it disappeared under our feet."

Scotty went to stand beside Bahadur at the edge of the chasm.

"I'll take the lower route with you, comrade," he said solemnly, putting his arm around the brown giant.

Bahadur smiled and gave a nod of deep appreciation. They walked back to where the others were.

"Let us begin to cross," said Bahadur, his voice deep with resolve.

Seeing that the old nun and brother were still resting on the chamber floor he added:

"We will begin by moving the equipment. Suora and Fra may continue to rest until we are ready to proceed."

CHAPTER 41

The five-hundred and sixty-one-foot Ohio Class submarine made its way through the dark waters of the Strait of Gibraltar, its enormous belly gliding mere meters above the sandy sea floor. Its crew had only just completed the last scans of the fault line, and they were steering the black goliath out into the Atlantic Ocean to take up their launching position. In the submarine's metal bowels, a ground-penetrating nuclear missile lay armed and ready for launch, specially modified, and a tactical twenty-five kilotons in size.

"The submarine will be in attack position in T-minus three minutes and counting," said the sultry voice of Christian's computer.

Christian glanced up at the hovering holographic planet. Across from him, and under the shadow of the enormous, blackened cherubim, Dr. Bennington's lifeless corpse had been propped up in its chair. Christian stared at it blankly, his face empty of emotion.

"As you can see, Doctor," he said, raising an eyebrow, "I feel no guilt or pain. I feel nothing whatsoever."

The chamber was quiet around him, the dark voices silent with anticipation. Christian felt sated. Killing the doctor was the best thing he could have done. He was in control of himself again. Nothing would stop him now.

"The missile is fully operational," said the computer. "Standing by for launch sequence."

Christian glanced up at the glowing holographic planet, his eyes panning over the banks of monitors that flanked it on all sides. Each one was showing its own live video feed, combining to form a flickering wall of war, carnage, and devastation. He shot a glance over at Bennington's slumped corpse, and for a moment he thought he could see it smiling.

"Fire," he said, a pang of self-doubt running suddenly through him. "Fire, God damn it. Fire, fire, fire!"

CHAPTER 42

Under the Mediterranean Sea.

Even after a long respite, Suora and Fra had still not managed to regain their strength. They were reclining on a blanket that had been laid out for them, watching the others as they gathered around a stone marker on the opposite side of the chasm.

"Have strength, my love," said Suora weakly to Fra. "There is only one kilometre left. We must try with all our might."

She was wrapped in her blanket with only her face visible, looking over at Miller who had remained behind to work the bridge mechanism.

The old brother was nodding wearily, knowing full well he would be incapable of such a feat. He had managed to sit up but he was still deathly pale, and try as he might, he could not stop shivering.

"One kilometre straight up, *mi tesoro*," he said hopelessly. "May God help-"

A booming blast shook the chamber, cutting off his words. It had sounded like a muffled thunderclap, and a moment later the entire gallery began to shake violently. From high above, large sections of stone began to fall in tumbling masses, disappearing into the void of the chasm.

Suora saw Miller jump to his feet, and in that moment turned to find Fra looking directly at her. For a timeless moment they gazed into each other's eyes.

"Could it already be time, my love?" asked Suora, a deep peace engulfing her.

"I believe it is, my darling," replied the old brother, smiling sadly.

No sooner had the ground begun to grow still again than another blast sounded, followed by yet another. This time it seemed that the explosive force was beginning to resonate within the stone itself. The chamber seemed to be lurching from side to side almost rhythmically.

At that moment the old brother rose slowly to his feet, pulling Suora up with him. He turned to face Miller, a newfound strength filling his body.

"Go and get Bahadur!" he ordered. "I will man the bridge!"

Within seconds he had stepped into the ovals and begun pumping them, the ancient mechanism shooting the long wooden catwalk out across the chasm.

Amid a rain of falling rocks they watched Miller arrive safely on the other side, just as the others appeared from within the tunnel mouth. Suora could see Natasha's face among them, and the expression of horror it bore when Fra stepped off the mechanism. The bridge retracted instantly.

"Suora!" cried Gabriel over the tumult. "Fra!"

There was panic in his eyes.

"Activate the bridge!" he screamed. "We're coming to get you!"

Natasha saw Suora move into Fra's embrace, and in that moment knew what was happening.

"No," she said quietly, her eyes filling with tears. "No, it can't happen here. Not like this..."

The ground shook again as the final shock wave detonated in the sea above them. The chamber was beginning to shudder in a peculiar way now, and across the chasm they could see Suora and Fra standing arm in arm, dwarfed against the backdrop of the massive rock formations.

"You will activate the bridge mechanism immediately!" bellowed Bahadur, moving dangerously close to the edge of the precipice. "That is an order!"

Those around him were not sure what boomed more deeply, the shuddering earth or the desperation in his voice.

"Leave this place now!" cried Fra with his last remaining strength. "Make haste!"

A tremor ripped through the chasm and were it not for the strong arm of Scotty Roberts, Bahadur would have fallen to his death. With a mighty heave, the smuggler drew the giant back from harm's way, bringing his battered brown face within inches of his own.

"Are you our leader?!" bellowed Roberts over the crashing tumult, and at that very moment, tumbling masses of seawater began to fall from above, partially obscuring their view of the brother and nun.

Like Gabriel and Natasha, Bahadur too was in a state of panic, wanting nothing but to leap the impossible distance and come to the aid of his dear friends. His heart went out to Suora and Fra in desperation. This had not been the plan. He and Scotty were to have taken the lower passage. It was they who should have been on the other side.

Bahadur looked down to see that he was still being clutched by the smuggler. He stared blankly into his eyes.

"Are you our leader?!" bellowed Roberts again, his face straining from the effort.

"Yes..." said Bahadur, at last regaining control of himself. "Yes, I am!"

"Then lead us out of this Godforsaken hole, God-damn-it!"

In that moment all hell broke loose. A force so powerful jarred the ground that it made the recent blasts seem tame by comparison. Mighty as they were, the other explosions had been manmade. What they were experiencing now was Mother Nature's tectonic response to their insolence, and it was by no means subtle.

"Come on!" bellowed Gabriel over the crashing of falling rocks and water. "We can't save them! We've got to go now!"

He had his hands wrapped around Natasha's shoulders, trying to get her to turn and run.

"Suora," whispered Natasha, suddenly seeing the frail little nun through a gap in the wall of falling water.

She stood next to Fra, but whereas he was waving his arms frantically, yelling out orders for them to flee, she was calmly smiling, and for an instant Natasha's eyes locked with hers and time seemed to stop. The chamber grew oddly silent.

"Run, my child," came her familiar voice. "Escape this place and complete the task you were born to do. Bring peace to the hearts of those who will make the crossing. Darkness surrounds us now, and you must be brave. We will meet again soon, my child. Run now. Run as fast as you can!"

In that instant a great churning mass of water descended on the nun and brother, washing them away in a fraction of a second. Natasha felt herself being turned around forcefully. The crashing tumult was deafening. Directly before her she could see Gabriel's face. He was drenched in seawater, but his eyes were calm with resolve.

"Natasha," he said in earnest. "They're gone. It's time to go."

* * * * * *

Najiallah Nasrallah threw down his bloodied knife and gripped a stone outcropping with all his might. His surroundings were shaking with indescribable violence, and already the rising seawater was beginning to cover the corpse at his feet.

He had been forced to run a considerable distance before arriving at a place where he could ambush the man who pursued him. The chase had led him into a formation of fractured rock, in the middle of a meter-wide gap that separated two towering sections of granite.

Nasrallah looked around in horror. He could clearly see that the rock faces were drawing closer together as they shook. If they continued to do so, it would only be a matter of time before he was crushed. He frantically looked around. There was nowhere to run.

"Dear, Allah!" he gasped, jerking his head from side to side. "Have mercy on me, I beg you!"

As if in response to his plea, a particularly violent tremor shook him to the core just then, and the rock walls jerked suddenly together with a grinding crunch. Nasrallah was swiftly pinned, and panic took hold of him.

"No!" he screeched. "Please!"

Very slowly, the rock face continued to close in upon him, and as his ribs shuttered and popped under the pressure, Nasrallah cursed Christian with every fibre of his being. The stabbing pain in his chest was unbearable, and things were about to get much worse. Without warning his flashlight slipped from his grip and sank into the frigid seawater, plunging him into an inky black hell.

For a long while Nasrallah struggled there like a pinned sewer rat, trying to keep his head above the turbulent water. In the end, however, his frenetic refusal to die ended in vain, despite his best efforts.

After what seemed to him like an eternity, the stone walls finally moved in to obliterate him, just as the seawater rose to cover his face. In this way Najiallah Nasrallah perished in the bowels of the earth, to be missed by no living thing that walked upon its surface.

CHAPTER 43

Under the Mediterranean Sea.

"We must move quickly!" bellowed Bahadur, shoving the others into the tunnel one by one. "The water will reach us the moment the lower galleries have been filled!"

Still in shock, Gabriel and Natasha found themselves first in line, leading the others through a narrow tunnel at a brisk run. It climbed steeply before them, a natural formation that looked to have once been an underground river. From behind them came a powerful current of air that was growing in intensity.

"Why's it so windy?" asked Natasha as she ran.

Mighty gusts were blasting past them now, pushing them forward with incredible strength.

"The seawater's forcing the air out of the lower galleries!" cried Gabriel over the tumult. "This must be the only way for it to get out!"

Luckily for the party, the compressed air was having a tremendous impact on the speed of their ascent. The wind was helping to push them up what would have otherwise been a very challenging incline. Because of its consistent flow, it became easier and easier for the party to measure its effect on them, and they were soon proceeding upwards in great leaps and bounds, the smooth tunnel walls speeding past them in a blur.

"We're going too fast!" cried Natasha over the buffeting air, her ears plugged from the rapid change in altitude.

"We'll be fine!" bellowed Gabriel from his place in front of her.

He was scanning the dark tunnel ahead of them.

"Just stay on your feet!" he cried. "And keep your flashlight trained straight ahead!"

Behind them the rest of the party was doing the same, each one focusing their jerking beams into the dark depths that rushed towards them.

Bringing up the rear of their procession came Bahadur, clutching the old bishop to his side. The buffeting wind was catching the enormity of his body and carrying him as though he were a tenth of his weight.

They had been ascending in this way for almost five minutes when Bishop Marcus at last began to feel a cold mist at his back. Shining his flashlight behind him, he could see hints of spray beginning to appear in the distance. There could be no doubt. The tumultuous seawater would soon reach them. If they did not find an exit soon, they would all be drowned.

It was only then that the tunnel opened suddenly into a wider chamber, and the flow of air lessened instantly. There was a stone marker in the centre of the space, and they gathered around it in the buffeting wind.

"We cannot stay here!" cried Bahadur.

He was bending over the stone now, reading it as best he could.

"The water is almost upon us!"

Gabriel joined him. It was imperative that they make the right decision. There were several openings to choose from, and a wrong turn would cost them their lives.

"It says that Gibraltar's directly above us!" cried Gabriel, looking back to see a wall of sea foam exploding from the tunnel mouth.

"Follow me!" bellowed Bahadur. "Now! Now!"

Within a matter of seconds, the giant had ushered the party through one of the portals and into a chamber. To their great relief the room had been equipped with a massive bronze door.

In an instant Scotty, Miller, and Bahadur were bent on closing it, but the ancient hinges were seized and not budging. Gabriel squeezed in to lend a hand. Outside, churning masses of white spume were quickly filling the chamber. The raging seawater would be upon them in a matter of seconds.

"Push!" bellowed Bahadur as the veins popped from his corded neck. "HEAVE!"

With a resounding crack the hinges at last gave way, and the massive door slammed into place with a boom, just as a deluge of seawater exploded into the chamber outside. With a final consolidated effort, a heavy iron crossbar was lowered into place. Outside, the angry seawater pummelled the bronze door violently.

Bahadur slumped to the ground, his back leaning against the door as a pool of shallow water formed beneath him. Natasha's anguished sobs filled the darkness. She had curled herself up in Gabriel's lap, crying uncontrollably as the reality of what had just happened set in.

Amir found a basket of torches nearby and lit one. In its flickering light the shocked faces of all those present could be seen with utter clarity. Two of their dearest companions had sacrificed their lives so that they all might live. The bishop stood swaying on his feet, the blow proving to be more forceful than all the explosions they had experienced.

"They were our dear friends," he said, his grief and fatigue overcoming him.

He fell to his knees.

"They were our family."

A long time passed before Bahadur ended his reprieve and stood up at last. He lit another torch and held it aloft.

"Take heart, comrades," he said bravely. "Our dear friends are with Allah. My faith tells me that they are well, and that we need not be sad for them. We must continue on."

And then looking down at Gabriel he said:

"Dr. Parker. I believe that only you can find a way out of this chamber."

Gabriel and Natasha glanced up at the giant, their faces still torn with grief. It was only then that they noticed they were in an exact replica of the antechamber they had found on the opposite side of the strait.

Gabriel kissed the top of Natasha's head and came to his feet, making his way over to an elaborately carved wall. It was identical to the one they had encountered in the original space. He cleared away a mass of cobwebs and dust to reveal the surface of the actuating mechanism.

"We're in a twin chamber," he said, looking back at the others. "If I'm not mistaken, the same stone that got us in will get us out."

CHAPTER 44

Los Picos de Europa, Northern Spain.

Their footfalls echoed hollowly off the dark stone masonry. The heavy monk was leading Isaac along the isles of a large gothic church and past a long row of life-sized statues. The effigies depicted angel warriors in full armour, and at their feet lay a long battery of flickering prayer candles. The shifting light cast shadows over their angelic wings, imbuing them with life.

Isaac moved forward in silence, his eyes scanning the strange house of worship. It was clearly of Christian denomination, but whereas most church altars had as their central element a crucifix, this one had instead a large tree of the purest white marble. Every leaf and stem was masterfully carved from what appeared to be a single piece of stone.

"The Tree of Life," said the monk, seeing where Isaac's eyes lingered. "To the early Christians it symbolized far more than a wooden crucifix ever could."

Isaac turned to find that the monk was looking directly at him.

"The cross was an instrument of death, dear Isaac," he continued, "while Jesus was, after all, concerned with life above all else. It is only the dark Vatican that is concerned with death, and it is for this reason that the crucifix has always been used as its primary symbol."

Isaac did not know how to respond. This was not the first hint of heresy he had heard in the few hours he had been in the monastery. Before their meal, Brother Bernardo had led him and a small group of monks in prayer, reciting the Our Father with slight variations to the version promulgated by the Church.

"And lead us in our temptations," he had said, *"So that we may deliver ourselves from evil."*

Isaac thought back on what he had read on the internet, and how this group of monks believed themselves to be the decedents of Jesus Christ. What could he expect to find here but heresy? Even still, doubt had somehow been instilled in his mind. It was not doubt in the existence of God, but rather in the Church itself. History was rife with far too many examples of the Vatican's corruptness, and of its murderous and hypocritical acts.

Leaving the church, Isaac followed Brother Bernardo into a long corridor, with Shackleton leading the way. He was amazed at how well the animal knew the monastery, and once again found himself wondering why the dog had saved his life. He considered the many strange synchronicities that revolved around the mysterious Cube, and now more than ever wanted to find answers.

"Brother Bernardo," he said on an impulse. "Could I ask you a question?"

"Certainly," said the monk, slowing to walk beside him.

"Does the name, *The Portal of Ahreimanius,* mean anything to you?"

The heavy monk stopped in his tracks and turned to grasp Isaac by the shoulders.

"Where did you hear that name spoken?" he asked, his brow furrowing. "Did Father Franco mention it to you?"

"Why, no," said Isaac, encompassed by guilt and shame. "I was made to go there by what I can only describe as a supernatural force..."

The monk continued to frown as he bent closer.

"By a demonic force?" he asked in a whisper.

Isaac bowed his head and shuddered at the memory of it all.

"Yes," he said quietly. "They made me do abominable things..."

"I see," said Brother Bernardo, and it seemed to Isaac that the monk somehow understood. "Were you made to do things to the corpse of your son?"

Isaac was taken aback.

"I was," he said. "How is it that you know?"

The monk looked deeply into Isaac's eyes.

"I was a fool not to heed my intuition. Follow me, please."

They changed direction and walked for some time before descending into a circular crypt. It had a low ceiling and was encircled by twelve arched openings, each emptying into dark, unlit corridors beyond. At the centre of the crypt was a single stone sarcophagus, unadorned and of simple construction.

"This is a very sacred chamber," whispered the monk, falling to his knees as he spoke. "Do not be fooled by its humble appearance. Please wait here. I shall not be long."

Isaac watched the heavy monk rise and disappear into one of the arched openings, then he turned to face the crypt. A powerful paranormal energy seemed to be radiating from the place, but unlike what he had experienced on the island, its vibration was utterly benign.

What is this?

The crypt was cold and damp, and its odour was that of antiquity, combined with the pungent bite of stale earth. Isaac glanced over to see Shackleton sniffing at the base of one of the stone arches, but when he looked away, he found that was standing at the foot of the sarcophagus now, though he could not recall having walked there.

At that very moment he was overwhelmed by a feeling of such warmth and safety; of such blissful peace, that he bent on an impulse and kissed the stone tomb.

"Dear Lord in heaven," he whispered, falling to his knees. "What joy is this that fills me?"

Isaac's heart was overflowing with a sensation of the purest love imaginable, and he could not understand why. It seemed to him that he was no longer alone in this world, and that the many tragedies that had befallen him in the past had all occurred so that he might be led to this very spot.

A sense of identity and purpose was welling up in him now, but more encompassing still was the feeling of unhindered redemption that permeated his soul. In that very moment, he knew that he had been absolved of all his actions at the Portal. He could only feel atonement now, perfect and complete atonement.

Isaac looked up with teary eyes to see that Brother Bernardo was standing next to him.

"Rise, dear Isaac," he said kindly. "You have passed the test. The *Logos* is strong in you."

Coming to his feet, Isaac saw the forms of what appeared to be twelve fully armed knights standing in each of the twelve niches that encircled the crypt.

"What is happening?" he whispered.

"Behold the sacred tomb of Jesus Christ," proclaimed the monk. "Few are those who have been given to drink of his Logos, as you have just done."

Isaac looked down at the sarcophagus in utter disbelief. Engraved into its top was the image of a sword with a single Greek word below its pummel.

Χριστός.

Isaac staggered backwards in shock. In his heart of hearts, he knew what the word meant.

The Anointed One. The Christ.

"Dear God," he gasped. "This cannot be…"

Throughout his entire life, Isaac Rodchenko had been taught that Jesus Christ had risen from the dead; that his body had vanished from his tomb only to come back in spirit after the third day. A sarcophagus claiming to contain the remains of Jesus Christ was heresy on every count.

A great conflict ignited in Isaac. A part of him could not accept what his heart was telling him, but at the same time, he could not deny the sublime reality of the events that had only just transpired. He was still overflowing with the love that had engulfed him upon kissing the sarcophagus, a love whose existence could in no way be denied.

After a brief moment the battle had ended. Religious dogma might be captivating, but experiential wisdom was irrefutable.

"Never in my life had I considered..." he whispered, running his hands over the tomb and falling to his knees again.

"Rise, dear brother," said the monk, smiling. "You are truly the *Consilio*. Long have we awaited your arrival, dear friend."

Isaac looked up at the monk, his brow furrowed with confusion as he rose slowly to his feet.

"Who did you say I was?"

"You are Rex Angelus, my brother," smiled the monk. "You have come to mend that which was split, and to assist the Two in their noble endeavor."

Isaac was going to speak, but Brother Bernardo held up his hands in a gesture of patience.

"The elders are gathering as we speak," he said. "The Final Council of the Apocatastasis has been assembled. All your questions will soon be answered."

CHAPTER 45

Gibraltar.

I just can't figure this out," said Gabriel, clearly stumped.

Having exited the twin chamber, he had led the group along a short tunnel only to find that it ended abruptly at a stone wall. After examining it he had found the hairline cracks of a concealed door but could find no way to open it. He had been searching for an activating mechanism for the past ten minutes.

"It just doesn't make any sense," he muttered, pushing back his wet hair.

He looked over his shoulder to see that the others had all seated themselves along the tunnel wall, taking the opportunity to rest while he plied his trade. Only Bahadur remained on his feet, pushing random bricks in the hopes of finding the actuating device.

"Perhaps we should return to the twin chamber, Dr. Parker," he said, coming to his side. "Is it possible that there might be another exit there?"

Gabriel turned to look at the giant, an idea suddenly occurring to him.

"I'll be right back," he said, vanishing into the shadows of the tunnel.

Not a minute passed before Bahadur heard a deep boom and saw the hidden door swing silently inward. A broad chamber lay on the other side. Gabriel returned a moment later.

"The mechanism was at the entrance of the tunnel," he said with a shrug. "Sorry about that."

He held out a hand and pulled Natasha to her feet.

"How are you making out?" he asked gently.

Natasha smiled sadly.

"It's so strange, Gabriel," she said. "It's as if I can feel Suora inside me. I feel even closer to her now than I did when she was alive."

The bishop interjected.

"That is because you truly are closer to her, my child," he said. "When our body dies, we do not go somewhere *out there*, but rather *in here*. We return to the great *One*, and that can only be found within."

He pointed to his solar plexus and gave a cheerful wink.

"We must not be sad even for a moment," he said. "Suora and Fra are very much alive. Do not be fooled by appearances!"

He gave a broad smile and turned to follow the others out of the tunnel.

"Death does not exist!" he added over his shoulder, and a moment later he was gone, leaving the two of them alone.

Gabriel took Natasha into his arms.

"Do you know what?" he said. "I think that crazy old man's right."

Natasha squeezed him tightly, her sorrow transforming.

"Come on," she said, her eyes bright and shining now. "We've still got to save the world."

Gabriel and Natasha found the others gathered in an open chamber. The walls here were bound by sturdy interconnecting arches made of ancient clay bricks. It was clear that they had found the foundations of Gibraltar's Moorish castle, and that their journey had at last come to an end.

No sooner had they passed into an adjacent chamber however, than an alarm sounded with piercing intensity. A blindingly bright light was suddenly illuminating the area around them.

"YOU ARE IN A RESTRICTED ZONE," boomed a computerized voice. "DO NOT MOVE OR YOU WILL BE SHOT."

Everyone looked up to see a crudely fashioned robotic bank of guns whir into position above them, its three gigantic barrels pointing directly into their midst.

The warning repeated itself again, and Bahadur turned to face the others, not knowing what to do. There was, after all, no enemy to be seen, only a makeshift bank of high-calibre guns seemingly aware of their every move.

Resigning themselves to their fates, Bahadur and the others lowered their guns and waited. It was not long before the alarm subsided and was replaced by an oddly familiar sound.

"Who are you, and what are you doing in here?" barked a hoarse and scratchy voice.

Gabriel and Amir turned to look at each other immediately, their eyes wide with surprise. There was only one person whose voice that could belong to.

"Peralta?" they asked in unison, amazed beyond belief. "Is that you?"

"All right," came the reply after a brief pause. "So you recognize my voice. Big deal."

Amir looked around the room for a camera.

"Peralta!" he said, pulling back his dreadlocks to expose his face. "It's me! Amir Mustafa. What the hell are you doing down here? And why the hell are you pointing those guns at us?"

All watched as the bank of weapons altered its position to face Amir, the lens of a camera that was hose-clamped to its frame buzzing as it zoomed in.

"Amir!" came the raspy voice again. "It really *is* you, man! What in God's name are you doing in here, and so close to the surface at that? Do you have any idea how much radiation there is up there?"

In an instant the robotic cluster of guns retracted, and the floodlights dimmed to a more comfortable level.

"Just stay where you are," came Peralta's raspy voice. "I'll come and get you myself."

It took about fifteen minutes before the stout and messy Peralta appeared wearing a white lab coat and green surgeon's pants. His glasses were exceptionally thick, and he possessed bushy white eyebrows that protruded out over their rims. Peralta had an uncommonly large head, with tangled white hair that proved beyond a doubt that he was his own barber.

Gabriel spoke into Natasha's ear.

"He's the crazy hacker we were telling you about in the caves," he whispered. "He'll know all about the matrices."

Natasha shook her head in amazement. She had just noticed that Peralta was walking amidst an entourage of miniature drones, each one whirring and buzzing around him.

He said nothing as he approached, but instead raised both his arms to exchange warm embraces with Amir, Bahadur, Miller, and Scotty Roberts alike. The latter hesitated a moment before returning the hug.

"I should shoot out your knees for what you did to my suppliers," said Scotty, pushing Peralta away but keeping hold of his shoulders. "But I'm too happy to see your sloppy face, mate!"

Peralta smiled back. In his eyes there was great affection for the smuggler, coupled with sincere regret.

"I had no choice, old friend," said the uncombed hacker. "I'll explain later. I'm really sorry."

Peralta turned to Gabriel, bowing his head respectfully.

"Dr. Parker," he rasped, shaking Gabriel's hand. "Always a pleasure."

When Peralta's eyes fell on Natasha his demeanor changed. His tight face seemed to relax, and his eyes opened a little wider.

"My name's Peralta," he said, shaking her hand. "But yours must certainly be Venus."

"I'm Natasha," she said, laughing.

She was instantly taken by the eccentric engineer and puzzled by the feeling of undefended familiarity that seemed to exude from him. If anyone could be said to be comfortable in his own skin, it was Peralta.

A tiny drone buzzed past them just then and Peralta produced an instrument from his pocket. There was a look of consternation in his eyes as he studied its display. He muttered something under his breath and stroked the side of the instrument as though it were a little mouse.

He looked up at the others.

"It's just as I thought," he rasped. "There are dangerous levels of radiation here. We've got to leave right away!"

"What do you mean?" asked Gabriel. "Why would there be radiation down here?"

Peralta cocked a quizzical eyebrow.

"Didn't any of you happen to hear a few little explosions around twenty minutes ago?"

He spread his arms and managed to herd the group down the passage he had emerged from.

"Do you mean the earthquake?" asked Natasha, stumbling forward as he pushed.

"No," said Peralta, perplexed by her ignorance. "I mean that silly little nuclear detonation that *caused* the earthquake!"

At these words, Bahadur, who was at the head of the procession, came to a complete stop. All bumped into him as he turned to face Peralta, his brow furrowed with severity. Bahadur knew well of his old friend's intellectual playfulness and was in no mood for it now.

"What are you talking about?" he said in his booming basso. "Be clear about it, man. We have been deep under the sea, navigating a tunnel that began in Ceuta. We heard many blasts. What is this talk of a nuclear device?"

It was only then that Peralta understood why he had found them where he had, and his eyes grew wide with amazement.

"You found it too!" he exclaimed; his voice particularly hoarse. "St. Michael's Pass! How the hell—"

"Of what detonation do you speak?" repeated Bahadur, and the firmness with which he asked the question seemed to take Peralta off guard.

"A nuclear device," stammered the engineer. "It must have gone off right above you. Not even an hour ago, I intercepted a coalition radio transmission warning that a terrorist attack was imminent in the strait. It ordered all personnel to prepare for a nuclear strike and the possibility of a resulting tsunami."

Everyone was speechless, and the horror in their eyes was more than enough to communicate their concern for all those who lived above. Peralta picked up on it immediately.

"Gibraltar's population is safe at least," he rasped solemnly. "There were still some people above, but they all got inside in time. The day before yesterday the governor called for an immediate evacuation into the galleries. It's a good thing he did too, or almost everybody on the Rock would be dying from radiation sickness right now."

They were partly relieved, but their concern hardly vanished. Hundreds of thousands of people along the coast would be dead or dying. Peralta tried to get them moving again.

"We've really got to go," he insisted, looking at the still stunned Bahadur. "We've already been exposed longer than we should."

Like Amir, the brown giant was thinking of his family, and praying that Tangiers had remained upwind from the blast.

"Where exactly are we?" he asked.

"Directly under the Moorish Castle's inner courtyard," rasped Peralta. "There's a hidden passage that leads up to the main entrance from here, but that's the last place you'd want to go right now. We need to head down, not up. Now come on. Please!"

With a grunt, Bahadur produced a flashlight and led them down the dark passage at a quick pace. He had to bend over so as to not strike his head on the low ceiling. Peralta took the opportunity to explain how he had come to be here.

"I always suspected there were natural caves on the Rock's eastern face," he began. "But I had no idea the military would have had so much interest in them."

Amir dodged one of Peralta's miniature drones and slipped a cinnamon toothpick into his mouth.

"What military interest?" he asked. "And how the hell did you get down here anyway?"

Peralta switched on his flashlight and trained its beam onto the roof of the tunnel.

"The Moorish Castle up there used to be Gibraltar's prison before it became a tourist attraction."

"So?" asked Amir.

"So, a long time ago, one of the inmates dug an escape tunnel…"

Amir frowned.

"Are you talking about Gavin's Hole? That's a smuggler's myth."

Peralta shook his head.

"It's not. I used it to get down here. I couldn't exactly take the hidden passage."

"Why not?"

"Because it opens onto the castle's main entrance. They nearly caught me when I used it to get out of here the first time. I couldn't take that chance again."

Amir looked back at the engineer in confusion.

"What are you guys talking about?" asked Gabriel.

Amir was shaking his head in disbelief.

"Gavin Binks was a convict back in the nineteen-forties," he said. "The story goes he spent years digging a shaft under his bed. One day he broke through into an old Moorish tunnel and supposedly used it to escape."

Peralta was nodding emphatically.

"It's all true," he said. "He tunnelled down here and then used the hidden passage to get out. I know because I found the old prison warden in the retirement home. He told me where Gavin's old cell was. As it turned out, it was in a part of the castle that's off limits to the public. I broke in and did some tunnelling after business hours. The rest was easy. I inherited this whole place."

As if to confirm Peralta's story, they arrived at an ancient brick wall that he claimed to have broken through. They had to bend low to traverse the short passage, but on the opposite side was a broad tunnel reinforced with concrete.

"And here we are," he rasped, sending the beam of his flashlight into the shadows. "This was all built by Canadian miners in World War Two."

He pointed the beam of light into the darkness.

"Down there's where the tunnel collapsed back in nineteen-fifty-three. The military never fixed it. I guess they figured the lost equipment was all outdated anyway."

Amir looked around through his dreadlocks. There was a three-wheeled service vehicle parked there. It had a flatbed trailer connected to it and resembled something from the nineteen-forties.

"Is that the equipment you're talking about?"

Peralta chuckled knowingly and approached the little truck.

"Hop in," he said, starting up the puttering engine. "It'll be faster than walking."

There was only space for one passenger in the little driver's cab and Peralta offered it to Marcus.

"God bless you, dear boy," said the old bishop, making himself comfortable. "It feels like I haven't sat in a proper seat for months!"

The other's piled into the trailer and they were soon bumping along the dark, humid tunnel.

"Where's he taking us?" asked Natasha, peering into the darkness behind them.

Gabriel produced a flashlight and checked his compass.

"We're heading east," he said. "Judging by our angle of decent, I'd say we were probably around sea level by now."

Ten minutes had not passed when they arrived at a single iron door at the tunnel's end. It had a large wheel at its centre and resembled something that might have belonged in a ship. Gabriel came up next to Peralta.

"Exactly what kind of military equipment were you talking about back there?" he asked.

Peralta gripped the rusty wheel at the centre of the door and gave it a turn.

"The kind that's been making me a fortune ever since I took possession of it."

After a short struggle with the mechanism, the door swung open to reveal an elevator-sized compartment within. Its walls were comprised of riveted iron, with another hatch directly in front of them.

"It's an old airlock," said Peralta, inviting them in and cranking the door closed behind them. "The military put it in to nullify the effects of the tide on the water level inside."

The old bishop was going to ask a question, but his words caught in his throat. Peralta had just opened the forward hatch to reveal a completely unexpected sight.

There, in an expansive subterranean cave, could be seen an old submarine. It was berthed in a dark, glassy pool, and was surrounded by a battery of pulsating electronic equipment.

Everyone blinked in amazement, their eyes scanning the tiny fifty-foot sub. It was dramatically lit; its dark hull rippling with reflections from the lapping waters beneath it. In its cavernous setting, it would have appeared to be part of an elaborate movie set, were it not for the smell of stale diesel fuel in the air.

"Bloody hell!" exclaimed Scotty, his eyes wide with surprise. "What the hell have you got going on in here, mate? You sneaky son of a bitch!"

Peralta was beaming with pride.

"It's a 1944 Royal Navy X-Class midget submarine," he rasped. "There are only two others like it in the entire world, and the one you're looking at is currently being used in one of the most lucrative smuggling operations in the entire history of the Rock."

The group shuffled their way into the secret military submarine port, with the entourage of miniature drones buzzing in ahead of them. The sight was impressive to say the least.

Set against a backdrop of old military crates and hanging cargo nets, were dense banks of electronic equipment, and dozens of monitors shimmering with rolling streams of data. A plethora of equipment filled the chamber, ranging from machining tools to laboratory devices. The gear occupied almost every square foot of available space, but the central attraction was most definitely the submarine.

"You're smuggling in that?" asked Amir, pointing to the vessel with a toothpick.

Peralta sat down at a workstation that looked like something Batman might have used.

"How else do you think I've been paying for all these toys?"

He began to type into one of the numerous keyboards before him.

"Cassano!" he bellowed unexpectedly, and instantly from out of the clutter there appeared a small man with a trimmed goatee, gold earrings, and a colourful scarf wrapped around his neck.

The latter looked at the group of visitors with wide eyes and removed the pair of oversized headphones that had prevented him from hearing them as they came in.

"Don't just stand there gawking," said Peralta, his voice particularly rough. "Go and make sure all the drones have docked into their stations!"

The scrawny pirate disappeared with a nod, leaving the others even more confused than before.

"That was Cassano!" exclaimed Amir. "Everybody thought he was dead; vanished on that run to Tangiers."

"He's been working for me down here," said Peralta, his attention focused on the monitors. "We've been moving tobacco, booze, hashish, marijuana, and pretty much anything else that's needed out there on the Med. The cargo gets brought down from the upper galleries through that."

Peralta used his thumb to point out a secondary airlock that led to an old service elevator.

"It really didn't take much to make it operational again," he said. "When seen from above, the shaft looked like it was caved in, but if those lazy military engineers had taken the trouble to go down and investigate, they would have found the damage to be quite minimal. The lift itself was in perfect nick. We use it all the time."

"But wouldn't they see you coming and going?" asked Amir. "The tunnels might be off limits to the public, but there are still military personnel walking around up there."

"Only occasionally," said Peralta, "and we've got hidden cameras that tell us when it's safe to go up. We're in a very isolated wing."

"This is brilliant, man," whispered Scotty in awe, his eyes scanning the miniature sub. "There's no way they can catch you."

"Not at sea," rasped Peralta.

He had just finished bringing up some images of the nuclear detonation.

"Any approaching customs boats or helicopters show up on the sub's radar, giving us plenty of time to dive. It's the perfect smuggling machine."

"And how exactly did you find out about this place?" asked Gabriel. "How did you know it was even down here?"

"I found out last year when Nasrallah had me locked up in his castle doing his dirty work," rasped Peralta. "I used his computers to hack into the S.A.S. mainframe one day and got a big surprise when I looked at their file on Gibraltar. The hard part was finding a way to get down here. After the tunnel collapse it was completely inaccessible."

"Until Gavin's Hole solved your problem," said Amir, shaking his head in amazement.

Peralta smiled impishly.

"But couldn't divers have gotten to it from the outside?" asked Gabriel.

"Nope," said Peralta. "They couldn't get through the bay doors. They'd been constructed to withstand direct hits from enemy torpedoes and could only be opened from the inside."

"Hang on a second, mate," said Scotty. "Back up. Tell me more about Nasrallah's dirty work."

Peralta scratched the back of his head as he recalled the events.

"When Nasrallah found out that Cassano and I had bought a shipment of hashish from his competitors, he nabbed us and forced me to plant RFID chips in every kilo of it. He made me put together a tracking network, and then return the hash, saying that I'd been found out, and that I couldn't distribute it.

"I gave Nasrallah's competitors five grand for their trouble, and then used the tracking data to find their warehouses and get them busted."

"That was a slimy thing to do, mate," said Scotty, leaning forward. "I lost fifty grand because of you."

Peralta looked down at his feet.

"I know," he said. "And I'll pay it all back to you. I just didn't have a choice at the time. Nasrallah was going to kill Cassano if I didn't do exactly what he said. It wasn't until a month later that I found out about this submarine port."

"So what did you do?" asked Amir.

"Cassano and I planned an escape. When we got back, I figured out a way to get down here and went looking for the old prison warden. You know the rest. We've been hiding down here ever since."

Peralta directed their attention to the monitors.

"Check this out. I just hacked into the dry dock security cameras, and this is what came up."

All looked over in time to see the massive detonation that had occurred not forty minutes before. A dome of seawater was rising over a thousand feet into the air.

"Good God," stammered the old bishop. "How could we ever have survived such a blast?"

All watched in amazement as Peralta replayed the video.

"Fortunately for everyone living on the coast, the detonation only triggered a minor earthquake," he rasped. "Anything larger would have wiped out coastal cities from here to Greece."

"That blast was aimed at us," said Gabriel to the others. "Whoever sent those military choppers was also responsible for this attack. I'm sure of it."

"But those helicopters were American," said Scotty.

Natasha turned to Gabriel.

"Are you saying that the American military would risk killing millions of people just to destroy the Cube? How could that be possible?"

Gabriel looked hard into Natasha's eyes.

"I don't know what I'm saying," he said. "A part of me still can't believe that any of this is happening."

"One thing is certain," said Bahadur, his voice sounding even deeper than usual. "Our enemy can track the artifact.

They will know that it has not been destroyed. They will come for us."

Peralta turned away from his monitors, a look of confusion transforming his features.

"Are all of you insane?" he asked. "This was a terrorist attack, just like the nukes that have been going off all over the world. Americans could never have done it. Besides, what artifact could you possibly have in your possession that would make them detonate a nuclear bomb to destroy?"

"This artifact," said Gabriel, producing the Cube from his duffel bag and passing it to Peralta. "We'd planned on looking you up as a consultant, but it would appear that you found us first, and for some crazy reason, that doesn't even surprise me. Very strange things have been happening lately. Inexplicable things..."

Peralta looked at Gabriel, straining to comprehend what he was being told. The scraps of information he had received thus far were disjointed, and difficult to understand. He took hold of the Cube and tried to piece together what he had learned.

"What could possibly be so special about this?"

Peralta gasped as the Cube burst to life, a strange blue light erupting from its core. He stared into it, struggling to understand.

"Believe it or not," said Gabriel, "the artifact you're holding is probably about two hundred and fifty million years old, and not only does it light up like a Christmas tree, it somehow interfaces with both Natasha's brain and mine. For the last thousand years it's been disguised as an unassuming medieval quadriform."

Peralta looked up over the rims of his glasses.

"With pictures of peeled apples on each of its sides?"

Gabriel and Natasha exchanged a quick glance before looking back at Peralta.

"Yes," they said in unison. "How did you know that?"

Peralta returned his gaze to the Cube.

"Because I've seen this artifact before," he said, frowning with confusion. "Nasrallah made me run some tests on it one night when I was his prisoner. It was emitting scrambled alpha-wave sequences. Human brain waves. Very, very strange. I didn't tell him a thing about them, but I think they made me dream things… It's difficult to explain…"

"What kind of things, mate?" asked Scotty, leaning closer.

Peralta looked up at the smuggler pirate, a distant look in his eyes.

"The morning after I'd examined it, I woke up knowing a way out of the castle," he said faintly. "There was a secret tunnel in the lower levels… Cassano and I used it to escape."

On hearing this, Bahadur took a step closer.

"That is very strange indeed, my old friend," he said in his deep basso. "Only Nasrallah and I knew of the existence of those tunnels."

"Look," said Gabriel, putting a hand on Peralta's shoulder. "We've got a big problem. If we don't get that Cube to the north coast of Spain before the winter solstice, this whole world is going to go to hell. As it stands, it might go there regardless. We needed to retrieve an Islamic codex that was supposed to be hidden in St. Michael's Pass, but we failed. It was the only thing that could tell us what we needed to do with the Cube."

Peralta tore his eyes from the artifact and looked up at Gabriel, his jaw hanging open with surprise. He was about to say something, but Amir spoke first.

"How the hell are we supposed to get the Cube up north?" he asked. "We can't exactly leave Gibraltar right now. The radiation would kill us."

Everyone looked at Amir in shocked realization. He was absolutely right. The levels of radiation outside would be lethal. Gabriel's eyes met Natasha's, a look of defeat coming over him.

"We'd have to wait at least two or three weeks," he said. "By that time, it'd be too late."

Peralta held up a hand.

"Hang on a second," he rasped, rising from his chair. "You said that you were looking for an Islamic codex in St Michael's Pass?"

Gabriel glanced over at Natasha and then looked down at his feet.

"That's right."

Peralta frowned and placed the Cube on the desk decisively. He walked to a nearby filing cabinet and opened a drawer, producing a medium sized package.

"Take it," he said, handing it to Natasha. "Consider it a donation to the cause."

Natasha took hold of the package, a quizzical expression on her face. She laid it down on a table and removed its wrapping, exposing a jewel encrusted book that was beautiful beyond description.

"The Book of Khalifah!" she gasped. "I can't believe it!"

Everyone looked at Peralta to find him oddly silent. His eyes were fixed on the golden book.

"Where did you find that?" demanded Bahadur, coming to Peralta's side.

The messy scientist looked up at him and shrugged.

"I found it in St. Michael's Pass," he said. "It was in a secret chamber not far from here."

Gabriel could not believe his ears.

"How did you find the chamber?" he asked. "And how the hell did you get into St. Michael's Pass to begin with?"

Gabriel looked over at the others, the answer to his own question coming to him at that very moment.

"He's the one who left the tracks on the stairs," he said, looking back at Peralta again. "They never belonged to Nasrallah. They were yours the whole time. What the hell happened?"

Peralta sat down in his chair and removed his glasses.

"When Nasrallah gave me the Cube to examine, he also gave me a scroll to look at."

He wiped the lenses with his lab coat and put them back on.

"I guess he figured he was going to kill me anyway, so it didn't matter if I knew about the secret treasure room. He desperately wanted to find the Book of Khalifah. I guess he hoped I might see something in the scroll that he'd missed."

Bishop Marcus could sense the scrappy engineer's distress as he recalled the events. He laid a comforting hand on his shoulder.

"All is well, my son," he said. "Go on."

Peralta looked up at the old bishop and smiled gratefully.

"I took a picture of the map with my phone when he wasn't looking. When Cassano and I escaped, we headed to Ceuta. We'd bought tickets for the ferry that morning, but I changed my mind at the last minute. I couldn't resist. I told Cassano I'd meet up with him in Gib and went to look for the treasure room."

"You sneaky little devil," said Gabriel. "And you figured out the way in."

Peralta shrugged.

"It wasn't so hard," he said. "All the clues were right there on the map."

Amir stared at the slipshod scientist in disbelief.

"And how did you manage to get into the Chamber of Khalifah?"

Peralta nodded as he remembered.

"That was trickier," he rasped. "The big wall of symbols reminded me of a trap I'd come across in a game of D&D once. Something about it just didn't feel right. I wasn't about to start lighting any lamps. When I found the runes on the opposite wall, I thought they'd be a much better bet."

"And how did you know which of the stones to push?" asked Natasha, still amazed. "There were six to choose from, and the others would certainly have triggered the trap."

Peralta shrugged.

"I pushed the one that had the highest electromagnetic reading."

"What?" demanded Amir. "How the hell would you know that?"

Peralta produced his smartphone. It was housed in a bulky case that had obviously been fashioned by him.

"I used this," he said, lifting up the device.

A slim rectangular sensor emerged suddenly from its side, buzzing momentarily. The screen of the smartphone showed a complex looking meter application.

"It's an electromagnetic field sensor," said Peralta. "It occurred to me that the mechanism behind the secret door's actuating stone might give off a different reading than the stones that would trigger the trap. There might be more bronze in there, or even a different kind of metal altogether. As it so happened, I did get a different reading in one of the stones, so I took a chance and gave it a push."

Gabriel was astonished by the device.

"May I?" he asked.

He had barely taken hold of the contraption when a sharp blue flame burst suddenly from its side. Peralta snatched it back.

"Sorry," he said, tapping the screen to extinguish it. "I should have told you about the blowtorch app."

Scotty laughed aloud.

"What else does that bloody thing do, mate?"

Peralta seemed suddenly self-conscious.

"Lots of things," he said bashfully, putting the gadget back into his pocket. "The case I built for it uses the phone's processor to drive all of its physical applications."

"All right," said Amir, beginning to pace. "So you used your special phone to get the Book of Khalifah. How'd you get across that chasm by yourself?"

"I couldn't," rasped Peralta. "I had to double back and take the lower passage. It really wasn't that difficult to get through. There were a couple of traps, but they were designed to kill people coming in, not going out."

Natasha had been leafing through the Book of Khalifah as Peralta spoke, and only now looked up from its gold encrusted pages.

"This book is not only the most beautiful thing I've ever seen," she said, looking over at Peralta, "It's also filled with important information about the Cube and our mission. I can't believe we have it. How can we ever repay you?"

Peralta picked up the Cube from where he had left it on the desk and held it up for all to see.

"Tell me everything you know about this artifact, and we'll call it even."

CHAPTER 46

Cassano took the rest of the party on a tour of the submarine after they had dined, leaving Gabriel and Natasha to relate the complex history of the Cube to Peralta. This in itself was no small task. Beginning with the story of their coinciding births, Gabriel and Natasha went on to tell him everything they knew.

Oddly enough, and taking into account the extent of their adventures thus far, Peralta was much less shocked and disbelieving than one might have suspected him to be.

Having briefly experienced the Cube's strange qualities himself, he could instantly appreciate the significance of the issues at hand. He took a particular interest in the events that had transpired in the Chamber of the Sphere, and the solar system's impending crossing of the galactic plane.

"I'm well aware of this hypothesis," he rasped, "but I had no idea that the actual crossing was so imminent. The last I heard; astronomers were saying it would happen in three thousand years. Not two days… It's quite scary really…"

He paused for a moment as though considering something.

"You know, Einstein would have had a field day with the Dark Rift," he said, shaking his head. "It's very likely that its gravitational field will cause severe temporal distortions in our solar system."

Gabriel and Natasha looked at Peralta, trying to imagine what this could possibly mean. Peralta had, in the meantime, picked up the Cube again. He was studying it closely.

"Speaking of Einstein," said Gabriel. "When we scanned the Cube, we found that it was comprised of thousands of layers, each one containing data encrypted in what appears to be Sumerian sexagesimal cuneiform.

"Suora had a chance to look at some of the scans we made in the tunnel last night. She said they were *matrices representing linear transformations in a state of quantum invariance.* Whatever that's supposed to mean."

Peralta nodded knowingly, his bushy eyebrows gathering together as he examined the artifact.

"I see," he said. "Did she say anything about them being arranged using different dimensional vector spaces simultaneously?"

"I think she did," said Natasha, looking over at Gabriel, amazed. "How did you know?"

Peralta turned his head to face them both, an excited smile spreading across his rumpled features.

"Let's just say I'm a fan of Heisenberg too," he rasped, rising to his feet with the Cube in hand. "Have you still got those scans?"

Natasha nodded and rushed off, returning with the 3-D scanner and her laptop computer. She placed them together on the table.

"Isn't that a cute little BIRIS," said Peralta, smiling.

"You know what it is?" queried Natasha, arching an eyebrow.

"Of course I know what it is," said Peralta, petting the machine's dome-shaped processor unit as though it were the head of a little animal. "I've got one myself as a matter of fact. Picked mine up in Switzerland..."

He pointed to her laptop computer.

"Why don't you boot up your little friend and follow me."

Peralta walked them over to an area that lay hidden behind a wall of empty WWII munitions crates. In amongst a tangle of wiring harnesses and other clutter, were various pieces of equipment, including an x-ray machine, a scanning electron microscope from the late nineteen-fifties, and a BIRIS that was considerably larger than Natasha's portable model.

He placed the Cube on a turntable within the apparatus and powered it up.

"What the hell have you got going on down here?" asked Gabriel, examining the vintage microscope.

"I've collected most of this equipment over a lifetime," said Peralta. "But I've also acquired some new pieces of late. I moved my entire laboratory down here shortly after I found the place."

"And what do you do with it all?" asked Natasha, peeking behind an adjacent wall only to find another grouping of machines.

"I explore, I resolve, and I build," said Peralta.

He was bent over and began typing into a keyboard as he spoke, absently reaching for a half-eaten sausage roll on the desk and popping it into his mouth.

"Let's take a look at those scans of yours while the BIRIS boots up."

Natasha opened her laptop and brought up the scans they had made of the Cube the night before.

"These are just of the first layer," she said, pointing to the screen. "I didn't have enough RAM to render anymore of them."

Peralta looked impressed.

"Great scans," he said, bringing the screen up to his face to get a closer look.

Gabriel peered over Peralta's shoulder.

"We used to have a sample page of conversions from the cuneiform into standard numerals," he said, "but it was lost in St. Michael's Pass."

"Not a problem," said Peralta, proceeding to upload Natasha's files onto a memory stick. "I've got AI software that'll scan and translate all of this."

Natasha turned to Gabriel while Peralta busied himself. Her face was troubled.

"Suora had your father's journal?"

Gabriel nodded in consternation.

"I gave it to her last night."

"What are we going to do without it?"

"I have no idea..."

It was just then that the bishop appeared from behind a pile of crates, having returned from the submarine tour ahead of the others.

"You underestimate Suora greatly, my dear children."

Gabriel and Natasha turned to find him with the professor's journal in hand.

"She gave it to me for safe keeping early this morning."

Natasha took the book.

"She knew she was going to die?" she asked solemnly, passing her hand over the battered cover.

The bishop smiled gently.

"She must have suspected something," he said. "But she was not fearful."

When they returned their attention to Peralta, they found he had already uploaded the scans and fed them into the AI. A scrolling array of glowing green data was tumbling down a monitor before him.

"This is certainly an algorithm," he said, nodding as he studied the speeding script.

Natasha frowned.

"What exactly *is* an algorithm, Mr. Peralta?"

The messy engineer turned to look at her for a moment.

"It's a series of instructions," he rasped. "In this case it's for completing a very complex task."

"And what task is that?" asked Gabriel.

Peralta squinted at the monitor.

"To activate some kind of transponder that appears to be housed within the Cube," he said. "All of this falls into the realm of *Algorithmic Information Theory*. The complexity of these strings is absolutely massive, and what's more, it looks like it requires some kind of universal decryption language to make it work."

Peralta stopped his typing and looked over his shoulder at them.

"If this artifact truly is capable of synching with your brains, there's a good chance that the decryption language is based on a combination of both of your alpha wave patterns."

"By that do you mean our thoughts?" asked Gabriel.

Peralta nodded absently as he scanned the rolling data.

"But that's not all..." he said. "There appear to be some other factors involved here as well..."

He resumed his typing for a moment and then sat back in his chair as the AI did its work.

"You mentioned a labyrinth," he said, his eyes glued to a different monitor now.

"Yes," said Natasha. "The Labyrinth of Sarras. We need to find it before the planet enters the galactic plane."

Peralta turned to face her.

"And what happens if we don't find it?"

Gabriel cleared his throat.

"Perpetual darkness..." he proffered. "That and the complete extinction of the human race."

Peralta shifted his eyes to Gabriel and held his gaze for a long moment before speaking.

"I see," he said at last, nodding. "That does in fact put a bit of a rush on things..."

CHAPTER 47

Natasha led Gabriel to the table where the Book of Khalifah lay. With the bishop having wandered off in search of a snack, and Peralta engrossed in his work, she thought it might be a good time to study the codex. She passed Gabriel his father's tattered diary and bent over the Islamic tome to get a closer look.

"I saw something in here about the *Ostium Sanctus...*"

"Latin for *The Sacred Gate*," said Gabriel. "The Chamber that lies at the centre of the labyrinth."

Natasha took hold of the book reverently. With the practiced hands of an artifact restorer, she made her way through the fragile pages until she had found what she was looking for. There, inscribed in what looked to be silverpoint, was an Arabic poem referring to a cube-shaped labyrinth.

"Here it is," she said, translating it as she read. "Listen to what it says."

In the belly of the mountain are two gateways,
Made by the ancients before the coming of man.
One is descending.
The other is ascending.
Like the cart that follows the wheel,
So are these two gateways married and joined.
Interdependent yet separate.
United yet divided.
So that in descending one may ascend.
And in ascending, one may know what it is to be free."

"Descending so as to ascend," said Gabriel, leafing through his father's journal. "That's a dualistic transcendency concept. A paradoxical contradiction."

He stopped at a double-page spread and tapped the diary. On it was a detailed diagram of the Labyrinth, depicted as a series of cubes within cubes. He held it out for Natasha to see.

"The only way to get out of the labyrinth is to go deeper into it," he said.

Natasha shook her head in confusion and turned her attention back to the ancient tome.

"Listen to this entry. It refers to *The Two*. And again there's that double meaning of the primordial-king-queen in its usage… Only this time it's in Arabic…"

Natasha read the excerpt aloud.

"For the mountain's belly is also a prison, and that prison is called the Firmament. Its walls are of earth and sky and flesh and bone, and the curtain of matter is drawn shut. The prison's six sides are equal. Its nature is impenetrable. But The Two are like the water that finds its way through to the other side. It seeps into the darkest of places where no man will enter, and breaches the six veils."

"I'm seeing a lot of sixes in this stuff," said Gabriel, and at that moment they looked at each other, the same idea occurring to them both.

"Each level of the Labyrinth corresponds to one of the six sides of the Cube," said Natasha, moving quickly through the ancient book until she found the page.

"Here it is. The translations of the proto writings that are carved into the Cube."

"Made by the Council of Six," said Gabriel, looking down at the book in amazement. "There's that number again."

At the top of the page, a page written solely in Arabic, were the Latin words *Illac Domus*.

"*The Path Home,*" he whispered, translating. "The way for the fallen angels to return to their place of origin."

He rubbed the back of his neck.

"A pathway to heaven..."

Gabriel's eyes locked with Natasha's. Once again, the same idea had just occurred to them both. Mapping this mysterious path was the Cube's primary purpose.

Natasha pointed to the line of text directly below the title. It was inscribed above a two-dimensional representation of a labyrinth, with the crude image of a man standing at its entrance. At its centre was an All-Seeing Eye.

To transcend the Cube is to see it in all things.

Gabriel opened his father's journal to the first page.

"That's the first thing he writes... What does it mean?"

Natasha shook her head and continued to read through the texts.

"Each side of the Cube appears to demarcate a spiritual milestone that's reached on the path of Illac Domus," she said. "They're calling them the *Six Divine Actions*, and each is directly linked to one of the six major world religions. It says here that a *Seal* will only open when we've fully understood the wisdom behind its corresponding Divine Action."

She held up the book, pointing out a collection of verses.

"These riddles hold the clues," she said. "But an intellectual understanding of the knowledge they relate won't be enough. We need to understand them experientially.

"It's like the difference between imagining that a flame can burn you, and actually being burned by it. The first way is knowledge by deduction—"

"And the second is knowledge by *experience*," said Gabriel, finishing her sentence. "...also known as *Gnosis*."

He skimmed over the verses. Above each one was a heading. He read each of them aloud.

"*Prajñā, Pu, Jihad al-akbar, Atma-Jnana, Logos,* and *Binah-Chokhmah.* Which is which?"

"*Prajñā* is Buddhist," said Natasha, drawing from her schooling in theology. "*Pu* is Taoist, *Jihad al-akbar* is Islamic, *Atma-Jnana* is Hindu, *Logos* is Christian, and *Binah-Chokhmah* is Judaic.*"

"And what do *these* mean?" asked Gabriel, pointing to a series of symbols that were drawn on either side of the headings.

"They represent the seven steps of alchemy and the seven Hindu chakras," said Natasha. "This is fascinating, Gabriel. The Cube draws on all the wisdom that humanity possesses, regardless of its place of origin."

"Six spiritual stages," said Gabriel, trying to understand. "Each one containing a key that can be used to get through each of the six seals, so as to arrive at the labyrinth's central chamber."

Natasha nodded slowly, her mind working.

"These Divine Actions are nothing less than the six fragments that the *Original Gnosis* was split up into," she said in awe. "Your father was right, Gabriel. At the root of each world religion lies a fragment of the *Original Knowledge.* The purpose of the Labyrinth is to unify all of those fragments."

"But what about the Seventh Seal?" asked Gabriel. "What about the key to the Ostium Sanctus? It says nothing about it anywhere."

"Perhaps that seal is always open," said Natasha, looking at the eye in the centre of the drawing. "There's no mention anywhere of it being locked."

Gabriel paused to think.

"And does anything in there talk about what actually happens if someone passes through that Seventh Seal?"

Natasha chewed her lip.

"According to this, one would gain entry to the higher spheres without having to actually die. Gutierrez refers to it as a kind of de-materialization."

"Like a transporter in Star Trek."

Natasha rolled her eyes and shook her head at Gabriel's nerdiness.

"He describes the Seventh Seal as the *Alpha and the Omega*. It could be a reference to the Book of Revelations."

"The apocalyptic prophecy that talks about a second coming of Christ?" asked Gabriel.

"Yes," said Natasha. "But Gutierrez interprets the second coming symbolically, referring to it as a higher *Christ Consciousness* that will be adopted by the collective consciousness, as opposed to Jesus actually coming down from the clouds."

Gabriel snapped his father's journal closed and crossed his arms.

"So there's our mission in a nutshell," he said. "All we've got to do is get to the north coast of Spain in the middle of a raging third world war, uncover the entrance to a long lost, proto-Celtic labyrinth, find our way through it by transcending duality, and then go to heaven without dying. And all this before a cataclysmic, extinction level event occurs just two days from now. Sounds simple enough. I don't think we should have any problems at all."

Natasha was looking for something to hit Gabriel with when she heard Peralta's scratchy exclamation.

"It's at the centre of everything!"

They turned to see the scruffy engineer pacing.

"What?" asked Natasha.

"The Labyrinth…"

Gabriel frowned.

"How so?"

Peralta was holding the glowing artifact out before him and shaking his head in amazement.

"The first layer of this Cube is a living testament to Gödel's Incompleteness Theorem," he began. "Your combined alpha waves won't be enough to satisfy it."

He continued with his pacing.

"My guess is there will be a master transponder located at the Labyrinth; one that'll provide the axiomatic systems needed to make the artifact fully functional."

Natasha and Gabriel exchanged a puzzled glance.

"There's only one problem," continued Peralta. "Even if we find this labyrinth, there'll still be something else needed."

"What?" asked Gabriel, moving closer with Natasha at his side. "What's missing?"

"It's a fourth factor," said Peralta, scratching his head. "I'm not completely clear on it yet."

He returned to his computer and scanned the rolling data.

"Is there somebody else involved in this? Somebody who can access the artifact with his thoughts as well?"

Gabriel and Natasha looked at each other.

"Not that we're aware of," said Gabriel. "What are you getting at?"

"It's difficult to say at this point…"

He shook his head in an effort to clear his thoughts.

"Either way, if we're going to try and figure out how this Cube works, it's going to take a huge amount of computational power to extract all this data."

"Is that a problem?" asked Natasha.

"A big one," said Peralta. "The only way I can think of pulling it off in such a short period of time would be to utilize a *Boink*."

Natasha glanced over at Gabriel in confusion.

"A *Berkeley Open Infrastructure for Network Computing*," said Peralta. "It's a middleware system for grid computing. It was originally developed for SETI."

"The Search for Extra-Terrestrial Intelligence?" said Gabriel. "They've got over two million PCs hooked up to that thing worldwide. How the hell are we supposed to put together a network like that in two days?"

"Well," said Peralta, looking down at his fingernails. "I'm sure they wouldn't miss a few Teraflops of processing power. I mean there's so much of it out there…"

"Are you suggesting we hack into SETI?"

Peralta looked intently at Gabriel.

"We've got to find that labyrinth right away," he said. "It's the key to everything."

Gabriel looked back at him hard. The nerdy engineer had touched on a problem that had been plaguing him since they had arrived back in Gibraltar.

"The Labyrinth is somewhere in the mountains of Northern Spain," he said. "How the hell are we supposed to even get there? We can't exactly leave Gib right now. The radiation out there would kill us. We'd have to wait at least two weeks, and by that time it'll be too late."

Peralta pointed to the submarine.

"There's a lot of lead in that hull, Dr. Parker."

"You think that old sub would make it all the way to the north of Spain?"

"I'm absolutely certain it would," said Peralta. "But there's one little problem. We don't have enough fuel to do it, and there's no way of acquiring any."

"I know a bloke who can get you the diesel, mate!"

All turned to see Scotty Roberts approaching.

Having completed their inspection of the submarine, he and Amir were making their merry way towards them enshrouded in hash smoke.

"And exactly who might this diesel-dealing gentleman be?" asked Peralta, propping his hands on his hips skeptically.

"My brother Richard, mate," said Scotty offhand. "He's practically the bloody governor, and he's in charge of the entire Gibraltar Regiment. If anybody's got access to fuel, it's him."

The smuggler snatched the chillum away from Amir and took a deep haul from it.

"I'll get him to give you all the bleeding diesel you need, mate," he said, releasing a billowing cloud of smoke. "Whether he bloody wants to or not."

CHAPTER 48

Central Jerusalem, Israel.

Christian entered his private chambers, overcome with frustration and rage. Even though he had obliterated most of the Mediterranean coastline, the Cube appeared to still be intact. To make matters worse, he had utterly lost his ability to pinpoint its location.

Oddly enough, the frenzied demonic whispering that had threatened his sanity up to that point was having no effect on him anymore. The reason for this was simple. There was nothing vulnerable left in him. Christian's reptilian self was fully in control now. Its demonic, multi-dimensional form had fully merged with his own. With the murder of his only friend, Christian had truly become the son of Lucifer.

He made his way to his desk. More disconcerting than his sudden inability to locate the Cube were the things he had learned from the Zurvanites in their last appearance. His brother had not died after all, but rather survived, and was on the verge of engaging in a plan that would assist the Two in their mission to unlock the gnosis contained in the Cube. The thought of his brother's betrayal made Christian's blood boil.

I will destroy him. I will drink his blood.

Now that he had embraced his dark, reptilian self, he knew it would always govern his actions, and he felt a certain comfort in this. At present, it was telling him that there was one more task for him to complete; one last element of an age-old agenda, which when enacted, would ensure the transference of all earthly power into his hands. He clenched his fists with resolve.

Let the will of Lucifer be done.

The Vatican church that Christian's forefathers had created as the seat of Lucifer's throne would now be destroyed, along with the entire city of Rome. The results of this *terrorist* attack would have global reverberations, affecting more than a billion Catholics worldwide. It would pave the way for a new world religion, one that would have at its root the cleverly hidden tenants of the left-hand path.

"Computer," said Christian dryly. "Activate *Terminus Sanctus*."

A holographic representation of Vatican City materialized suddenly over his desk. Located deep in a crypt beneath St. Peter's Basilica could be seen a massive nuclear device awaiting detonation. Christian smiled darkly. The Vatican, as it so happened, had been doomed since its inception.

In 1139, during an audience with Pope Innocent II, the Irish Archbishop St. Malachy had experienced a 'holy mystical vision' and shortly after named the one hundred and twelve Popes who would reign from that day until the Day of Judgment.

His predictions had of course been fabricated by the Church, but they would over the centuries prove to be forebodingly accurate, adding to the Vatican's multi-armed campaign to achieve subservience through fear.

To the very last Pope, Malachy had given the name, *Peter the Roman*, and it was a Pope by this very name who currently resided in office.

Christian studied the hologram. According to Malachy's prophecy, the utter destruction of both the Vatican and *The City of Seven Hills*, which was Rome, would come to pass under the reign of the last Pope. It was an ominous foreshadowing of an event that had, in reality, been planned since the Vatican was first created in the fourth century.

"*Terminus Sanctus* is armed and ready to deploy," came the computer's sensual voice. "Awaiting further instructions."

Christian could not help but marvel at the size of the explosive. Built during the Soviet era, it was a one hundred megaton version of the fifty megaton *Tsar Bomba*, the most powerful explosive ever to be detonated in the history of humanity.

That an artifact such as this had been sitting in the bowels of the Vatican since the early nineteen-sixties was incomprehensible; that it was on the verge of being detonated, unthinkable.

A sensation of baleful ecstasy encompassed Christian. This would be the event that would mark the world's transition into darkness and misery.

"Computer," he said with perfect equanimity. "Let us fulfill the holy prophecy that St. Malachy so graciously gave to us. Detonate *Terminus Sanctus* at sunrise, local Rome time."

Here ends **Book Two – The Lost Labyrinth.**
The Last Artifact Trilogy *concludes with:*
Book Three – The Sacred Chamber

www.ingramcontent.com/pod-product-compliance
Lightning Source LLC
Chambersburg PA
CBHW030919050726
47498CB00003BA/818